Remember RAMSEY

New York Times & USA Today Bestselling Author

CYNTHIA EDEN

PROLOGUE

Observation notes: Day one. Initial observation begins tonight. My goal is to slip into the bar and assess the subjects inside. My sources have told me that a great deal of illicit activity occurs within the confines of the bar owned by the mysterious Ramsey Hyde. Everyone knows about Ramsey's reputation.

If I'm lucky, he'll never even know I'm there.

***

Dr. Whitney Augustine took a deep breath and offered a tentative smile to the bouncer who sat on the old, wooden stool just outside of the bar.

He didn't smile back. He glared. "Lady, what the hell are you doing here?"

"Looking for a drink?" Her brows climbed. "This is a bar, isn't it?"

His gaze slid over her. He took in her loose, flowing top. Her jeans. Her high heels.

"Uh, is there like...a cover fee or something that I have to pay?" This was getting awkward. She'd watched other people slide inside the bar with no problem. The bouncer had barely glanced at them. But when she'd tried to stride boldly past him, he'd lifted up his hand to halt her progress.

"We're at capacity." He pointed over her shoulder. "You should get back in your ride and head down the road. I'm sure there are more bars open. Try finding a place on the beach."

Her shoulders squared. "I don't want another bar. I want this place." Whitney released a long breath before saying the phrase she was about ninety percent sure would get her inside. "There is business I must conduct in Ramsey's. I'm looking to hire someone for...a bit of work that I have."

He stared back at her. Just stared.

He was in his early twenties, with long, brown hair and clad in a black t-shirt.

Whitney kept her chin up as she waited for his response. The intel she'd obtained had told her that Ramsey's bar was a front. Inside, all sorts of dark deals were arranged. If you went in Ramsey's, you were either a criminal or someone looking to hire a criminal.

Despite the words she'd just given to the suspicious bouncer, Whitney did not actually want to hire a criminal. She just wanted to study one. Or a few. Up close.

It was her job, after all. She was a psychologist, and her major area of focus was criminal behavior. She needed to understand the criminal mind. Needed to learn as much as she could and—

"I've got just the guy for you," the bouncer surprised her by saying.

"What? You—you do?" Excitement pumped through her blood. *Yes.*

"Uh, huh." He rose from the stool. "Follow me."

She scrambled to keep up with him. "You're just leaving your post? Is that all right? Your boss won't get angry?" She didn't want him to get in trouble because he was helping her.

The bar was packed. Music blared. And excitement had her whole body shaking. She'd planned for this immersive experience for weeks. To actually *be* in Ramsey's had surges of nervous energy pumping through her.

"Oh, I don't think the boss will be angry with me at all."

She barely heard his words because a large, hulking figure had loomed in her path. Whitney quickly side-stepped that figure, only to draw up short when she realized the bouncer had stopped. He stood next to a man with thick, black hair. A man who wore an absolutely ancient-looking jacket.

"Got someone for you to meet," the bouncer drawled. "A lady looking to hire someone to do some *special* kind of work."

Her stomach twisted in knots. She'd done her research ever so carefully. Now this, *this* was finally it. It was one thing to just do research from the safety and comfort of her office. It was quite another to be in the field and get first-hand exposure. And it had been far too long since she'd journeyed into the field. *Definitely time to get busy again.*

The man at the bar slowly turned toward her, and every single bit of breath seemed to leave her in a *whoosh*. Whitney could not look away from the darkest, deepest eyes she'd ever seen in her life.

The noise around her seemed to mute as her heart launched into a triple-time rhythm. The man before her was dangerous. The waves of danger seemed to roll off him. He was also drop-dead gorgeous. His head tilted as he studied her, and he lifted a shot glass to his sexy mouth. His hand gripped the glass easily, and he drained the clear liquid in one gulp. Tats covered both of his hands. Swirling, fierce tats.

He put the glass down with a soft clink.

His gaze swept over her. Slowly. The bouncer had studied her, too, but this man's gaze was different. It *felt* different. It felt like he was undressing her.

And she should have been completely pissed off.

She had never in her life been attracted to dangerous men. She studied those sorts of men. Wrote research papers on them. Lectured on them to her students at the college. She didn't feel attraction to men like that. She certainly did not sleep with men like that.

Whitney had a rule. When it came to her personal life, she preferred nice, safe men.

One look at the stranger, and she knew there was nothing nice or safe about him.

"So...I'll just leave you to business." The bouncer. She'd almost forgotten he was there. "Have fun." He sauntered away.

The stranger kept staring at her. At least his gaze had returned to her face. That was something. And her breathing was semi-normal again. That was something else.

He quirked one brow at her. "You gonna stand there or you gonna hop up on the stool and have a drink with me?"

She liked his voice. She should *not* have liked his voice because she wasn't there to get drawn to some dangerous man. But his voice was low and rumbling and sexy. The kind of voice that would whisper to a woman in the dark and—

Nope. Stop it. Focus. You are a professional.

She'd never, ever had a reaction like this to someone she had just met. What in the world was wrong with her?

He leaned forward and patted the stool next to him. "I promise, I won't bite."

"Well, of course not," she rushed to say as she hopped up on that stool. "I certainly didn't think—"

"Unless you want me to bite. I mean, if you're into that." He gave her a slow, sensual smile. "Not quite sure what you're paying me to do yet. Is it to fuck you? Is that what you want? You came in, and you're looking for a guy to—"

"No!" Heat burned through her cheeks. This was so wrong. She grabbed his arm. *Hello, muscles.* "I am most certainly not here to hire someone to—to—"

"To fuck you?"

"Yes, that. Thank you."

He laughed. "Too bad. For you, I would have offered a discounted rate." He winked.

Her flush got worse. She yanked her hand away from his muscled arm and gave herself a quick fan with a flutter of her fingers. "It's rather warm in here, isn't it?"

"Not particularly." *His* tattooed fingers drummed on the bar.

Trying to be casual, Whitney slid her hand into her purse and pulled out the four twenties she'd prepared. Then she inched that money toward his drumming fingers.

His eyebrows lifted. "What in the hell is that?"

"Eighty dollars. Eighty dollars is worth an hour of your time, isn't it?" Surely it would—

"Not normally, no."

Oh. She'd rather thought eighty would be a good starting point. "Maybe I should tell you about the job."

He grunted. "Maybe you should."

She risked a glance around. No one seemed to be paying them much attention, yet she had the weird feeling that everybody in that place was aware of her conversation with the stranger. Crazy, of course. But...

She pulled her stool closer to his. Their shoulders brushed. "I just want to sit with you."

"Excuse me?"

"It will be the easiest job of your life, I promise." Her words came out in a fast, soft rush.

"You smell like raspberries."

"I—" She got caught by his eyes. "Scented soap."

"It's fucking delicious."

Whitney swallowed. Her gaze drifted over his face. A line of stubble covered what was truly a phenomenal jaw. Strong. Hard. His thick, dark hair was swept back from his high forehead. And his eyes weren't just brown. They were golden brown.

"Back to business," he murmured.

Oh, crap. Had she just been *staring* at him? How embarrassing. And unprofessional.

"You want to pay me eighty bucks so that you can sit with me. That's a new kink."

"It's not a—" Her breath huffed out. "If I'm with you, then no one will look twice at me."

"Don't be too sure of that."

"They'll think we're conducting business, and I'll be left alone." Her brilliant plan. She'd figured she'd be the one who picked out her partner-in-crime, so to speak, but the helpful bouncer had done the job for her. "Then I can do my work."

His face hardened. "And what exactly *is* your work?" A new note had entered his voice. A low, harsh note that sent chills skating down her spine. "You a cop?"

"No! Nothing like that!" Once more, she glanced around. "And I don't think you should be throwing out the 'C' word in this place. You don't want to get us in trouble. If Ramsey hears you saying that, he'll probably throw us both out."

"Doubtful. I'm pretty tight with him."

"Well, I'm not."

"Obviously."

Her gaze darted back to him.

He was watching her. "You don't look like a cop. Don't have cop eyes."

"That's because I'm not a cop."

"Then what are you?"

She leaned in even closer to him. "I'm a psychologist."

"Bullshit."

"No, I really am. And I want to have the chance to observe the behavior in this bar because I am—"

"Crazy?" he interrupted.

"Uh, no."

"Delusional?"

"No, not that, either. Thanks for asking."

"You sure?" He hadn't taken her cash. He *had* turned fully toward her. "To me, it seems like you must be nuts. Because otherwise, why the hell would you walk into this place? You must know how dangerous it is."

Of course, she did. "That's why I'm here." This wasn't an official study. Not sanctioned through her college. This was an observational process that she wanted to do for herself. She'd been shut away in the classroom too long. She needed to get out. To experience the real world.

"You know the bar is full of criminals."

"I have heard that, yes." Which went back to...*That's why I'm here.*

"And you want to play with them? What the hell? You get off on screwing dangerous people?"

"I'm *not* here to screw anyone! Why do you keep getting fixated on that point?" Her breath huffed out. "Never mind. You are obviously not interested in helping me. I'll just take my money and find someone else." Her fingers closed around the cash.

His fingers closed around *hers*. A surge of heat flew from her fingertips all the way through her body. One of those electric jolts that people wrote about in books but that had never happened to Whitney before in her entire life.

"You're not finding anyone else."

Their heads were close. Their mouths were close. Why was she thinking about kissing him?

She licked her lips. His gaze followed the movement of her tongue, and she could have sworn that his stare heated. Whitney tried to de-escalate what felt like a majorly tense situation. "I'm not looking for trouble."

"Could have fooled me."

"I just want to sit here. I want to observe."

"You want to run a freaking experiment on the people in the bar. People who are armed and dangerous and could hurt you in the blink of an eye. Did you even think about that? Did you think about how easy it would be for you to be hurt before you sashayed in here in those tight jeans and those screw-me shoes?"

"I have mace in my purse."

His eyes squeezed shut. "Not going to fucking help you much."

"I'm not helpless." Her spine stiffened. "I know self-defense. And I've been in plenty of dangerous situations."

His eyes opened. "That does not reassure me." A pause. "Your name." It was an order.

"Whitney Augustine." She stared at him. Nothing.

"Uh, this is the point where you are supposed to tell me *your* name," Whitney prompted.

"How about we take a walk?"

"But I just got here. If you're not going to take my job—"

"A walk." He closed his hands around her waist and lifted her off the stool. "We're going to take it now."

"I am not going *anywhere* with you!" Whitney snapped even as she tried to ignore the heat that his touch had just generated. Why was she reacting this way? "Kindly take your hands *off* me."

His hands dropped from her waist, but he didn't back away. "You think this is the type of place where some white knight will rush to your rescue if you get in trouble?"

Actually, no, she rather believed the opposite. She suspected this was the kind of place where people ignored most types of trouble.

"That's what I thought."

Wonderful. He seemed all smug and satisfied. Good for him.

"How about this..." he murmured. "How about I promise to be on my best behavior with you? I will keep my hands off you, and we can go into the back and have a polite, private conversation. Sound good to you?"

No, it most certainly did not sound good. "*You* must the crazy one if you think I'll just wander into a back room with a stranger." Especially one as muscled and dangerous as he appeared. "My job was simple. I wanted you to just act like we were conducting business. We would have stayed right here where we were surrounded by plenty of other people. It should have been easy." Then he'd gone and complicated things.

"I don't think anything about you is easy..."

Was that an insult? Or a compliment? She couldn't tell. "Just forget it. I'll find someone else." Whitney marched a few steps away from him.

"I don't think I can forget you."

"Try. Try really hard." Her gaze was already scanning the room. Who would be her partner? Who could she pay to—

"*I don't want anyone fucking touching her.*" His voice boomed out behind her.

Horrified, her head—and body—whipped around, and Whitney gaped at him.

"She's mine, and no one will put a finger on her, no matter what wild shit she says."

Whitney could only shake her head at him. "Do you have some sort of...issue? Like, should I call someone for you?"

She thought his lips might have twitched. Before she could say anything else—

"Sure thing, boss," one guy called out. "We hear you."

Boss.

Her heart slammed into her chest.

Boss.

Another hard slam.

This couldn't be right. No, no, no, this had better be wrong. The handsome devil with the tatted hands and taunting, sexy grin...he could not be the boss. Granted, there were surprisingly few pictures of Ramsey Hyde online. The man had *no* social media presence, and the mug shots she'd found had been taken when he'd been barely legal. Those old photos looked nothing like the guy in front of her. This man could *not* be—

"I guess this is the part where we finish the introduction bit." His grin stretched. "I'm Ramsey Hyde, and your sweet ass does not belong in this bar."

CHAPTER ONE

Observation notes: He let me stay. Ramsey is an arrogant, controlling—never mind. He agreed to let me stay. Reluctantly. He agreed to let me do my "research" in his bar. Except he told me eighty bucks just wasn't going to "cut it" in his book. Instead, he offered me another deal.

Why the hell did I accept it?

***

"Uh, lady?" The bouncer eyed her warily. "Did you hear me? I said you don't belong in this bar." He cleared his throat and lifted his hand to point back toward the dark parking lot. "You should go back to your car and get the hell out of here."

Whitney Augustine straightened her shoulders. "It's a public bar. Anyone should be able to go inside."

The man seemed to be sweating. Odd, it was a surprisingly crisp night.

"This is really, really not a good place for you."

It didn't seem to be a good place for anyone. The bar looked like a hole in the wall. Music screeched from inside. A moment ago, she'd seen two men get tossed out—literally, thrown into the air before they slammed onto the ground. It certainly wasn't what she'd call a family-friendly spot. No matter. She *was* going inside. "Do I need to pay some sort of cover fee?"

The bouncer blanched.

"Are you all right?" Whitney asked in concern. Her hand rose and gripped the man's shoulder. He'd nearly fallen off his wobbly stool. "Are you feeling sick?"

He jumped off the stool—and away from her. "You should not be touching me."

She blinked. "Sorry." Her hand fisted. "Look, I just need to go inside and see if—" But Whitney broke off. Mostly because what she had to say was too crazy to be believed.

I just need to go inside and see if anything about this bar is familiar to me. I need to see if anyone in there comes and talks to me...if anyone knows me.

"You should leave," he urged her. "Now. Run away. Fast."

But her shoulders just rolled back with determination. "I'm going in this bar."

"He is *not* gonna like this."

What? "Who won't?"

A long exhale. "Come with me."

Then she was scrambling to follow him. They pushed through the heavy crowd inside, and the too loud music had her temples aching. But there was something about the scene, about the atmosphere of the place, that nagged at Whitney. Something that felt...familiar.

And familiar wasn't something that she was too used to experiencing, at least not lately.

But as Whitney followed the brown-haired bouncer through the crowd, she became aware of the fact that conversations were stopping. The noise level fell off, and even the screeching band...paused.

She looked around and realized that people were staring at her.

Yeah, right. Not like that was the first time she'd been gawked at by strangers. Unfortunately. Her face had been splashed all over the news in the last few weeks, and she couldn't even go to the grocery store these days without people in the aisles whispering about her. Or snapping pics of her with their phones. Talk about something that made her stomach knot and twist.

"The boss is up here," the bouncer told her.

The boss? *Ramsey*. The name slid through her mind and rattled her nerves. Ramsey was the man she was there to see. It was his bar. His place. And, according to the notes she'd found, he was the one who'd given her permission to visit the bar over and over again in the past. *Before* her life had become a nightmare.

When Whitney thought of her life, she divided it into two main parts.

Part one...life before she'd been left for dead in the Gulf of Mexico.

Part two...life when she'd come back...with too many holes in her memory.

Back in part one of her life, she'd visited this bar. The visits had been part of an unofficial research activity that she'd been conducting in criminal psychology. Since Ramsey had been aware of her visits during that time, Whitney hoped he might be the man who could help her fill in some of those holes in her memory.

Oh, she *hoped* he could help her.

The bouncer stopped near a man who sat at the bar. His broad shoulders were covered by an old, battered coat. His dark head was bent forward.

"Uh, boss." A tap on the boss's shoulder. "It's *her*."

The boss—Ramsey—slowly stiffened. Then he turned his head, and deep, dark eyes met hers.

She couldn't speak. Her whole body kind of jolted as she stared at him.

"Fuck me." Ramsey grabbed a shot glass and drained the contents. His hold on the glass was so tight that Whitney was surprised he didn't shatter it.

"Um, okay. I'll leave you to it." The bouncer fled.

The bar stayed uncomfortably quiet.

"Play some damn music!" Ramsey roared. "And everyone—look the freaking other way!"

Music started playing. Whitney didn't glance around, but she was certain everyone started looking the other way, too. She rather thought that when Ramsey gave an order, most people jumped to obey it.

"And you..." Now he swiveled his body so that he was angled completely toward her. "You need to get out of here."

Right. As she'd thought, *most* people probably jumped to obey his orders. She wasn't most people. And she was also super, super desperate. So instead of backing away, she moved closer.

His eyes widened. Whitney realized they weren't just dark brown. They were golden brown and—

And I knew that.

"You came to see me when I was in the hospital." The words burst from her, but they were true. When she'd been in the hospital, this man had rushed into her room. He'd seemed frantic. Desperate to talk to her. And then...

Then everything had changed. As soon as he'd become fully aware of her—ah, her *condition*—he'd left.

For some reason, his departure had gutted her. It shouldn't have mattered. He was a stranger. But...

It had hurt.

"You have me confused with someone else." His voice was low and rumbling and rough, and it made the fine hairs on the nape of her neck rise.

"I don't think that I do." She risked another step closer. She was so close now that Whitney could reach out and touch him. Her fingers wanted to touch him so badly that she clenched them at her sides. "You're Ramsey Hyde, and you know me."

His gaze slid over her body. "I know lots of people."

"You came to the hospital. You came to see *me*." That had been weeks ago. And he hadn't come back.

"You're a celebrity." He shrugged. "Lots of people want to see the woman who cheated death. Not every day that someone comes back from a watery grave."

Whitney flinched. He didn't know it, but his words had immediately summoned a nightmare memory for her. The damn flashes would hit at the weirdest times. And right then, she had a sudden flash of her hands clawing through water. Of her lungs burning, and the heavy water trying to pull her down...

"Hey." His hand was on her cheek.

And his touch...*familiar*.

"You okay?" Gruff. As if the question had been torn from him.

Whitney was one hundred and ten percent *not* okay. She blinked away tears and shook her head. "If I was okay, I wouldn't be here." But desperate times had led to some desperate measures.

His fingers smoothed over her cheek. Was it her imagination, or did his fierce expression soften just the faintest bit?

"I'm an asshole," he told her bluntly. "A selfish, diabolical bastard who has no business being near you, much less *touching* you." His hand dropped. "This bar isn't the right place for you. The bouncer shouldn't have let you past the door. Jimmy knows better."

Now why did those words hurt? She didn't know for sure, but they just did. Time for her to bluff and see what happened. "I've been here plenty of times before, and you didn't mind then."

Now his expression definitely changed. Shock flashed across his features.

"In fact," she continued because his response had just given her more courage, "you were more than happy with our arrangement."

"You...remember?"

If only. Immediately after her attack, Whitney had lost all of her memories, but as the swelling in her brain had decreased and she had slowly recovered, the memories had returned...Except for the six months before her attack. *Before* she'd been left for dead in the Gulf of Mexico. Those memories still eluded her. Her dark time. It was frustrating and maddening. She could remember growing up. Going to college. Teaching at the university.

But those six months had been erased.

She didn't know if she would ever get those memories back.

"Whitney." He stood. Towered over her because he was at least six-foot-three and all solid muscle. "Do you remember me?"

She wanted to say yes. But even as she opened her mouth—

"No." Ramsey shook his head. "No, you don't remember a damn thing." He turned his back on her. "This place isn't for you. You need to get the hell out of here."

All of the air left her like she was some kind of deflated balloon. First, she felt shock, then...*anger*. No, no, he would *not* do this to her. Whitney grabbed his shoulder and swung him around to face her. "You know me."

One brow rose.

"I found *notes*. I wrote about us."

A muscle jerked along his jaw. "What?"

"We worked together here. Now you're acting like I'm a stranger. I want to know why. I want to know why you left me in that hospital. Why you didn't come back. Why you—"

"First, lower your voice." His own voice was barely a rasp. "You don't know who is listening. And this crowd isn't the sort I'd trust with anything valuable."

Her lips clamped together.

"Second, you're far too damn pale. Why the hell are you so pale?" He curled his hands around her hips and Whitney gave a startled gasp but—

He just lifted her onto the barstool and immediately released her, as if touching her had nearly burned his fingertips.

She hunched forward, and the loose tunic top she wore slid over her thighs.

"You want a drink? Hell, I could use about four more shots." He tapped his fingers on the bar.

Her gaze darted to his tattoos. There were lots of different tats on his hands and sliding up his wrists, and when he opened up his right hand—

A rose.

There was a rose tattoo on the inside of his palm. A black rose.

"I've heard that palm tattoos can be one of the most painful tats to get." Her voice was low. A little stilted. "Your palm is supposed to be more sensitive, I think something like four times more sensitive than other places to get tats on your body—"

His hand fisted. "I don't mind pain."

"Oh." Whitney wasn't exactly sure how to respond to that statement. "Well, um, good for you?"

His brow furrowed.

The bartender sidled up toward them.

"Tequila," Ramsey snapped.

The bartender glanced at Whitney. She should order something. Check. "Could I have a water, please?"

He squinted at her. "You don't want your lemon drop?"

Her what? Then Whitney's eyes widened. *The bartender knows me. I've come in here so often that he remembers the drink I like.*

Ramsey growled, "We don't serve those drinks anymore, remember? It's beers or hard alcohol. Not a freaking thing else."

"Water," Whitney said again. "I'll just have water, and thank you."

The bartender swung away.

Whitney's gaze darted back to Ramsey. She found him staring at her. And his expression was so stark and savage and...hungry. No, maybe hungry wasn't the right word. But it sure as heck looked as if he wanted to eat her alive.

The bartender was already heading back to them—

"Fuck it," Ramsey suddenly snarled. "You're coming with me." He locked his hand around her wrist and hauled her off the stool. Then he was tugging her through the crowd. Everyone seemed to jump out of their path, and in moments, Ramsey shoved open some door in the back. He ushered her over the threshold. Slammed the door behind them. Then threw the lock.

Her breathing heaved in and out. Whitney found herself backing up until her shoulders brushed against the nearby wall. Ramsey stalked toward her. His arms rose to cage her as his hands pressed into the wall on either side of her head. "You shouldn't be here."

"You know me."

"You should stay the hell away from my bar. Away from me. You don't belong here."

Why did his words *hurt?*

"And why the fuck," Ramsey rumbled, "are you so pale?"

He'd asked her that question before. The man seemed obsessed.

"Are you sick?" What *could* have been worry slid into his voice. "I thought you'd recovered. I thought—"

"You *know* me." This was said with more confidence because he'd just given himself away. He'd been following her progress—somehow. Maybe keeping tabs on her through the media. Maybe even talking to someone who was in her life. But Ramsey wouldn't do that if they didn't have some sort of relationship, right? He wouldn't bother if they weren't connected.

His gaze dropped to her mouth. "Yeah, I know you."

She wet her lips. Why had she just done that? Why was her head tipping back and her toes pressing against the floor as if she wanted to get closer to him? Did she *want* him to kiss her?

Utter madness.

"I know that you used to come into my place because you liked to run your little experiments." His gaze lifted to meet hers. "But you stopped doing that. I told you the bar was off-limits, and you stayed away."

"I...that wasn't in my notes." Her heart lurched. "When did you tell me to stay away?"

He swallowed. "What notes?"

He'd just answered a question *with* a question. There couldn't be a more obvious diversionary tactic.

"What. Notes?" Ramsey pushed.

"I was able to recover some observational notes that I had created on an old computer. Some info about my trips to this place." She would be as honest as possible. "Unfortunately, the files were corrupted so I couldn't read everything." If only. "Just bits and pieces. But they are bits and pieces from the time in my life that I lost."

"I see."

Did he? "I don't think you do." Anger hummed in her voice. "I don't think you see anything at all about me because you don't know what it's like to *be* me. You don't know what it's like to have a giant hole in your life. A blank space during which anything could have happened. I lost time. I lost my life. I want it back."

He leaned in even closer.

He's going to kiss me.

And if he did, his mouth would be hot and hard and so sensual. He'd tug on her lower lip. Thrust his tongue past her parted lips. He'd have her moaning and arching against him, and she wouldn't care who was outside of his door.

"Have you ever thought..." His voice had gone lower. Rougher. "That you're better off not knowing what happened?"

Then, before Whitney could respond, he shoved away from her.

"It's *my* life," Whitney told him grimly. "I think that means I should make that decision."

He'd turned his back on her. "And it's my bar. So when I say that you won't be allowed entrance here again, I mean it."

"You are a bastard."

He didn't look back at her. "I've been told that before." He headed for a desk. Ran his fingers along the edge. "Go back to your quiet, safe world, Whitney. You've always been too obsessed with danger. It's time to put that obsession to bed."

She didn't move. "I have some questions for you."

"And I don't have answers for you."

"You don't even know what the questions are!" she exploded.

Slowly, his head angled toward her. His gaze met hers. And once more, she had the wild thought...

He looks like he wants to eat me up. His stare seemed to burn with intensity as it raked over her. There was too much knowledge in that stare of his.

"I'll answer one question. Just one."

"Oh, wow, aren't you the super generous one." She stomped toward him.

"No, I'm not. No one has ever accused me of being generous. Or kind. Or any of those other annoying and useless traits. I'm dangerous. I'm deadly. I'm the bastard you don't want to face in the dark."

"Are you trying to scare me?"

"Is that your one question?" Mocking. Maddening.

"No!" She stopped in front of him. Straightened her spine. "I want to know..."

One dark eyebrow rose. He was all cocky and confident and arrogant and she wanted to shake him because there was so much more beneath his surface, Whitney was sure of it.

"What do you want to know?" His hand rose, and his fingers curled under her chin as his thumb brushed gently over her cheek.

She stared straight into his eyes. She wanted his control to shatter. She wanted to see the real man that he was hiding beneath this cold mask. "How do I know what it feels like when you kiss me?"

The darkness of his eyes seemed to get even deeper.

"If I don't belong here, if I'm supposed to stay out of your bar and your world, then how come when you were leaning toward me just a few moments ago, I suddenly knew exactly what it would feel like if your mouth took mine?"

CHAPTER TWO

Observation notes: I don't think Ramsey Hyde is as bad as the stories say.

Or...is he? Maybe I just hope he's not that bad...

***

Whitney Augustine stared up at him with her gorgeous, green eyes. Her lashes were thick and dark, and her gaze seemed to bore straight into him. Her hair—blond, silky—teased her shoulders, and her lush red lips were parted.

She seemed fragile. Almost breakable. Back when she'd first started coming to his bar, she'd just strode right in as if she didn't have a care in the world. She'd always smiled. Laughed freely. She'd gone toe-to-toe with him and showed no fear.

But now, fear clung to her. And she was too fucking pale.

His thumb slid over her cheek again. Beautiful Whitney. The woman who damn well haunted him. All he wanted to do was drag her closer. Hold her tight. Never, ever let her go.

She had no idea how close to the edge he was. Had no idea that for once in his miserable life, he was actually *trying* to do the right thing...for her.

"How do I know how you taste?" Whitney whispered.

His cock shoved hard against the front of his jeans. He'd been turned on ever since he'd seen her. Whitney had that effect on him. He saw her, he wanted her, and, usually, he took her.

Not that she remembered any of that. If she'd remembered all the times—all the ways—they'd fucked, she wouldn't be staring at him with faint confusion on her face. She had no clue that he'd had her against the door. On the nearby couch. On the desk.

No matter how many times he took her, Ramsey always wanted more.

She'd become his obsession.

A weakness that he could not afford.

"How do I know?" she pushed in that sensual, husky voice that haunted his dreams.

He wanted her mouth. Wanted to drive his tongue past her plump lips and take and taste and have her giving that little moan in the back of her throat that always drove him insane. But if he did that, if he crossed that line...

It's taking all of my strength to give her up. I can't taste her again.

Because...he'd just want to keep her.

Fuck me, I already want to keep her.

"Have we been lovers?" Whitney searched his gaze. "Were we involved?"

"You've asked a lot more than just one question." His voice was too gruff. Her scent had wrapped around him, and it flooded him with too many memories. Raspberries. She still smelled like sweet raspberries. Whitney must still be using the same scented soap. He'd bought her a ton of that stuff one day because he loved the way it smelled on her body and—

"And you haven't answered *any* of my questions."

No, he hadn't. "Pick one. I'll answer it." He shouldn't. He should be walking her outside. Sending her away. This was too dangerous. His life had always been too dangerous to include someone like her.

She nearly died once. Nothing like that can ever happen to Whitney again. But as long as she stayed in his life, in his twisted world, she would be a target. The only way for her to be safe—it was for him to keep his hands off her. For *him* to stay away.

For him to be the utter bastard that everyone knew him to be.

Her breath whispered out. "Were we lovers?" She pulled her lower lip between her teeth. Waited.

He could lie. Say no. Tell her that he'd never had her. But... "Of course," he replied casually.

Her eyes widened. "We—we were?"

"Oh, yes." His hand slid away from her. Went back to his side. Clenched into a fist. "We fucked dozens of times. Maybe even a hundred times. I wasn't exactly counting." He'd just been focused on sinking into her as deeply as he could go. "I had you in so many places. Once I fucked you on the bar top outside. On the pool table. I've had you in this room." He rapped the desk with his fist. "Right here."

If possible, her eyes got even bigger.

"I fucked you in my old car. On my motorcycle. On the beach. At your office. I fucked you in your bedroom, and we nearly broke your bed. I fucked you so many times that your body was tuned to me and only to me."

She barely seemed to be breathing.

He should stop. He didn't. *I'm a bastard.* "You like it dirty and rough, and you like to screw the worst criminal you can find. You get off on that, you know? The danger. Having sex with a man others say is a killer. You like to—"

"No." Fast. Hard. "Stop it."

Ramsey shrugged.

"You're lying to me."

He smiled. "What did you expect? For someone like me to tell you the truth? Where the hell is the fun in that?" His laugh was mocking and bitter. She wouldn't get that he was mocking himself. "You really think someone like you hooked up with me? You practically scream innocence, while, baby, I'm more in the mood for sin."

She put a hand to her stomach. "Coming here was a huge mistake."

"Absolutely. I tried to tell you that."

Her hand dropped. "I thought you could help me. You knew me."

Those damn notes of hers. He'd have to get his hands on them and see just what she'd uncovered. "You want to know about our past? Fine. Once upon a time, you came into my bar. You wanted to observe the people here. It was for some damn research you had going on. I allowed you to stay for a while. End of story."

"Why did I stop coming? Was I watching anyone in particular? Did I get involved with anyone here?"

His gut churned. "Lots of questions, and I'm pretty sure I only agreed to answer one."

Her lips thinned. "You're doing that thing again."

Don't ask. Don't ask— "What thing?"

"Where you pretend to be an extra special type of bastard. I wish you'd stop."

His lashes lowered to conceal his gaze. "Sweetheart, I'm extra all the time. Just as I am the worst bastard you will ever meet." He had to get her out of there. It was taking all of his self-control not to reach out and touch her again. But if he touched her again, he *would* be kissing her. And if he kissed her, he *would* be keeping her.

It's too dangerous. You have to get her gone.

"You don't date the types of guys in this place, Dr. Whitney Augustine. You like safe guys. You even told me that shit once." That part was true. Over the years, he'd found it was always easier to tell a blend of truth and lies.

"As far as you know, was I seeing anyone?"

Me. Only me. Because I wouldn't let any other man get close to you. He shrugged. "Not like I was gonna keep track of your social life."

Her hands went to her hips. "You are an exceedingly unhelpful man."

"You're welcome."

She glared.

Stunning. Color had finally come back to her cheeks. She was sexy as hell, and he wanted her more than he'd ever wanted anyone or anything in his entire life.

"Why won't you help me?" Whitney demanded.

His chest burned. She was lost and he knew she was scared, and he wanted nothing more than to pull her into his arms. He wanted to protect her from every dangerous thing in the world.

That is exactly what I am trying to do. And he was helping. It just so happened that his helping routine made him look like he was an, ah, extra special type of bastard, as she'd put it. "There is no Prince Charming for you here. Is that what this is about?" He kept his voice mocking. "You read some bit in your notes about me, and you thought we'd shared something magical?"

"My notes. Yes." A jerky nod. "I had notes saying you were a dangerous SOB who couldn't be trusted."

What? But his expression didn't alter. "Yet you're here...?"

"I told you, the files were corrupted. I thought there might be more to you—to me. To us." She raked a hand through her hair. "I was desperate. Desperate times call for crazy measures, but I've learned my lesson. I won't be bothering you again."

You never bothered me. You just obsessed me. "I'll have you escorted out to your car."

"Not necessary." She opened the door. "I can leave on my own."

Then she walked away without looking back. As soon as she was gone...

He dropped his hands on the desktop. His body hunched forward.

No one had ever told him that being *good* would hurt so friggin' much.

***

Whitney was blinking away tears—actual *tears*—as she rushed to her car. The parking lot was even more crowded than it had been before, and she was pretty much stumbling through people. Whitney ignored them as she beelined for her ride. Coming to Ramsey's had been such a colossal mistake. She should have known better.

I needed help. And I was so sure...

Her hand swiped over her cheek.

"Hey, pretty lady!" A loud voice—loud and way too close—called out to her. "What's the rush?"

She cut a glance to the side and saw a man with lots of piercings in his nose and ears start to swagger toward her. *I do not need this now.*

"Why don't we go inside?" He hurried closer. Lifted his hand and curled it around her arm. "We can dance." He rolled his hips.

God, I do not need this.

"Or we could just get straight down to business, and we could—"

"Get your hand off her. *Now*." Ramsey roared.

The hand was immediately yanked off her. The guy swung toward Ramsey. "What—who—she—" He couldn't seem to manage to put his words into any comprehensible form.

"She's not touched. *Ever*. You put your fingers on her again, and I will break every single one of them."

Whitney backed up. Rammed her ass into the bumper of her car.

"Sorry!" A squeak from the man with all the piercings. "I'm—"

Gone.

The guy had just full-out run across the parking lot.

Ramsey lunged as if he'd chase after him.

"Stop!" The order burst from her, and, surprisingly, at her cry, he did. Ramsey froze instantly. His hands were clenched. His body tight. And she could practically feel the fury crackling in the air around him.

"I could have handled him," Whitney said, and her voice only trembled a little. "He just was being a nuisance. I don't think that you needed to go full hulk on him and threaten to break his hand."

He spun to face her. "Did he hurt you?"

She shook her head. "No."

He stalked toward her.

There was no place for her to go, not unless she jumped into her car. Maybe she should consider that option. Because in the shadows, Ramsey looked scary and savage and the fury around him just seemed to grow and grow.

He jerked to a halt near her. His body brushed against hers. "I told you...I wanted to have an escort come outside with you."

Her mind was trying to process everything as fast as she could. "You followed me."

He didn't deny the charge.

"*Why?*"

"Another question. Do you truly think I'll answer it?"

"I think—" No, she didn't think he'd tell her the truth. She thought he was lying and tricking her. Words could deceive. Actions couldn't. He'd just *acted* like some kind of primitive, jealous, out of control...lover? Boyfriend?

What was it? What were they to each other?

"You wouldn't have broken his fingers." At least she'd finally found something to say.

He didn't respond.

"You wouldn't have done that." He was just trying to seem scary and intimidating.

Ramsey laughed. "You don't know me. You don't remember a damn thing about me. How could you determine what I would or wouldn't do?" He pointed toward the driver's door of her car. "Get in the vehicle and get out of here. You can't trust the people at this place. They will hurt you."

"That man, he—"

"That man has a record a mile long. He's gone to prison for assault twice. Hell, yes, I would have broken his hand if he'd hurt you, and I would not have even given the act a second thought."

Her breath shuddered out.

"Get in the car, Whitney."

He was protecting her. Scaring her, but protecting her. Why? "You're wrong."

"The hell I am. I know these people. I understand them. If you don't show strength, then you get destroyed. Believe me when I say that I would not hesitate to—"

She put her hands on his chest. *Mistake. Mistake. Mistake.* But she was practically going crazy, and she had to know if she was right. "I do remember something about you. I remember how your mouth feels against mine." And to prove it— to him and herself—she shoved up onto her toes. One of her hands grabbed the back of his head and she pushed her mouth against his.

Her movements had been awkward and too fast, and this was probably such a bad idea. An even worse idea than going into Ramsey's in the first place, but she just had to know, and—

He wasn't kissing her back.

His body was granite hard. So unyielding. And he wasn't kissing her back.

Her lips brushed against his. Carefully. Tentatively. She'd been so sure...

A shudder ran the length of his body.

Whitney realized she'd squeezed her eyes shut. She cracked them open. "Ram?" The shortened version of his name slipped from her.

"Fucking...*tried*..." His hands closed around her hips. He lifted her up. Put her on the trunk of the car, and then he stepped between her spread legs. "Need you."

This time, his mouth took hers.

Her lips were open, her body bow tight. His mouth brushed against hers, and then he tugged on her lower lip. A sensual pull that had her tensing all the more just before his tongue thrust into her mouth. He tasted her. He teased. He took. A moan built in her throat, and his mouth grew even harder on hers.

He was pulling her closer. His hands were sliding over her.

Everything was familiar. His mouth. His tongue. The way he touched her. The way he felt. The way hunger and need and lust whipped through her. Everything was familiar. Everything was—

I fucked you so many times that your body was tuned to me and only to me.

The words he'd said earlier rang through her head. She'd thought he was mocking her, but he *felt* right against her.

His hand slid to the front of her—

"Stop!" She'd torn her mouth from his. Her breath heaved in and out. Her heart raced far too fast.

His hands slapped onto the car's trunk.

"We've kissed before." She was definite on this.

He still stood between her legs. His gaze pinned hers. In the dark, she couldn't read him, and she hated that.

He didn't deny her words. How could he?

"What you said before..." She pressed her lips together and could still taste him. "About us. About all of the stuff we did together...was that true?"

"I told you to stay away."

"Was that true?"

"You should have listened to me." He shoved away from the car. Turned and seemed to sweep his gaze around the lot. "We could have been watched."

Like she cared about anyone watching her at that moment. "We were lovers. That was why you came to the hospital that first day. We were involved."

"Thought we already established that I wasn't the type of guy you'd get involved with. You weren't the type to screw dangerous men." He whirled toward her. "Whatever we were...it's all ancient history."

Not to her, it wasn't.

"You need to let the past go."

She couldn't. "Ramsey..."

"Drive away. Do not come back."

Well, that was brutal. They'd kissed and he was still kicking her to the curb. She slid off the car. Tried to ignore the fact that her knees did a little jiggle. "Was I seeing someone else?"

"What. The. Fuck?"

Her chin lifted. So what if his voice had just gone all low and lethal? *He would never physically hurt me*. And that thought was as crazy as everything else that had happened that night. He was a crime boss. He'd threatened to break a guy's hand just moments before. How the hell could she know if Ramsey would physically hurt her? She should be absolutely terrified of the man. Yet, she wasn't. "Was I involved exclusively with you or was there someone else?"

"You have no idea what you're doing." Grim. Flat. "You do not want to push me right now."

She did because she had no choice. He didn't understand what she was facing. "If there was someone else, I need to know about him."

He backed up a step. Another. "You...and some other jerkoff? Not really a picture I want in my head. Not something you should be throwing at me."

"So you *are* at least confirming that you and I were involved?"

His arms crossed over his chest. "You ever wonder why you forgot that lost time?"

Of course, she did. "Yes. Every single day."

He looked away. "Maybe it's because you wanted to forget what happened."

Bull. "Retrograde amnesia is a tricky bitch. After a traumatic brain injury..." Like she'd had. "Some people permanently lose years of memories. I lost six months." One doctor had said she should consider herself lucky. "I don't *want* my memories gone. No one wants to miss a giant chunk of life."

"You do if that time is something you'd rather erase. If deep down, you wish the shit that had happened then...you wish it had never occurred. If you know it was a mistake."

Mistake. "Are you saying that's what we were?" Why was her chest aching so much?

"I'm saying there is nothing to tell you about us. Have we made out before? Sure. You've got one sexy mouth, and I wanted a taste." A pause. "Not like you and I were hot and heavy. Not like we were planning a future and we were going to run away from everyone and everything else out there." Another of his mocking laughs. "I mean, really, do I look like the type of man who'd do that?"

No, he didn't. He looked like the type of man who didn't care about much at all. And he'd told her—over and over again—to leave. She needed to take her tattered pride and get out of there. "As I said before, I won't be bothering you again."

With slow steps, she headed for the driver's side. Her fingers pressed the button on her key fob, and the vehicle unlocked as the headlights flashed.

But before she could open the door, Ramsey beat her. He opened the door. Held it for her. Without a word—because there truly wasn't more to say, not after he'd basically told her they'd been a colossal mistake—Whitney slid into the car. Her hands curled around the steering wheel.

"Promise me that you won't come back here." A new note had entered his voice.

She didn't look his way. "Why would I possibly come back? Obviously, there is nothing for me here."

He didn't shut the door. Just lingered. Mixed messages much?

Whitney cranked her car. The engine growled.

"I'm damn glad you're alive." His words were low and ragged, and when she heard them—or, thought she heard them—her head automatically whipped toward him.

"Ramsey?" Had he really said—

"You don't belong here. Stay on your safe side of town from now on."

He slammed the door. Backed up.

Locking her jaw, she reversed and shot out of the lot. But she could not help glancing just once into her rearview mirror.

He was watching her leave.

***

He didn't move. Not until her taillights had vanished down the road. Ramsey stood absolutely rooted to the spot. He swore that he could still smell her sweet scent. Could feel her lush curves against him. Could taste her.

Kissing her had been a colossal mistake. He'd been weak, and he'd given in to the rough lust he felt for her. Whitney had always been able to break his control.

A dangerous thing.

But she wouldn't be back. There was no reason for her to come back. He'd played the bastard to the utmost level even though all he'd wanted to do was put his arms around her and hold her close. To never let go.

It wouldn't work. We wouldn't work.

He had a new enemy out there. A prick who thought he could move in on Ramsey's territory. In addition to that jerk, the Feds were still jonesing for him. Hell, the Feds were always after him.

Then there was the matter of Ramsey's not-so-long-lost brother being in town. Jinx was gonna be a major pain in the ass. He always was.

Ramsey had more than enough crap on his plate. He had—

All I want is her.

Jinx had told him to go after Whitney. To tell her the truth. But Jinx didn't get just how far down the rabbit hole Ramsey had truly gone. When your hands were as bloody as his were, you weren't supposed to put them on someone like Whitney.

I thought she was dead once. That nearly broke me. Needing Whitney so much made him weak. He couldn't be weak. Not now.

Gravel crunched as the bouncer edged closer. "Boss...you mad?"

"Mad isn't the right word, Jimmy."

"I just—you used to always want her inside. You gave orders that she was to be brought straight to you. You seemed kind of, you know, down the last few days, so I thought that you might want to—"

"Did you just tell me I seemed 'down'?" Jimmy had better be freaking kidding him. Ramsey spun on the bouncer and marched for him.

Jimmy did a fast and desperate retreat. "I, uh, I just thought she might make you happy—"

She did. "Whitney Augustine is not to be allowed in my place again." Each word was spoken through gritted teeth. *He said I looked freaking down.* Down? What was he, Eeyore? Sonofabitch. "If she shows up, you escort her back to her car and you make absolutely sure she leaves the premises. I don't want to see her again."

"Uh, yeah, yeah, okay."

"I don't want her near me."

"Sure, whatever you say, boss."

"I don't want her."

Dammit. I am such a liar.

Because he wanted her—wanted her so badly that he thought he might be close to losing his mind.

"And I'm not fucking down." He spun away and stormed back for his bar. "I'm a freaking ray of sunshine. Ask anyone."

CHAPTER THREE

Observation notes: Ramsey is disagreeable, arrogant, and can't be trusted. He also...

He gave me a rose today. It was random, and I just...

I love that stupid rose. And why am I including this in my notes? Irrelevant. Completely irrelevant.

***

"Closing time."

She glanced up at his voice. There was something about his voice. That low and rumbly voice that seemed to sink right into her core.

Ramsey stood at the edge of her table. "Time for you to leave."

Whitney didn't want to leave. She wanted to stay with him. That was becoming more and more of a problem. "I...I found a rose at my office."

"Did you?"

"I don't know how you're getting past the security there, but I do know the roses are coming from you."

"The security at your college is shit. It should be upgraded."

He hadn't denied giving her the rose. "Why?"

His brows climbed. "Because anyone who wanted could get inside. Because sometimes you work too late, and you need better protection than the security guard who looks like he's pushing ninety and can barely shuffle through the building."

Her breath caught. "That description was very specific."

"I'm a pretty specific kind of man."

He was a pretty interesting kind of man. "When I asked why, I wasn't talking about the security upgrade." Her gaze darted around the bar. Everyone else had left. She'd watched them all leave. She'd wanted to be alone with Ramsey. "I wanted to know why you were giving me roses like some kind of secret admirer." A pause. "Or secret stalker."

His lips curled. "Do you think I'm stalking you?"

No, if anything, she was stalking him. Did he know that? Did he know that she sometimes snuck off to tail him? Because surely, Ramsey wasn't as bad as the stories said. Before she'd met him, yes, she'd feared him. But the more she got to know him...

The more I want him.

"I'll take the silence for a yes." His hands were loose at his sides. "You don't have to worry." His voice had softened. "I would never do anything to hurt you."

She believed him.

"You're like a rose," he told her, surprising her with words that were sweet. Not his style. "Beautiful on the outside. Vibrant and so bright, a fucking light drawing me in."

Her breath had frozen in her lungs. And when he gave her a slow grin, she could have sworn her heart jumped right out of her chest.

"But you've got thorns, don't you, my Whitney?" He leaned toward her and put his palms on the top of the table. "Beautiful but strong, and if someone comes at you too hard, I think you just might cut them..."

She forced a laugh. "I'm hardly armed with a knife." *Or thorns*.

"Um. Force isn't the way to go with a rose. You don't just grab it. Don't hold it too hard. You do that, you'll crush the rose. Destroy the petals. And you'll bleed."

There was no way she could look away from his eyes.

"You have to be careful if you want to touch a rose. Go slowly. Carefully. Be more tender than you've ever been with anything in your life."

Holy crap. He was hot. His words were seducing her as he leaned forward and rumbled to her in that deep, sexy voice of his. She was craning up toward him, and all she wanted was his mouth on hers.

But if he kissed her, what would happen next?

Whitney couldn't wait to find out. Her lips parted, and she could practically taste him.

"Do you want my mouth?" he rasped.

Wasn't it obvious?

"If you do, then ask for it."

Fine. "Kiss me."

His lips brushed over hers. Careful. Tender.

Whitney wanted a lot more. "I'm not going to make you bleed," she whispered against his lips. "I won't hurt you." Her lashes lifted, and she stared into his gaze. "I want you."

His mouth came back toward hers again. He caught her lower lip with his teeth. Tugged. Then his tongue thrust inside, and desire exploded within her as—

***

Whitney jerked upright in bed. Her breath panted in and out, and she put her hand over her racing heart. For a moment, she was lost as she stared into the darkness around her.

The dream was fading. Only bits and pieces remained. But she wasn't convinced it *had* been a dream. She thought it might have been a memory.

Sensory memories.

Her therapist had told her those might be coming. Of course, she'd already known about sensory memories. Memories that could come from the five senses. Like when you smelled something and then that scent got associated with an event. Or a particular sound could stir a memory of a place. Or a person.

She could remember kissing Ramsey. When she'd kissed him that night, had it triggered something in her mind? Triggered the flashes she'd had while she slept?

Because for a while there, everything had seemed so real. She struggled to hold on to the pieces. To pull them back to her.

Roses.

Whitney shoved aside the cover. Jumped out of bed. Her bare feet flew across the hardwood floor as she bounded into her kitchen. She hit the lights.

A red rose waited in a vase on her kitchen table. A single red rose. She'd found the rose on her doorstep the previous day.

Had Ramsey left that rose for her? If so, why had he turned her away when she'd been at his bar? What game was he playing?

***

The kitchen light had just flashed on in Whitney's house. Ramsey's eyes narrowed as he stared at that light. It was close to four a.m.

Why was she awake? He knew why the hell he was awake. When she'd first disappeared, he hadn't been able to sleep at all.

At first, he'd thought that she'd just left him. Changed her mind about them.

Then...then the truth had come out.

Whitney Augustine had been the presumed victim of a serial killer. *His* Whitney had been taken. When he should have been protecting her.

Eventually, a confession had come. A confession about her murder. Her body had been dumped in the Gulf. And all he'd wanted to do was rip apart anyone and everyone who'd ever hurt her—

I hurt her. I let her down. I pulled her into my world.

When he'd learned that she was alive, that she'd survived—because his Whitney was such a fucking amazing fighter—

He stopped the thought. *She's not mine.* He had to stop thinking of her that way. He had to—

Movement caught his eye. Someone was sneaking toward her house. A shadow creeping carefully forward.

Fury pumped through his body. Some asshole intended to break into Whitney's place? Oh, hell, no. Without making a sound, Ramsey left his spot beneath the heavy branches of a nearby tree and rushed toward that figure. The jerk dropped something on her porch and spun to bound away. He wasn't even looking where he was going.

So Ramsey just lifted one arm, and he let the creep plow straight into it. The guy was rushing so fast and hard that when he hit Ramsey's arm, he immediately flew backward and slammed down onto the sidewalk.

He also screamed.

Ramsey bent and grabbed him by the shirtfront. "Hey, asshole. What the hell did you think you were doing?"

The front porch light turned on, almost blinding in its brightness. The pad of footsteps rushed across the porch. "What is happening out here?" Whitney's shocked voice.

She'd actually just run outside? Run straight to danger? "Get in the house," Ramsey snarled.

"Help me, lady!" The guy on the ground twisted and heaved beneath Ramsey's hold. He didn't get free, though. No way would he get free. "This psycho just attacked me!"

Ramsey studied the man in his grasp. Early twenties. Thinning hair. A stupid, bright shirt with a big, red bird on the front. "You tried to break into her house."

Whitney gasped.

She still hadn't gone inside. "In the house," he ordered.

"No, thank you," Whitney snapped back as she came even closer. "I'm calling the cops!"

"Yes!" From the man on the ground. "Please, do it! He attacked me! I was just doing my job and he—"

"*What job?*" Ramsey demanded.

"D-delivering the flower. Just like last time. I was—"

Ramsey hauled the jerk to his feet. "Who the hell delivers flowers at this time of night?"

"Uh, I do?" Fearful. "Guy said it was a surprise. W-wanted them here for his lady when she went to work first thing. Was just easier for me to stop after my shift, so I brought the rose now and—"

"There's a rose on my mat," Whitney said.

Finally, Ramsey's head whipped toward her. Mostly because the woman just would not listen to reason and go inside like she was supposed to do so she could be *safe*. And when he saw her...

Legs for days. Long, perfect legs.

Whitney was clad in a loose, silky robe. The robe stopped at her thighs and showed off her gorgeous legs and her bare feet. One of her hands clutched a phone.

From what he could tell, she hadn't made a call yet. Not that he needed the cops to handle this prick. But first... "*Clothes.*"

Her brow furrowed.

"Could you put on clothes?" he managed to grit out.

"I have on a gown *and* I'm wearing a robe. Those are clothes. Focus on the important matter, would you?" Whitney snapped right back at him. "In case you don't know what that matter is...it would be the man you're currently holding captive."

Like he'd forgotten the SOB. Ramsey turned his focus back on his prey. "You were hired to deliver a rose."

"Y-yes. So please, pretty, pretty please, let me go?" His glasses were slipping off his nose. "*Please?*"

"Who hired you?"

"I, um, I don't know."

Ramsey growled. "Not good enough—"

"OhmyGod. You're going to punch me, aren't you? You're about to break my nose. Or my jaw. Or all of me." He was shaking. "Please, God, don't." His head bobbed toward Whitney. "Talk your boyfriend down, lady! I'm begging you! I swear, I didn't know that you were involved with someone. I took the job off the freelance site. It was a delivery job. Paid one hundred bucks for the delivery of just one rose. That deal was too sweet to pass up." His chin sagged down. "I *knew* it was too good to be real. Should have realized she'd have a jealous lunatic of a boyfriend who would want to wreck my face because that is just the luck that I have—"

"*Stop rambling*," Ramsey blasted.

"I can't! You're scaring me and when I get scared, I talk a lot! Oh, God, please, can we just call the cops? I don't think they'll let you hurt me."

Whitney's steps shuffled closer. "Let him go, Ramsey."

The hell he would—

"He's a delivery person. I'm sure he'll tell us everything that he knows if you just stop terrifying him."

"I like terrifying people." His flat reply. "It's half the joy I get out of life."

The man whimpered.

"Ramsey..." Whitney sighed.

Fine. He let the bastard go. "Tell me your name."

"R-Ronald Rudolph. But my friends call me Rudy—"

"Are you shitting me?" Ramsey's hands went to his hips. "Does it look like we are friends?"

Rudy shoved his glasses back up his nose. "No." Low. Miserable. Rudy rubbed his chest. "I think you bruised me."

"You're lucky I didn't do more than that. You were sneaking onto her porch in the dead of the night. Like that shit doesn't look seriously shady?"

"And he's done it before," Whitney added.

Ramsey's shoulders stiffened. "Are you kidding me?"

"Just once!" Rudy rushed to say. "I was hired to do it last night, and then now and—"

"Give me your driver's license," Ramsey cut through the man's words.

Shaking, nearly dropping the ID four times, Rudy handed Ramsey the license. Because Whitney's porch light was so bright, he had no trouble reading the info on the license—or instantly memorizing everything there. Grunting, he handed the license back to Rudy. "I know where you live now."

"Oh, God."

"You're going to tell me everything you know. I'm going to check out your story. And if I find out that you told me so much as one small, white lie, I will come to your house, and I will make you sorry."

***

Ramsey strode into her house and slammed the door shut behind him. He'd grilled Rudy for a good half hour before letting Rudy go, and she knew Ramsey had watched every single moment until the other man had vanished in the ride he'd parked down the road.

"Where is the other rose?" Ramsey demanded. "He said he delivered one last night."

"It's in the kitchen."

Without another word, he turned to the right, slid down the little hallway, then took a left into her kitchen. Whitney sucked in deep breath and followed him. "Well, that answers one question."

He was glaring at the rose in the vase. But at her words, he looked up. "What question?"

She wrapped her arms around her waist. "The 'have you been here before' question. Because you're walking around my place like you own it."

His stare snapped back down to the rose. "Why'd you put it in a vase?"

"Because it was a pretty flower that I found outside, and I just—" Her lips pressed together. "It felt familiar." Another sensory memory? "Finding a rose. Pulling out the vase. Putting it in water. It all just felt familiar, so that's what I did." She licked her lower lip. "I had actually thought...just a little while ago...that you were the one who might have left it for me." She'd had that thought before the whole scene with the ever-so-nervous Rudy.

"Me?" His brows climbed. "Why the hell would you think I left it?"

"Because you used to do that...didn't you?"

His low laughter filled the room. "Sure. Because I'm the type to wine and dine a woman with roses. Just call me Mr. Romantic."

Anger flashed through her. Whitney marched across the room. Marched right up to him. "Stop it."

"Excuse me?"

"Stop pretending. Drop the bastard image. I had a dream about you tonight—"

His grin was absolutely sexual. "Dreaming about me, huh? What were we doing and where were we doing it?"

She was grinding her back teeth. "It would all be easier if you just told me the truth."

"Fair enough. Here's truth. I didn't hire that prick Rudy. I haven't left roses for you last night or tonight. Looks like you have another admirer out there." His darkening expression indicated he wasn't pleased about that fact.

Neither was she. In fact, goosebumps rose on her arms.

"Don't worry," he promised, all confident. "I'll find him. He won't be leaving you any other unwanted gifts."

The unease settled around her shoulders like a heavy weight. "Why would a stranger send me flowers?"

"Someone could have seen your story on the news. You're a beautiful woman." Said simply. As if it was the most basic truth in the world to him. "People get hooked on things they see. Maybe some guy thought he'd be able to get in your life. So he hired that prick for the deliveries."

She thought about what Rudy had told them regarding his employer. "He did everything online. Sent the money through a secure app. There was no person-to-person contact." A shiver slid over her. "That doesn't seem right."

"Just because he's online, it doesn't mean he can hide. I've got contacts who can help me. I'll find him. Let him know that his *gifts* aren't appreciated. That, in fact, they scare you and if he does it again—"

"You're trying to protect me." Her hand lifted to press to his chest. "Seems an odd thing for you to do."

He looked down at her hand. "Shouldn't you be asking why the hell I was even outside of your house in the first place?"

Okay. She could do that. "Why the hell were you even outside of my house in the first place?"

His lips twitched.

"That's not an answer."

"I was on my way home. Just driving by on my motorcycle. I always come this way."

"No. Try again. You don't always drive through a cul-de-sac on your way home."

He was still looking at her hand. "I was...concerned that you were too upset when you left. Just wanted to make sure you'd gotten in safely for the night. I looped around your cul-de-sac. Saw the man on your porch and figured it would be a good idea to find out what the hell he was doing."

If he hadn't stopped, she wouldn't have ever seen Rudy. "Thank you."

His eyes lifted. "You won't be hurt again." Gruff. "I'll make sure of it. Because maybe it's just some guy who saw you and lost his heart, but it could just as easily be some freak with an obsession. I'll find out what's going on. I'll make sure it stops."

The last thing she wanted was more danger in her life.

It was odd, but standing right before him, Whitney felt safer than she'd felt since she came home from the hospital.

"Do me a favor?" he murmured.

She nodded.

"How about you don't run outside—in your robe, without a weapon—when you hear people fighting?"

"I ran outside because I heard *you*."

His incredibly thick lashes flickered. "You shouldn't run to me."

"Then why do I feel like I should?" This was what drove her crazy. "Why do I feel like everything about you is pulling me closer, even as you *tell* me to stay away?" Which hurt. Gutted. Messed with her head. "Why did I feel like I had to go to your bar? Like I had to kiss you? Why do I dream about you when I don't dream about anything else but water that drags me under and floods my mouth?" Tears pricked at her eyes. "I usually wake up choking as I try to breathe, but right after I saw you, I woke up and I was almost crying out your name. Why—"

His mouth crashed onto hers.

CHAPTER FOUR

Observation notes: I know the bar is dangerous. I know Ramsey is dangerous. I know he's bad. Except, I'm not sure he's bad...for me.

***

He was making a mistake. Ramsey knew it. He should not have his hands on Whitney. He should not be kissing her. Should not have his lips pressed so hard to hers and should not be thrusting his tongue inside to taste every single bit of sweetness that she had. He should not be thinking about lifting her up onto the kitchen table. Spreading her thighs. Putting his mouth on her hot core and licking her until she screamed his name.

He shouldn't...

But he was.

The pain in her voice had broken something in him. Hell, he was already more than broken enough as it was. But when she'd talked about clawing through the water, choking on the water...

That shit happened to her. She'd had to face that terror alone.

His mouth was too hard on hers. His hand was under her chin as he tipped back her head and took and took and took—

Her fingers pressed to his chest. She gave that little moan that drove him absolutely wild, and his whole body shuddered.

This isn't putting space between you. This isn't staying the hell away from her.

This is you...doing what you always do. Taking what you want.

And he wanted nothing—no one—more than he wanted her.

Her mouth pulled from his. Her breath gave a little heave. "You are the king of mixed messages, you understand that, don't you?" Her voice had gone all husky and sensual. It was the way she sounded when he had her in bed. When he'd driven her to be just as crazy and hungry as he was.

Ramsey locked his jaw. "I want you."

"Yes, I can, ah, feel that."

She would be referring to the giant cock shoving toward her. Check. His gaze sharpened on her face. "I never denied wanting you." It would be impossible to deny that basic truth. "You're gorgeous. I'm sure most men you meet want to fuck you."

Her brows rose. "I...don't think that's the case."

"Then they're morons."

"Again, I don't think—" She broke off as she delicately cleared her throat.

"If you want me to be honest, I wanted you from the first moment I saw you," Ramsey told her flatly. Her hand was still on his chest and seemed to burn through his t-shirt.

Her green gaze held his. "And when was that?"

"When you came into my bar, saying you wanted to do some research." The memory was so sharp and vivid, mostly because it had haunted him too many nights. "Knew from the first look that you didn't belong there." *That you didn't belong with me.* "But you insisted. Even offered me a bargain."

Now her lashes flickered. "What sort of bargain?"

He couldn't stop the quick smile that spread across his face. "Well, first you offered me eighty dollars." He hadn't thought she was serious.

She had been.

She'd also been intriguing as hell.

He was used to people lying to him. Trying to deceive him. Threats were everywhere he turned.

Whitney had seemed too good to be true. An angel, cast down in his hell. He'd wanted to get his hands all over every inch of her delectable body. Eventually, he had.

"I'm guessing you didn't take the money."

"Can't say I needed it." What he needed was her mouth beneath his again.

"Then why did you let me stay?"

"Because I wanted to fuck you."

Her eyes flared wide. "Is that...no. There is no way I would make a bargain that involved me sleeping with you in exchange for you letting me stay in your bar."

"You wanted to observe the people who came into my place. In case you missed it, they aren't exactly the sort that like to be watched. You were so determined to do your big experiment or field research or whatever you wanted to call it..." He paused. "Are you so sure you wouldn't have agreed to any terms I offered you?"

She swallowed. "I didn't sleep with you as part of a deal."

"No? But you don't remember..."

"And you're trying to make me mad at you again. Is this some kind of self-sabotage thing? One step forward, and three steps back."

"You're shrinking me." Ramsey had to shake his head. "You used to do that to me all the time when..." *Shit. Stop talking.*

But a little furrow had appeared between her eyes. "Were we *friends*?"

Now he laughed. "I don't have friends."

"I could swear, the way you just acted..."

Was kissing her like a madman a sign they were friends? He didn't think so. "Like I told you already, I wanted you from the first moment I saw you. A normal reaction, no big deal. I still want you. So kissing you when you're wearing a sexy robe and standing in front of me shouldn't be anything unexpected." He took a step back from her. His gaze darted down, and he saw that her tight nipples were thrusting against the silky fabric of her robe. "But what *you* might want to consider, with your ever so impressive psychology background, is why *you* are so hot for the bad guy?"

"Because I don't think you're bad." An immediate response.

One that he hadn't expected.

And, judging by the sudden parting of her lips and widening of her eyes, it was a response she hadn't expected to give, too.

Ramsey pulled in a deep breath. "You'd be wrong on that score. You don't remember..." His hand lifted and his knuckles slid over her cheek. "But I am very, very bad. I've done things that would give you nightmares."

"I already have plenty of nightmares."

Yes, she did. "And that's why you don't need me." Another light brush of his knuckles over her cheek before his hand fell away. He had to get out of there. If he stayed longer...

I will put my mouth on her again. My hands. I'll have her on the kitchen table and get her screaming my name as she comes over and over.

Ramsey turned away.

"You don't know what I need." Her low, angry words stopped him.

His shoulders stiffened.

"You don't know because you haven't been in my life since I came back. I vanished, and it seemed like *I* was forgotten."

The hell you were. His hands clenched into fists as he faced her once more.

"No, correction, let me amend that statement. My friend Maisey hunted for me. Everyone else just seemed to think that I'd left town."

I thought you'd left me. That you had gotten tired of the danger and the crime, and you'd run from me.

"She hired a PI to figure out what had happened to me. Maisey didn't give up. But there was no one else. No devoted boyfriend who rushed out to find me. Even my own sister just closed down my house and started making arrangements to sell everything I owned."

Each brittle world felt like a knife stabbing into him—and he should know. Ramsey had gotten plenty of knife wounds over the years.

"Then when I came back, I thought...I don't know. That *someone* would be there. It's like I've had a hole in my chest because something—someone—was missing. And if someone was missing for me, then I had to be missing for someone else, right?" She heaved out a frustrated breath. "Am I even making any sense?"

She was making plenty of sense. And yes, he understood having a hole in his chest. His heart had been carved out when she'd first gone missing. "Why don't you just think of this as a do-over for you?" His words rasped out. "Whatever you had before, whoever you had, maybe it just wasn't worth remembering."

"I *have* to remember! You don't know what's at stake."

He did know. Her life was at stake. Too many people had realized she was a weakness for him. And those dangerous people wanted to use his weakness against him. Until Ramsey eliminated those threats, he couldn't afford to feel this pull for her. "I shouldn't be here." Truth.

But she took a step back, as if his words had hurt her.

Dammit. He didn't *want* to hurt her.

He'd tried to be careful when he drove to her place. Ramsey had checked for tails and hadn't seen any, but even he could make mistakes. "I won't be back." At least not until he'd taken care of the threats.

Wait. Shit...am I planning to claim her again? He knew that was wrong. He knew she would be a hundred times better off without him.

Her chin lifted. "I don't want you back. Go. I can handle things just fine on my own. In case you missed it, *I* survived. I'm the one who stayed alive in the water until I could flag down fishermen. I'm the one who didn't let that water take me. I can handle anything that comes my way. I am more than enough."

"I don't need to be told that. You've always been the strongest person I ever met." His stare swept over her because he just had to drink her in. To have this memory to get him through the hell that would come. "How about you don't take flowers from strangers for a while?"

"How about you stick to being the big, bad, crime boss and you don't worry about me?"

"Worrying about you is what I do. A habit that I don't think I can ever break." His nostrils flared. "Lock up behind me."

"No, I'm going to leave my front door unlocked *and* open. That way, any would-be thieves or stalkers in the neighborhood can just sweep right inside."

He loved her bite. "You're even sexier when you're a smartass."

"And you're a secretive, controlling, apparently *nightmare*-inducing bad guy who likes to give mixed signals."

She was so beautiful. "Good-bye, Whitney."

He left. And it *hurt*. Because he wanted to stay with her so badly.

***

Trouble for Hire Private Investigations. Whitney took some nice, calming breaths and hoped they would help to slow her racing heart. They didn't.

And she could not afford this level of stress. It wasn't good. The doctor had told her to eliminate as much stress from her life as possible. Then what had she done?

Gone to Ramsey.

That had turned out to be a colossal mistake.

This time, she was going to the professionals. The PIs at Trouble for Hire would help her. She hoped.

When Whitney had been missing, her friend Maisey had gone to Trouble for Hire. Maisey had hired Odin Shaw. She'd also fallen in love with Odin, but that was a whole other story...

Whitney sat in the chair in front of Odin with her back perfectly straight as she tried to do her breathing exercises. *So not helping*. Her palms were all sweaty as she sat there with her bag near her feet.

More than a few moments had passed. She knew that. Whitney also knew that she should speak. The whole thing was just so awkward...

Odin—a giant of a man with blond hair and fierce features—cleared his throat. "Is there anything in particular I can do for you?"

The silence must have gotten to him, too. "Yes." The word came out like a hiss.

He waited. Waited some more. His fingers drummed on the desktop.

She should say more. Whitney scrambled. "Maisey said you were the best." She remembered her friend. They'd been tight for ages. Of course, Whitney didn't remember anything she and Maisey might have done in the missing six months but...

"Did you tell Maisey you were coming to see me today?"

Miserably, Whitney shook her head. She'd really wanted to solve this problem without giving all the details to Maisey. Whitney had quizzed her friend to try and learn what she needed, but it hadn't worked.

"Why not?"

"It's...private." Because after the careful questions she'd put to Maisey, Whitney had realized that Maisey couldn't help her. Maisey simply didn't have the information that Whitney needed.

"Well, we *are* a private investigation firm."

Obviously, she knew that. Why else would she be—oh. Right. He'd been making a joke. She'd said the business was private and he'd followed up with his line. Maybe she was supposed to laugh?

Only Whitney very much didn't feel like laughing. There had been nothing at all in her life to laugh about for a while.

"I can't help you if I don't know the problem." His brows lowered over his piercing eyes.

Without thinking about it, one of her hands moved over her stomach.

And those piercing eyes of Odin's widened. "Whitney?"

Just say it. "I'm pregnant."

Oh, hell. Oh, damn. This was a mistake. The minute the words left her mouth, she knew she should have stayed quiet. If she kept working at it, Whitney was sure she could figure things out on her own. She jumped to her feet and whirled for the door.

"Stop!"

Her feet seemed to glue to the floor.

"Whitney, let me help you."

Those words sounded wonderful. Tears pricked her eyes. She was crying over nearly everything these days! Slowly, Whitney turned back toward Odin. "It's a miracle." She knew that. Was grateful for her gift. "After what happened to me...the baby was safe all that time. The doctor said that's what the body does. It protects the baby. A perfect design." They'd done tests. So many tests. When she'd gone into the water, the doctors believed that her baby had only been a few days old. He'd told her some technical stuff about when the egg had been fertilized. Measurements could be taken of a fetus during the ultrasound process so he'd narrowed it down as best he could.

When I went in the water, I wouldn't have known I was pregnant. It had actually been several weeks later before she'd learned the truth.

And...

She'd been scared. But also, elated. *I'm not alone.*

When she'd been taken ashore by the kind fishermen, exams had been performed on her. There had been no signs of sexual assault, and when she'd found out that her pregnancy had occurred *before* she went into the water...

I knew someone had to be waiting for me. Someone back in my real life.

"Then I came back here, and I thought—surely the father will make an appearance. He *has* to be someone in my life. Someone I-I knew, but the attack made me forget him."

Odin was still sitting behind the desk and looking pretty stunned.

"But no one showed up." Her voice lowered. "No man came to tell me that we were involved or that—that we..." Whitney crept closer. *For a bit, when I found my observation notes, I wondered if maybe...* "It could have been a one-night stand."

"I don't think so," he said quickly.

His words gave her pause. "Um, why do you say that?" When he'd been working her case before, had he turned up a list of men she'd been involved with? Whitney hoped so—that was the main reason she'd come to Trouble for Hire. When he'd been hired by Maisey, Odin's job had been to dig into her life, so maybe he'd created a nice file on her personal relationships. A file that he could slide her way so she could figure things out. Time to woman up and cut to the chase. "Look, that's why I'm here, okay? Because I'm pregnant and I can't remember who the father of this child is. This child that is so tiny and precious inside of me and...I just—can you help me?" She was close to begging. So what? She'd do anything for this baby. "Can you help me to figure out what was happening to me during that period of my life that I forgot? Help me to find the man I forgot?" Whitney held her breath.

"I can do better than that."

He could? Great. Wonderful.

"I'm taking the case. Pro bono."

That wasn't necessary. She could easily cover the costs for the case. "But, no, I will pay—"

"I'm taking the case," he told her grimly. "And I think I may know the father."

"Already? How?" But—she knew. It must be in her case files—

"You might want to take a seat."

Oh, no. "That doesn't sound good."

He motioned toward the chair she'd used before. "Please, why don't you sit down again?"

She fell into the chair. "I-I had a crazy hunch about who the father might be." It felt like she was rambling. Probably because she was. "I found some old notes I'd made when I was doing some field research, and I went to, ah, see a certain individual. But that turned out to be a dead end."

Actually, she didn't know if she and Ramsey had been together or not. She'd asked. Over and over. He'd lied.

Not exactly reassuring.

"You know I looked into your life before."

A nod. *That's why I came to you.*

"I can tell you—right now—that I know the identity of one man you were seeing before your disappearance." He raised his right hand. "However, I'm not saying he is the father of your child. Are you sure that the baby..." His face darkened. "Have you talked to the police and—"

"I was not raped. I was pregnant before my attack, my doctor said it would have just been too early for me to know." She'd also talked to the cops, yes, and they'd grilled the individuals who had been guilty in her attempted murder about every aspect of the case.

"I can't say for certain you were only involved with this individual. He was the one who appeared to play most prominently in your life during that time but..."

"The people at my office thought I wasn't involved with anyone." She'd done careful questioning there.

"You kept your relationship secret."

"Why?"

"Because...he's a complicated man. And a bit of a dick," he muttered darkly.

She leaned forward. "Excuse me? I didn't hear that last part." She didn't *think* she'd heard him correctly.

He let out a rough exhale. "Does the name Ramsey Hyde mean anything to you?"

A fist squeezed her heart. "I am aware of him, yes."

Odin winced. "You've probably heard the stories that circulate about him."

"You mean the ones that say he's a criminal mastermind who is under investigation by the FBI?"

"Uh, huh. Those stories."

"I've read them." Her lips pressed together.

"You were doing some research at his place before your disappearance. My understanding is that you and Ramsey grew...close during that time."

Ramsey's voice blasted through her head. *We fucked dozens of times. Maybe even a hundred times. I wasn't exactly counting.*

"Whitney? Are you okay? You look a little flushed."

I had you in so many places. Once I fucked you on the bar top outside. On the pool table. I've had you in this room.

"Do you want me to get you a glass of water?"

"No." She swallowed twice. "I'm fine." She was not. Ramsey hadn't been playing a mind game with her. He'd been telling her the truth. Maybe. "Your investigation showed that Ramsey and I were intimately involved?"

"The two of you were planning to run away together."

"*What?*" It was a good thing that she was sitting down. Otherwise, she probably would have fallen. "That's wrong. Your information is incorrect." She was speaking too quickly. "Maybe we—we hooked up. I could see that happening. He's sexy in a dark and brooding kind of way—"

"You don't usually hook up with men like him."

"But I sincerely doubt we were going to run away together and—" She stopped. "What did you say?"

The faint lines near his mouth deepened. "When you were missing, Maisey talked about you a lot. You're her best friend. You know she loves you."

And Whitney loved her.

"She said you had rules about the men you dated. You research criminals, but you only date safe men. The upstanding good guys are your type."

That did not describe Ramsey.

"So maybe there *was* someone else. Maybe there is some safe guy who was in your life, and I will consider that option. I'll get started digging, and we'll just say that Ramsey is—"

"I spoke with Ramsey recently." She should probably try the breathing routine again. Deep breaths. Shallow breaths. Ah, screw it. "He made it clear there was certainly nothing permanent between us. I find it hard to believe that we were running away together."

"Ramsey is a very good liar."

Why did those words make her flinch? "I need to know if there was any lover other than Ramsey. You just said there could have been someone else. We should find out for certain." *Ramsey. Ramsey.*

Odin opened his mouth to speak, then stopped.

"What?" Whitney nearly jumped toward him.

"From what I know about him, Ramsey isn't exactly the type to share...not anything. If you were involved with him as deeply as I suspect, he would have been possessive as hell."

"Okay. Then that proves you're wrong. Excellent." *Ramsey.* She sniffed. "If he was 'possessive as hell' as you put it, then wouldn't he already be back in my life?"

But he was outside my house last night...

No, no. *No.* "Wouldn't he have rushed to my side?"

He did rush to the hospital in town. The first day I came back, he rushed in...only to leave moments later.

Whitney cleared her throat. "Wouldn't he be staying with me?"

Silence. She was realizing that Odin was a man who liked a lot of silence. Or maybe he just didn't have a good answer for her last question. Or any of her questions.

"Ramsey is a complicated man." His response came very slowly. "And his life is complicated."

"Yes, well, so is mine. Super complicated."

"I'll talk to him."

"And you think he's just going to open up and tell you all the private details that went on between the two of us? Hate to burst your bubble, but I went to him and tried to find out. He wasn't the sharing sort and—" Hell, she'd basically just backed up what Odin had told her moments ago, and she could see the truth of that in his eyes. "What I mean was...he wasn't very forthcoming," Whitney carefully corrected.

"Uh, huh."

"He *wasn't*. And I doubt he's just going to be a big sharer with you."

Odin tapped his chin. "Maybe not with me, but we do have another PI here at Trouble for Hire who can get the truth from him, if you don't mind me passing along this case. Be assured that I will still work it, too, but I think Jinx's unique relationship with Ramsey may help us get to the truth faster."

She knew Jinx. Big, muscled, and with a devilish grin, their paths had crossed a few times lately. "Just what sort of relationship does he have with Ramsey?"

Once more, Odin started to speak. His lips parted, but no sound emerged.

She tapped her right foot against the floor. Waited. Waited—

"Complicated," Odin finally announced.

Her eyes narrowed. Odin must love that word.

"Sorry. That's a shit answer, isn't it?"

It was. "Everything is complicated these days."

He rose and strode around the desk toward her. Odin towered over her with his expression all earnest and concerned. "You are Maisey's best friend."

A nod.

"You matter to her, so that means you matter to me. I want to help you. Trust me to do this. Trust me and trust Jinx. We'll find out the truth for you."

It wasn't like she had much choice.

Odin's hand closed over her shoulder. "Everything is going to be all right."

Dammit. Stupid tears filled her eyes again. She didn't contradict him, but Whitney knew Odin was wrong. Nothing had been *all right* in her life for a very, very long time.

***

Damn. Damn. Damn. Whitney had left his office. Odin had felt the woman's pain battering at him, and if there was one thing in this world he just could not stand, it was a woman hurting.

He pulled out his phone. She'd given him the okay to bring in Jinx on this case, and he could definitely use the other man's, ah, special touch.

Jinx picked up on the second ring.

"Personal day, man!" Jinx seemed abnormally happy. Sure, the guy was *usually* happy, but this was a whole other level of joy. "I am taking a personal day and living my best life with my lady—"

"Whitney Augustine was just here," Odin cut in before Jinx could tell him more about that best life he was living.

"Yeah, yeah, I know you had a visit with her planned." Not overly interested. "Even told Ramsey about it when he—"

Yes, he would have mentioned the appointment to Ramsey...since Jinx was Ramsey's *brother*. "She's pregnant."

"*What?*"

He winced and had to pull the phone away from his ear. Who would have known that Jinx could make his voice get that high? When the ringing in his ear subsided, Odin brought the phone back and bluntly asked, "Is the baby your brother's? Because she wants us to find the father. The woman has no memory of that time or who she was involved with, and she just hired *us* to solve the mystery for her." He didn't mention he'd insisted on doing the case pro bono. No point. He knew Jinx would have wanted the same thing.

"Oh, damn." Now Jinx sounded shaken. "Ramsey will lose his mind."

Yep, that was Odin's thought. "Guess who gets to break the news to him?"

"What? Aw, man. Come on. Did you miss the part where I was having my *best* life?"

"I heard it and good for you."

"Thanks, I appreciate that. I—"

"But we both know you are one of the few people who can get an immediate audience with Ramsey."

"Uh, he keeps kicking me *out* of his life."

"You're his brother. He'll see you. And when you deliver the news about Whitney, he won't shoot the messenger because the messenger will be *you*."

"Don't be too sure of that," Jinx muttered. "He's more likely to shoot because it *is* me."

"If the baby is his, that will make the kid your niece or nephew."

Silence. Then... "Well, that's just fucking sweet. You know I will be an amazing uncle. I will let the kid get away with so much shit. I'll be her favorite person. She will love me more than she loves anyone else and will want to spend all of her time with her Uncle Jinxy."

His temples were throbbing. "It may not be Ramsey's baby. If it's not..."

"Yeah, I don't think you quite get just how obsessed the man was with her. Even when we were kids, the guy would beat the ass of anyone who tried to take his toys."

"Don't think Whitney is a toy."

"Of course, not, but you see where I'm going."

Not really.

"I'd bet on the child being his," Jinx added confidently.

"We need more than a bet. We need certainty. There are tests that can be done. We'll get proof. *After* you break the news to him."

"Right." A sigh. "Once more, I'm telling you, he will lose his mind."

"Yeah, well, good luck with that."

CHAPTER FIVE

Observation notes: They're afraid of him. Even the people with the worst reputations and worst records tend to steer clear of Ramsey. When he's at the bar, no one approaches him. They're too wary.

He's alone, unless he's with me.

***

"You have a death wish." Ramsey stared down at the drink in his glass and didn't look at the man who'd just taken a seat next to him. "Obviously. Because we have been over the fact that you are supposed to stay out of my bar. Over it again and again."

"It is wonderful to see you, too. I'm doing well. Thanks for asking. My lovely Ali is doing well, too. And, again, when the wedding comes, we plan on you being there."

Ramsey finally turned his head toward Jinx. The brother he kept *trying* to protect. He'd told Jinx it was too dangerous to be in his world. Ramsey had told the guy that he wasn't the person Jinx remembered.

Once upon a time, it had been the two of them against the world. They'd been thrown in the foster care system. They'd had no one else.

And then...

Then he'd overheard their case worker talking. Saying some shit about how he had trouble connecting with people. That he was exhibiting oppositional defiant disorder and that he was scaring away potential foster families.

Hell, yes, he'd been defiant. He'd been a pissed-off teenager who had no control over his life. He'd been watching as strangers were paraded in front of him. People who looked at him and had fear flashing in their eyes.

But...

Those people hadn't looked at Jinx the same way. Jinx with his quick grin and twinkling blue eyes. Jinx with his ready jokes and easy attitude. Those people had liked Jinx. They'd wanted to offer him a home.

But they hadn't wanted to bring Jinx's screwed-up, younger brother along for the ride.

Ramsey had known that Jinx would never choose to leave him. Instead, Jinx would have given up opportunity after opportunity for Ramsey.

So...Ramsey had made the decision for him. He'd left Jinx.

And this is the life I made.

"Earth to Ram." Jinx waved his hand in front of Ramsey's eyes. "Can you zone back in? Because I have some pretty big news that I want to share with you."

"You already told me you were getting married. What's bigger than that?" he growled.

"Well..." Jinx pursed his lips.

Ramsey rolled his eyes. "Just spit it out already."

"I think it would be better if we discussed this privately. I had actually hoped fewer people would be here since it's fairly early in the evening, but I guess folks just can't stay away from your place."

"What can I say. It's popular."

Jinx hadn't taken a seat, and his body seemed oddly tense. "It would really be better if we took this conversation into your office." His eyebrows rose. "I am assuming you have one of those around here, yes? Some nice, soundproof room where we can have a quick chat that might just change your whole life."

A muscle jerked along Ramsey's jaw. Jinx damn well knew he had such a place. "I'm not in the mood to be jerked around."

"Excellent." Jinx's hand snaked out, and he snagged Ramsey's drink. In a flash, he'd downed it. "Because I am not here for that particular activity."

The SOB had taken his drink.

"Rather important," Jinx said. "Time's ticking."

Fine. What-the-hell-ever. Ramsey glanced across the bar. "Jag, keep an eye on the place, got me?"

His first in command nodded. Jag didn't say a word. He didn't, usually. He kept quiet and did what he was told, and he eliminated any problems that appeared at the bar. He and Ramsey had been together seemingly forever. When Ramsey had first taken to the streets, he'd found Jag getting his ass kicked.

He'd intervened. Kicked the asses of the three guys who'd been jumping Jag, and he'd had the man at his side—in one form or another—ever since. *Gang member, friend, bar manager, trouble eliminator.* Jag had worn many different hats over the years.

Ramsey turned on his heel and made his way to the back. Yes, there was a sound-proof room back there, and after a recent visit from the FBI, he'd even had some extra tech and hardware brought in to make the place even more secure. The bar patrons got out of his way as Ramsey led Jinx through the crowd. And in moments, they were alone.

The band's music had vanished. The murmur of voices had disappeared.

Ramsey crossed his arms over his chest and propped his shoulder against the wall. "Talk."

"This is kind of awkward."

Ramsey lifted a brow.

"I am trying to decide if I should be tactful and build up to the news or if I should just drop it like the bomb that it is." His fingers spread out in the air. "Boom."

"You've never been tactful."

Jinx's shoulders straightened. His bright blue eyes glittered. Jinx had their mom's eyes. Ramsey had their dad's. *And I hope that's the only thing I got from the bastard.* Hoped, but he knew he was wrong.

"First, I am *always* tactful. I'm tactful and charming and super likable. Ask anyone."

"*Jinx.*" A note of anger hummed in his voice. "You don't have to do your fun routine. This is me. Just say whatever the hell it is and be done." Because he was starting to get mildly worried. He could have sworn that Jinx actually seemed nervous, and that was odd. Jinx was rarely nervous about anything.

"Right." Jinx blew out a breath. "It's just...this is big."

"Spit it out already—"

"Whitney is pregnant."

Ramsey blinked. Shook his head. There was no way he'd heard correctly. "Say that again."

"Whitney. Is. Pregnant." Spoken very slowly and clearly.

Ramsey surged away from the wall. Caught himself right before he grabbed Jinx. His hands fisted. "Who is the lucky sonofabitch?" *Who touched my Whitney? What lucky fucking bastard gets to have the life that I always dreamed of having? Who—*

"So...that's the interesting part. She doesn't know."

Ramsey's eyes narrowed. His heart was racing so fast his whole body seemed to shake.

"Remember how she can't remember the six months before her attack? Well, since she can't remember, then Whitney doesn't know who the proud papa is."

Now he did grab his brother. Ramsey clenched his hands in Jinx's shirt and hauled him forward. "*Don't lie to me.*"

"I never have. That is just insulting—"

"I've seen Whitney. I've—" *Kissed her, touched her, pushed her out of my life when I just wanted her close.* He cleared his throat. "She's not showing. The pregnancy has to be new—"

"Yes, look, don't strain yourself doing math. We both know it was never one of your strong suits."

Ramsey growled.

Jinx winced. "If you will let go of my shirt— because it is one of my favorite t-shirts—"

"It's a cheap piece of shit."

"Then I can explain the birds and the bees to you, and you will understand what's happening with your precious Whitney."

"You are *such* a pain in my ass." But he let go. Only to realize that his fingers were trembling. Not wanting Jinx to see that telling tremor, Ramsey shoved his hands into the back pockets of his jeans. "Tell me everything that you know."

Whitney. Pregnant. Had he been careful enough when he touched her? Had he been gentle? Had he—

"Whitney came to Trouble for Hire because she wanted to pay a PI to help her figure out who the father of her baby is. See, according to her doctor, she was pregnant *before* her attack."

Ramsey fell on his ass. Just fell.

Jinx's eyes widened. "Holy shit, are you all right?"

No, he was not all right. His world was shattering around him. *I told her we were done. I told her that she hadn't mattered. I told her...*He grabbed the edge of the nearby couch and hoisted himself back to his feet. "The floor was slippery."

"No, it's not. It's dry as a bone."

"We spilled whiskey in here yesterday. It's *slippery.*"

Jinx snorted. "Whatever you need to tell yourself."

His knees were still feeling weird. "*Finish talking.*" Jinx was about to drive him mad.

"So, back to my story..."

Another growl broke from Ramsey.

"The doctor said Whitney couldn't have been far in the pregnancy when she was attacked and had her life-or-death struggle in the Gulf. Said she was probably only a few days along at that point. And then he told Whitney that the body does a fabulous job of protecting the baby, even though Whitney went through so much hell. I mean, personally, I think it's a miracle..."

Ramsey turned away. His eyes were all gritty. He squeezed them shut.

"Uh, Ram? You okay?"

"*Finish the damn story.*" His hands were clenching and releasing. He kept seeing Whitney's face in his mind. The way pain had flashed across her beautiful features when he'd said...

I won't be back.

He turned and drove his fist into the wall.

"That is not normal," Jinx noted. "What did the wall do to you?"

Ramsey hit it again. He wanted to pound and pound until his knuckles were bloody.

"Dammit, Ramsey, *stop*." Jinx grabbed him and whirled him around. "I knew it would be bad, but get your shit together. She's going to need you."

"I am the last man she needs." Whitney needed someone good. Upstanding. Someone without wire taps and Feds stalking him. Someone who could give her the world.

Because that's what she deserves.

"Oh? So you're just gonna let her go and allow some dumbass out there to eventually marry her and become a father to *your* child? Because it is yours, isn't it, Ram? I mean, unless Whitney was cheating on you before she vanished—"

"Whitney *wouldn't* cheat."

"How can you be so sure? What, were you following her? Getting a tail on her twenty-four, seven? There are tests that can be done on the baby. Tests that will let you know—"

"The baby is mine." The words echoed through him. "And no, I wasn't tailing her. I *know* her. Whitney is loyal and honest, and when she said she loved me, I fucking knew it was true. She wouldn't be sleeping with me and someone else at the same time. That's not her."

Jinx's mouth dropped open. He gaped for a good two minutes.

Ramsey shoved him away.

"She *loved* you? She said she loved you?"

A jerky nod.

"Then why the hell didn't you *run* to the woman when she came back here? I haven't understood that this whole time! She came back, and fine, her memory is gone, but you could make her love you again."

A bitter laugh tore from Ramsey. "I highly doubt that. I got lucky the first time."

Sympathy flashed on Jinx's face. "Is that what you think happened? That you got lucky or somehow tricked her the first time? And you thought she couldn't feel the same way about you again?"

Jinx just did not understand. When they'd been kids, he'd gone off to be all he could be. He'd been special ops and he'd saved thousands of lives. Then he'd started doing work for the government. Side jobs.

"You think *I* don't know?" Ramsey charged, voice gruff. "Know what you did? You traded your life for me, brother. You worked the most dangerous cases out there in exchange for making my crimes vanish."

Jinx's gaze cut away from his.

But Ramsey wasn't done. "Your hands aren't covered with blood. Mine are. I'm the one who took to the streets while you were out saving lives. I'm the one who was in the gangs. I'm the one who broke the law." Over and over. "And despite *your* efforts, it's not like all of that can be erased."

"Says who?" Now Jinx's gaze jerked back to him. "The Feds have nothing on you. Even without me, they don't have evidence. You were too good at keeping your secrets."

No, he'd just been good at not leaving evidence behind because even as a kid, he hadn't wanted to wind up in jail, like their dad.

But Jinx was staring at Ramsey like he'd just discovered some big secret. "You thought she'd be better off without you. I heard that story before from you—it's the same story you tried to sell to me when you ran away from the group foster home we were in."

Ramsey's back teeth clenched. He gritted, "You *were* better off without me—"

"No." Flat. Hard. Snarled. "I was never better. I wanted my brother with me every damn day, and know this...this baby? This baby will want his real dad. Just as I know you want him. I can *see* it in your eyes and on your face. The longing isn't going away. You want a family. You *have* one. You just have to step out of the shadows and take them."

He did. He wanted the baby. Of course, he wanted the baby. Just as he wanted Whitney. "You don't know what it was like when I thought she was dead."

"She's not dead. You still have a chance. The question is, are you gonna be man enough to take it?"

Jinx was taunting him? "Why do you want an ass kicking so badly?"

Jinx shrugged. "I'm older. I can kick *your* ass."

No. Not even with his special ops skills. Jinx might have been the military guy, but Ramsey was the man who'd learned to fight hard and dirty in back alleys. He'd been in cage fights before he was even eighteen because he'd needed to earn money. He hadn't cared about the danger. He'd had so much fury in him, it had just needed to come out. "I hurt her."

Jinx's eyes widened. "How?"

"I told her..." A lot of stupid things. "I pushed her out of my life."

"Then go out and *charm* her right back!"

It wasn't going to be that easy. Charm had never been his area of expertise.

"I can help," Jinx rushed to say. "I can help you woo her."

Woo? "I don't need your freaking help."

"Uh, I think you do."

"And I think our heart-to-heart is over. Time for you to go." Because Ramsey had a million plans to make. And a whole lot of dirty jobs to close. He was also barely holding onto his control, and he needed Jinx to get the hell out of there.

"Fine. But you need me—and you *are* definitely going to need me, by the way, especially when you realize you require serious help in the charm department—then call me. Day or night. I'll be there for you." Jinx closed his hand around Ramsey's shoulder. "This is a good thing."

For Ramsey, yes, it was. It was his dream. To have Whitney. To have a link with her, an unbreakable bond. A family.

But he didn't think it was going to be such a happy ending for her. "She deserves better."

"What the hell are you talking about? My brother *is* the best."

The best criminal. The best at killing. At making problems go away.

I can do more. I can be more. For her, he would have to be.

Jinx left. Ramsey stayed put and sucked in deep breaths.

***

"So, I think we just solved a case in record time." Jinx had his phone shoved to his ear as he stalked through the bar's parking lot. "You're welcome, by the way."

"He confirmed the baby is his?"

"Oh, I'd say his reaction was definitely a confirmation." Jinx cut his gaze to the left. He'd felt eyes on him. He squinted and saw one of Ramsey's shadows, Jag, glaring back at him. "I'll call you back soon. Something just came up." He shoved the phone into his pocket. "You might want to run back inside," he advised Jag. "Something tells me your boss might need you tonight."

"What the hell did you do?"

He got that Jag didn't like him. He'd gotten that from the beginning. "Oh, not much. Just showed him that there was more to the world than..." He waved with one hand toward the ramshackle building. "This."

"He's told you to stay away."

"Yeah, but he doesn't mean it."

There was a crash from inside the bar. Jinx winced. "You really might want to check on that."

Swearing, Jag whirled away.

Jinx pulled out his phone. Dialed Odin again. When his buddy answered... "Where were we?"

"You were telling me about Ramsey's reaction."

There were screams. Shouts. People flooded out of the bar.

"Uh, yeah. His reaction? It was very positive. In fact, I do believe his joy is contagious..."

***

"Get the fuck out of my bar!" Ramsey roared.

Most people were already running to obey. When he'd come out of the back, he'd seen some dick try to pull a knife on a woman.

Seriously? What in the hell? Ramsey had rules in his place. Everyone knew his rules. You either followed the rules or he fucked you over.

He'd already broken the jerk's wrist. Smashed it hard against the bar and bloodied the guy's nose. Now he wanted this prick—and everyone else—*gone*. "You won't come back to my bar," he snarled to the fool. "You will never enter again. If you try, you'll get more than just your hand broken."

"Uh, boss?" Jag cleared his throat. "There a problem here?"

"Yeah, there's a problem. This dick broke one of my rules." He shoved the guy toward Jag. "He's done." He motioned toward the doors. "*Fucking closing time. Everyone out!*"

But the dumb dick just had to stagger back toward him. "I'm not scared of you!"

You should be. Obviously, you suffer from low intelligence.

"You're old news. Don't even pull jobs anymore." The dick smirked even though blood dripped over his lips. "I ain't scared of you, and I'll pull a knife anytime I want to—"

Ramsey grabbed a pool cue from the nearby table. He slammed it up against the man's head, then drove it right at his crotch. The guy's pain-filled howls filled the air.

"Are you scared yet?" Ramsey wanted to know. "Because I am about to give whole new meaning to the term 'racking balls' for you."

A whimper. The man scrambled back.

"Throw his ass out," Ramsey barked at Jag. "Everyone *out!*" They needed to leave, and then he needed to get to the one person who mattered most...

Whitney.

What would he have to do in order to get her back?

CHAPTER SIX

Observation notes: I know the tattoos that I see people sporting in Ramsey's bar have many different meanings. Some are old gang symbols. Some have religious significance. Some are even to...mark kills.

Ramsey got a new tattoo today. He got it on his palm. I heard Jag say that palm tattoos can hurt the most, that they were real bitches. He even warned Ramsey that it might fade. That he'd have to get another.

Ramsey said he didn't care. The pain had been worth it.

The tattoo was of a rose. It looks so much like the roses he's left for me.

I think the tattoo was for me, too. I teased him and asked exactly what it meant, asked if he was trying to say he had me in the palm of his hand.

No one usually teases Ramsey, but I did. I wasn't surprised he didn't laugh. Getting Ramsey to laugh can be nearly impossible. But he told me...

He said the tattoo was to remind him that beautiful things had to be held carefully. Treasured.

I think...I think I was the beautiful thing he was talking about.

And none of this belongs in my notes. Later, I need to delete, delete, delete. But typing right now helps me to think. Because...when it comes to Ramsey, I think—

***

"What did I think?" Whitney glared at the computer screen. "Did I actually think that he cared about me? What was happening?"

She'd been unable to sleep, feeling too wired after her visit to Trouble for Hire earlier in the day, and she'd pulled up her old notes to see if maybe there was something she'd missed. Only half of the files would open for her. And the text would sometimes be cut off by random numbers and letters.

The entry she'd been reading just stopped with a sequence of zeroes and ones. She needed help. Maybe someone in her college's computer science department could work some magic to help her retrieve more information? After her disappearance, the cops had taken her laptop for a while. They'd apologized when they gave it back to her and said someone had spilled some coffee on it one day.

Her fingers tapped on the keyboard just as her doorbell gave a loud peal. The sound jolted Whitney, and she jerked.

She thought of the mystery deliveries she'd been getting. Whitney pulled out her phone. She'd had one of those video doorbells installed earlier in the day, and a swipe of her finger brought up the feed of her front porch to show her that the visitor was—

Ramsey?

She shoved the phone into the left pocket of her comfy pajama shorts and stormed for the door. As fast as possible, she flipped the locks and wrenched open the door. "What in the hell are you doing here?"

His hands were shoved into the pockets of his battered coat. "Hello to you, too, sunshine."

Whitney's eyes narrowed. "Not even twenty-four hours ago, you very dramatically told me, and I quote, 'I won't be back.'"

His lips pressed together.

"You're back." Whitney pointed out the obvious. What wasn't so obvious? "Why?"

"We need to talk."

"You could pick up a phone and call me if we need to have a conversation. You can text me. Email me. There are lots of ways to communicate."

"In person," he gritted.

Her arms folded over her chest. "Fine. Talk."

Ramsey glanced over his shoulder, then back at her. "Could we talk inside?"

"No. We can talk outside. There's no need for you to come inside. As you've pointed out to me many times, we were not friends before. We're not friends now."

"I'm a bastard."

A quick nod from Whitney. "Yes, you've pointed that out to me several times, too. Seems unnecessary to rehash it yet again."

A muscle flexed along his jaw. "Would it help if I said that I came to apologize?"

"Not particularly." But her eyes had narrowed. "Though I am curious about just what you'd like to apologize for."

"Oh, you know, the usual."

"I have no idea what your usual would be."

His lips appeared to almost curl, but the smile—or what *could* have been a near smile—vanished in the next instant. "Being a heartless, controlling, arrogant jerk. That usual routine."

"Fine. Apologize."

"Can I do it inside?"

He just kept pushing to come in her house. She thought that was a terrible idea, especially considering the way things had ended for them before.

"I'm sorry," Ramsey announced before she could tell him that hell, no, he wasn't bringing his sexy and arrogant ass into her house. "I'm sorry that I pushed you away. I'm sorry that I wouldn't let you get close." He stepped forward.

She stiffened her spine and refused to back up.

His voice deepened even more. "And, mostly, I'm sorry that I didn't grab you tight the minute you came back to the area. I'm sorry that I let all this time go to waste because I fucking thought I was doing the right thing when I wasn't. When I was just leaving you on your own."

Then...his gaze dropped to her stomach.

He swallowed.

"I'm sorry you were alone...when you do *not* need to be alone at a time like this," he added gruffly.

Oh, no. Nope. Her hand immediately flew to her stomach. She touched the silky material of her pajama top. When he'd barged in, she'd been dressed for bed, wearing the blue pajama top and matching shorts. "Who told you?"

"It's true?" His gaze lifted. The light on the porch shone down on him, but she could not read his expression to save her life. "You're pregnant?"

"Who told you?" she repeated. "Was it Odin? I didn't want to go to him, but I was running out of options, and he seemed to already know so many details about my life..."

"I know more about your life than he does." Ramsey's hand lifted. Tenderly tucked a lock of hair behind her ear. "I know more about you than anyone else ever could."

His tender touch *hurt*. Tears pricked her eyes. "You sonofabitch."

He flinched.

"You know so much?" His words infuriated her. Made her want to scream and rage. "I have been in the dark for *so long*. I was desperate to find out what happened in my lost time. You knew, and you didn't tell me? You left me alone!"

"I thought you were better off without me."

Now a cry of fury did burst from her. "That isn't your call to make! It was my life! I had a big void where memories should be. You *knew* and you didn't come to me!"

Lights flashed on at the house next door.

His head turned toward the suddenly bright illumination. "Your neighbors will be calling the cops if you keep yelling at me."

"Good. Let them come. They can haul you off in handcuffs and that will be an awesome end of the night for me." She exhaled on a hard sigh. *He'd left her. Just abandoned her.* Until...

Until he'd found out about the baby, and only then had he come back.

Ramsey didn't come back for me.

Her chest burned.

"I deserve that." His shoulders squared. They'd already been square because they were awesomely wide and strong, but he rolled them back as if preparing for some big battle. "Jinx told me. You know he works with Trouble for Hire."

"Yes."

"He's also my brother. Though very few people realize that. I keep it secret. If Jinx had his way, he'd blab to the whole world about us."

Her eyebrows rose. "Why are you keeping it secret?"

"Because bad things happen to people who are close to me. I have more enemies than you can possibly imagine, and sometimes, those enemies try to hurt people that I care about in order to hurt me." His gaze didn't leave her face. "You want to know why I didn't come to you and hold on as tightly as I could? Even though I fucking dream and fantasize about you twenty-four, seven?"

No, that wasn't right. He didn't—

"It's because as much as I want you, I want to protect you even more. Staying out of your life was the best thing I could do for you. When I stayed away from you, that protected *you*."

Back to that song, was he? "You don't get to tell me how to live my life. I decide what's safe and what isn't."

Her neighbor had crept onto her porch and was peering over at them.

"Shall we let the lovely lady with the rollers in her hair call the cops or will you let me come inside and talk to you for five minutes?" Ramsey asked.

"Everything okay over there?" Her neighbor called out.

"Fine!" It wasn't.

Ramsey turned toward the other woman. He gave what looked like a friendly wave. "She was just overwhelmed with surprise and joy when she opened the door and found me on her doorstep. That was a cry of pure happiness you heard moments ago."

Hardly.

"Maybe take the joy inside," her neighbor grumbled. "People are trying to sleep." She marched back in her house and slammed the door.

"New neighbor?" Ramsey asked, voice turning silky. "Because she wasn't here before. You had the talented jazz player who would sit on his porch and play his sax all night. After we were done fucking for hours, we'd open your window and let the music drift inside."

She reached out and grabbed his coat. "Get inside. And *stop* talking about us having sex."

"Why? Our having sex has led to the current situation."

His voice was loud and strong, and she did not want her new neighbor hearing all of these details. Whitney hauled Ramsey inside and slammed the door shut behind him.

Before she could flip the locks, he beat her to the punch. Once the door was secure, he turned back toward her. His gaze slid over her. "Are you feeling well? Eating enough? Taking vitamins? Because I read that it was extremely important to be on prenatal vitamins."

Her hands went to her hips. "I'm feeling great." No, she was feeling furious. "Eating perfectly, thanks. And, yes, I am on prenatal vitamins, so you can mark that off your check list." Hold up. He'd *read* that it was important to have prenatal vitamins? What had he done? Researched pregnancy?

"No morning sickness? No late-night nausea?"

"Oh, I'm feeling pretty nauseous right now," she muttered.

He immediately bounded toward her. "Crackers."

What?

"Crackers can help with nausea. I can go get you some. I can—"

"*Stop.*"

His mouth closed. His eyes glittered.

She pulled in a deep breath. Let it out slowly. "How do you even know the baby is yours?"

"Because *you* are mine."

That wasn't a real answer. And why were chill bumps skating down her arms?

"We were involved before you disappeared, Whitney."

"Yes, I managed to figure that out. Despite *your* efforts to stop me."

His head inclined toward her.

Her chill bumps got worse. "So we slept together once."

"More than once."

"Twice?"

He shook his head. "I told you the truth before. You just didn't realize it."

We fucked dozens of times. Maybe even a hundred times. I wasn't exactly counting. I had you in so many places. Once I fucked you on the bar top outside. On the pool table.

"I know every inch of your body, and, once upon a time, you knew mine the same way."

I fucked you in my old car. On my motorcycle. On the beach. At your office. Her gaze darted toward the hallway—toward her bedroom. *I fucked you in your bedroom, and we nearly broke your bed. I fucked you so many times that your body was tuned to me and only to me.*

"Jinx told me that you were pregnant before your attack. That means the baby is mine. You were with me and only me."

"Hate to shatter your ego, but you don't know that. You *can't* know if I was being faithful to you." She could be logical and think this through. "There are tests that can be performed. I spoke with my doctor about them. For one, I-I will just need to get a cheek swab from you in order to get your DNA. The doctor can take a sample of the DNA in my blood and compare it to yours. He told me this one can be done as early as seven weeks, and I'm certainly past that point now so there is..." Her words trailed away because his expression had become even more fierce.

"I don't need a test. I know I'm the father."

"Yes, well, *I* want to know, how about that? You may have this magic faith that you were all-knowing about my faithfulness, though I don't get why you're so trusting on that point. You hardly strike me as an overly trusting individual. Quite the opposite."

"True. Except when it comes to you." His hands lifted as if he'd touch her, but then he seemed to catch himself. "When it comes to you, all of the rules are different. Besides, I know one irrefutable fact that you don't."

"Oh, really? Then please, enlighten me. Tell me about this 'irrefutable fact' of yours." Like it was going to be a game changer.

"You were in love with me, Whitney. You wouldn't have slept with someone else while you loved me."

Now she jerked back as if he'd burned her. "*What?*" No, he had to be playing some kind of mind game with her. "You said it was casual sex!"

"I never said that." A line appeared between his eyebrows.

"You sure implied it! What with your whole we-were-fucking-everywhere routine! It was like fuck city, but you didn't mention love!"

His lips lifted. "Fuck city?"

"Do not dare laugh at me right now."

Instantly, he sobered. "I would never laugh at you." His nostrils flared. "There are lots of things I would do for you."

"Oh? Like what?"

"Like lie. Steal. Kill."

Her chill bumps were so bad.

"But I would never laugh at you. You're far too important for that."

"How am I supposed to believe you?"

"I can prove myself to you, if you just give me time."

She had to focus. *Get back to DNA.* "The second type of test is more invasive. There's a risk."

"Forget it."

She ignored his interruption. "There's a small risk of miscarriage because a needle has to be inserted through my abdomen to collect a fluid sample..." Just the mental picture had her squirming. "I'd prefer not to do that method because I don't want to do anything that might have a chance of hurting the baby."

"I don't want to hurt the baby or you. I *know* this child is mine. But if you want a DNA sample from my cheek, take it so *you* can know what I already do. But please, don't do anything that risks you or that child."

His *please* sounded rusty. "You want the baby?"

"I want the baby and the baby's mother. Let me be very clear on that." His stare didn't waver from her face. "I want you both."

"Do you? Because I didn't see you saying that yesterday. I only see you saying it now that you know about the child." She put her hand over her stomach. "I can take care of this baby just fine on my own. I just—I contacted Odin because I wanted to know the truth."

"The truth is that you were mine. That baby is mine. And I want you to be mine again."

He was unbelievable. "You didn't seem to want me last night."

He surged even closer. So close that the heat from his body seemed to wrap around her. "I wanted you last night. I knew kissing you was a mistake, but my lack of control around you has always been an issue. I've been dreaming about you, fantasizing, craving you, and then you just walked right back into my life. I kissed you because nothing has ever tasted as good as you do. I kissed you, and I wanted you naked. I wanted to have you on your kitchen table or against the nearest wall. Wherever I could get you."

Her breathing had hitched.

"But I was trying to be a gentleman. Something I am very much not. Walking out was the only way for me to keep my hands off you."

His cocky arrogance was astounding. "I don't remember inviting you to have sex with me. We were just talking in the kitchen. And we kissed. So what?"

Now he did smile. A full smile that tilted his lips, that lightened his dark eyes, and made the gold hidden in the depths gleam. "When it comes to the way we react to each other, your control is as weak as mine."

A lump rose in her throat.

"You don't remember," he murmured.

No, she *didn't*.

"But I do. That will work to my advantage. I remember everything that you like. I know how to drive you wild with need. I know how to make you shudder with pleasure. And believe me, I will."

Utterly astounding. "You think I'm going to take you back with open arms? If so, you're delusional." She ignored her racing heartbeat and the way her whole body suddenly felt way too sensitive and hyperaware. "I *might* have been involved with you before—"

"You *loved* me before."

Don't focus on that. "But that was then. I have no memories of you now. I know nothing about you except that you're some sort of super criminal. That information hardly makes me want to fall at your feet." If anything, she thought he needed to be at her feet. A good grovel would probably do wonders for him.

But he didn't look as if he was anywhere close to groveling. In fact, the gold in his eyes gleamed all the more. "Then I guess I'll just have to make you either remember me..."

Like it would be that easy. Didn't he think she'd *tried* to remember?

"Or...I'll follow Jinx's advice."

"What the hell?"

"I'll just have to get you to fall for me again."

"Not happening," she fired right back. The man could just keep dreaming on that one.

A loud, growling reached her ears. A sound that seemed to vibrate from outside.

His head immediately jerked to the left.

"Some wanna-be drag racer," she said, dismissing the noise even as it grew louder. Closer. "Probably just a kid spinning through the cul-de-sac." Super annoying and loud. "He'll be gone in a few moments."

The growl turned into a rumble. As if...as if the car had stopped. Right in front of her house.

Tension poured from Ramsey. "I don't think it's a kid."

Well...

Before she could answer, the glass of her big picture window—the window in the front of her house—exploded inward as something hurtled through toward them. The glass shattered, and she automatically brought up her arm to protect herself, but Ramsey was already there. He'd moved in a flash and his body curled over hers.

Whoosh. There was a weird rush, sounded like wind, and when she peered around him, she saw fire eating its way up the billowing curtains that had surrounded her favorite window. "Ramsey?" Alarm had her voice breaking.

A second projectile hurtled through the window.

And more flames erupted.

Before she could scream, Ramsey had her in his arms.

CHAPTER SEVEN

Observation notes: The people in Ramsey's world are dangerous. Not just the individuals I've watched in the bar, but the ones in his inner circle. I had a friend at the police department show me their rap sheets. The people who smile at me so easily when I am with him hide pasts that are scary and brutal.

Can people change? I've always believed they could. When I look at Ramsey, I have to keep believing that.

***

He scooped Whitney into his arms and ran away from the flames eating up her den. He'd seen attacks like this before, usually in turf warfare when someone wanted a message received. If he ran out the front door, an attacker could be waiting.

He wasn't about to risk Whitney. So he tightened his grip and rushed toward her kitchen. He knew exactly how to get to the rear door of her house—to the door that led off her laundry room. "Cover your mouth, baby," he urged her. He didn't want her inhaling the smoke. And he sure as fuck was not about to let the flames so much as touch her skin.

As he raced with her toward the laundry room, she jerked in his grasp. "No, wait!" Whitney cried. "My laptop. I have to get it!"

Was she freaking serious? "The house is on fire. We just need to get you *out*."

"Ram!"

He could see the laptop. He snagged it with one hand and pushed it toward her. "Hold it tight."

Then he had her in the laundry room. He swung the door that led back to the kitchen shut, then he carefully lowered Whitney to her feet.

She clutched her laptop like the thing was made of gold.

His hands flew over her.

"What are you doing?"

"Making sure you're not hurt." Fury pounded at him.

"I'm not."

She could have been, though. She could have been killed. Someone would be paying—in blood. "I'm going outside. He's probably in front, waiting for us, but if I'm wrong and he's waiting near the back door, you stay behind me, got it?" He yanked a knife from the sheath he'd strapped to his ankle.

Her wide eyes followed the movement.

"Whitney, promise to stay behind me."

A jerky nod. Then... "And promise you won't get hurt."

"I promise that I'll be the one doing the hurting." Then he yanked open the back door. He rushed out, looking to the left and the right for a threat, but he didn't see anyone. The growling roar of an engine reached his ears. "Sonofabitch." He rushed toward the front of the house just in time to see taillights vanishing down the road.

The attacker hadn't stuck around. He'd fled.

Like that was going to save him. Ramsey would find him. With his resources, there would be no escape.

"Ramsey?"

He whirled toward her. The knife was still gripped in his hand. He immediately shoved it down and away from her. "He ran."

"My house is on fire." Her voice was low and sad. She clutched the laptop to her chest. "We need to call the fire department."

Yeah, they did. But first...

He sheathed the knife and scooped her into his arms and ran for his ride.

"Uh, Ramsey?"

His grip tightened. "We're getting the hell out of here." If the attacker came back, she wasn't going to be anywhere near the scene.

"Whitney!" A shrill cry from her neighbor. "Whitney, are you all right? What's happening?" And the woman was rushing toward them. A roller fell out of her hair and hit the ground.

"Call nine-one-one, Jenny!" Whitney yelled at her. "And stay away from the fire!"

Ramsey lowered Whitney near his motorcycle. He'd be ditching that bike at the first opportunity and getting a different ride. Whitney and the baby would need something different. For now... "Climb on and hold on tight."

She looked at the bike, then at him. "We should wait for the cops."

The fire was crackling.

He put her laptop in one of the saddle bags. Then he carefully settled the helmet on her head and secured it beneath her chin. "We should get the hell out of here," he told her. "*Now.*"

She bit her lip. Looked at the burning house. Looked at him.

"Time is kinda of the essence here," he murmured as he climbed onto the bike.

Whitney slid on the bike. Wrapped her hands around his waist. He revved the motorcycle and shot them away from the scene.

The heat of the flames seemed to follow in his wake.

***

"We fled a crime scene." Whitney paced in front of the massive floor to ceiling windows that overlooked the beach. Waves pounded and the glitter of stars shone in the dark sky. "Why did I do that? I'm a law-abiding citizen. I always do what I'm supposed to do." She turned and marched back toward him. "What was I thinking?"

"That you wanted to stay alive?" He lounged on the couch. His pose was deliberately relaxed...when relaxed was the last thing he felt. Fury pumped through his body, and all he wanted to do was go out and hunt.

Destroy.

Kill.

Because *that* was who he was. At his core, he was a monster. A killer. An eye-for-an-eye bastard who did not stop until he'd gotten vengeance on those who had wronged him.

Someone had gone after Whitney. Made the worst mistake possible.

And isn't this what you feared would happen? Isn't this why you tried to stay away? But it was too late for all that now. "I'm sorry."

She squinted at him. "Was that an apology? Because it kind of sounded like a curse."

It had felt like a curse. "I brought the danger to your door. That's on me."

"Uh, you have *no* idea that you caused this! You don't have a monopoly on danger. In case you've forgotten, I had killers after me before, and from what I learned, you had nothing to do with all that." She glanced around his den. "Where's the phone? I need to call the cops." Then she spied his cell and immediately rushed toward it.

He rose and stepped into her path. "Sorry, that's gonna be a no."

"What?"

"You're not going to call the cops."

"But—but we can't just—" She sputtered to a stop.

"We can. We did. It's handled, don't worry." His gaze swept over her. He'd been doing that over and over again. Checking her out. Ramsey wanted to be absolutely certain that she hadn't been hurt.

"Handled? How?"

"I made some phone calls."

"When?"

"When you were in the bathroom."

"I was in the bathroom for all of two minutes."

"And my calls were very fast. I'm amazing like that."

Her head cocked to the right. "Who did you call?"

He wanted to touch her. Because he wanted it so badly, he backed up and put more space between them. "The police. Happy now?"

"No. I want more information."

Ramsey let loose a long-suffering sigh. "Fine. I called one of my many contacts at the PD. I informed him of the events that had happened, and I told him that I had removed you from the scene for your safety." He thought that all sounded very reasonable. How could she have a problem with that? "See? I handled things. Now you don't have to fret that you did something wrong by fleeing. Your good-girl complex is maintained."

She rushed to close the space between them. Whitney jabbed him in the chest with her index finger. "First, I do *not* have a good-girl complex."

"No?"

"*No.*"

"Then do you have a bad-girl complex?"

"I'm not a girl. I'm a woman."

"Absolutely, you are." The woman of his dreams. Not time to address that situation, though. "My mistake. I forgot, you have a bad-*guy* complex. You know I'm dangerous, but you just can't turn away from the wicked thrill that I give you."

She jabbed him with her index finger again. "I have *never* had a bad-guy complex in my life!"

His brow furrowed. "No?"

"No." Adamant.

"Then how do you explain us? Some would say I'm the baddest of the bad..."

"Oh, and *someone* sure is bragging right now..."

He fought the smile that wanted to spread over his face. *There you are.* The strong, snarky woman who'd obliterated his world. The hell she'd lived through hadn't dampened her fire. He didn't think anything could. Whitney always said and did the unexpected. She'd never been intimidated by him. And she could throw him off his guard—or get way under his skin—with just a few simple words.

But her hand suddenly jerked back. "Why are you looking at me like that?"

"Like what?" His voice had gone gruff.

"Like you want to kiss me." Hers had turned soft.

Ramsey nodded. "Fair enough. I'm looking at you this way because I want your mouth." A pause. "I want you."

He noticed that her breaths heaved out faster. "I don't know what you think our past was about—"

Lots of hot sex. A desire that could never be sated, no matter how many times he had her.

"But I wasn't with you because I wanted some kind of danger high. I've interviewed plenty of criminals. I've gone in maximum security prisons and had one-on-one discussions with some of the most infamous killers out there. Do you remember Murphy the Monster? He sat down for a heart-to-heart with *me*."

He knew full well about all of the work she'd done. When it came to criminal behavior, Whitney was at the top of her game. She'd written several best-selling books and gone on speaking tours across the country as she lectured about the criminal mind and motivations for criminal behavior. He knew all this about her because he'd made a point of knowing everything.

And when he'd discovered just how close she'd been to some of the most brutal killers out there, it had chilled his soul. Very little scared him. Whitney sitting down for a fun chat with a convicted serial killer?

Fucking terrifying.

"I've had the chance to get close to plenty of dangerous men," she continued doggedly. "I never slept with any of those others. I studied them."

"Because they were your experiments."

Pink tinted her cheeks. "No, that's—that's not the right word."

He thought it was. "When you started getting...close...to me, I asked if I was an experiment to you."

"You're not." An immediate response.

That had been her response back then, too.

"I've had lots of women sleep with me because they liked the thrill of screwing the bad guy."

Now she surged toward him. "It's not my fault you have bad taste. You should try sleeping with women who want to be with you because they think there is something more to you than just that tough, criminal persona you present to the world."

He could not look away from her mouth. "I tried that." *Got addicted to it*. "It pretty much ruined me for everyone else."

Her eyes narrowed.

"In case you don't quite get what I'm saying, I'll try again." He released a long breath and then confessed, "There has been no one else for me since you."

"But...but I vanished..."

"There has been no one else." There couldn't be. No one could fill the hole she'd left in his life.

Her gaze searched his. "What am I supposed to do with that?"

"Whatever the hell you want." He wasn't going to pressure her. "I didn't bring you back here so that you would have to sleep with me. Though, let me just go ahead and make sure you know, sleeping with you—fucking you—is always at the top of my to do list."

Her cheeks flushed even darker. "Good to know?" Her words were tremulous. A question when they should have been a statement.

But he let that go, for now. "I brought you here because you're a target."

"Me?" Her mouth gaped. Then closed. "Why am I a target?"

"Because your house was just set on fire?"

"But I thought that attack was about you! You arrived at my place and then just minutes later we hear the revving engine, and the bottles came hurtling through my window. Someone followed *you*!"

But Ramsey had to point out, "You received the mystery rose deliveries."

"Yes." Grim.

"I'm thinking your place was scoped out." *Full disclosure*... "And, yes, it could damn well be due to our connection." He could have put her in the crosshairs. "Maybe I was followed to your place—"

"But you just came by last night! And I received the first rose—"

Tell her. "I came to your house before last night."

"Oh." She bit her lower lip. "You mean that you came to my home before I lost my memory—"

"I mean I've been by your house every damn night since you've gotten back to the area. I would drive by on my way home from the bar and just pause to make sure everything looked safe." He hadn't been able to stay away from her.

She didn't speak.

Was she shocked by his confession? Freaked out? He had to trudge on. "I came by every night, so if I was followed one of those nights, then, yes, I would have led the bastard right to you. He would have easily seen what I valued most, and now he could be targeting you as a way of hurting me." *The sonofabitch.* "Know that this is the *last* thing I wanted. I tried to protect you, but because I want you so fucking badly, I did nothing but put you in harm's way." He spun from her. Started to head toward the mantel.

Her hand closed around his arm. "You came to my house every night?"

A jerky nod.

"Why didn't you ever come to the door? I mean, last night you did, but..."

"Last night, you'd come to *me* at my bar." That had changed things. Broken through his already weak control. "When I want something too much, it's dangerous. You should know that there is nothing I want more than I want you."

But she shook her head. "I'm supposed to buy that?"

Yes, because it was the truth.

"I was alone for weeks. I was pregnant and I kept thinking...surely, if I was involved with someone, he'd be here. Only you weren't there. And you only told me the truth when you found out about the baby." Her hand dropped to protectively rest over her stomach. "So pardon me if I don't trust what you're telling me. I think you want this baby more than anything else. I think you brought me here to protect the baby, not me. I think—"

"I want the baby," he growled. "Make no mistake. I want the baby because the baby is *yours*. There is no part of you that I don't want. Staying away isn't an option any longer. Protecting you *and* the baby is my priority." Which was why... "I want you moving in here."

"Uh, *no*."

He'd expected an argument. That was why he already had his defense ready. "Your house was torched. Hardly a safe place for a pregnant lady."

Her delicate jaw hardened.

"I've got top-of-the-line security. I will make sure that you are safe twenty-four, seven." He would eliminate all the threats to her. No sense in telling her that he would have to get violent with his enemies. That news could come later. Or never.

"Am I supposed to become your prisoner?"

Prisoner wasn't the right description. *Cherished lover* was way better. "You will be free to come and go as you wish. I'll just make sure you have a bodyguard with you when I'm not close."

"*What?*"

He winced. Her voice had gone shockingly high.

"Don't you think that's a little over the top?" Whitney demanded. "For all we know, the cops could be hunting down our pyro right now!"

"When it comes to you, I am over the top."

"I have a job! I can't have a bodyguard trailing me when I'm lecturing! I can't—"

"Please."

Her head tilted. "You think that is some kind of magic word? That I'll just cave when your voice gets all low and sexy and you say *please* to me?"

"A guy can hope." He made a mental note that she still found his voice sexy. That was a good sign.

"Look, let's not worry about bodyguards yet. How about we just focus on getting through the rest of the night, hmmm? Can we do that?" She nodded resolutely as if she'd made her own plan. Knowing Whitney, she probably had. "I'll stay here tonight. As you pointed out, my place was torched. And, obviously, there are a million rooms here."

Not quite a million.

"So I should be able to stay out of your way."

Why do that? "You're welcome in my bed."

"Yes, slow down. That's not happening. I'm *staying* here. We'll see what the cops turn up, and in the morning, we'll go from there." Then she yawned. An adorable little stretch of her face.

It was late. She probably was tired, no, exhausted considering the additional strain of her pregnancy and—

He yawned, too.

"Well, that's good to know." Her tone brightened. "Your odds of being a psychopath just plummeted."

"Come again?"

"Catching a yawn like that is linked to empathy. Psychopaths often don't experience empathy. They can't. They can fake it, but not actually feel it. There was a study conducted a few years back that said if you scored high on a checklist for psychopathy, you would have a lower chance of responding to contagious yawns."

"So I'm not a total psychopath. Good to know." His fingers tapped against his thigh. "Any other tests you want to perform on me?"

"No, because you aren't my experiment." She turned on her heel. "And I'm very tired. If the cops arrive and want to question me, please wake me up."

If the cops arrived and she was sleeping, he damn well would not disturb her. She needed her rest.

Whitney disappeared down the hallway.

She'd given him that yawn test before. He'd known how to pass it because they'd had that exact discussion before.

Did *she* remember? Was the past coming back for her, too?

His gaze trekked to the laptop that she'd left sitting on his couch. He was curious about just why it had been so important to her. When she was asleep, he'd be sure to check it out.

For now...

He crept carefully down the hallway after her. He just wanted to make sure she was settled comfortably and—

A door shut on the right.

He stilled. She'd picked her room for the night.

A slow smile spread across his face. She'd picked *his* bedroom. Satisfaction flooded through him.

He *had* gotten her back in his bed, after all. Just where he wanted her to be.

CHAPTER EIGHT

Observation notes: Ramsey took me to a house on the beach tonight. His home. I don't think that he allows many people inside his sanctuary. I actually don't think he allows many people close at all. He has a wall up to keep everyone out.

I want to shatter that wall into a million pieces.

***

"This place isn't what I expected." Whitney stared down at the dark beach below. She could hear the thunder of the waves. Her hand was curled around the stem of her wine glass. The taste of the sweet wine lingered on her tongue.

"What did you think? That I lived in some kind of mobster's paradise? A house behind a giant wall with dozens of guards?"

She felt the light breeze brush over her skin. "I'm sure you have plenty of security here." She'd caught sight of the cameras. "And, no, I was hardly expecting you to be surrounded by a seven-foot brick wall or to have Dobermans running around your property."

"Dobermans are great dogs. Intelligent. Loyal. Fearless." He came closer to her. His arm brushed against hers as he looked over the balcony.

"When I said the home surprised me, it's because you don't strike me as someone who is big on material things. I know you own your bar, but you mostly drive that motorcycle that has to be at least ten years old, and I've never seen you waste your time at the trendy spots or gala events."

"Why the hell would I go to places like that? People would just stare at me and whisper. Or they'd try to photograph me, and then I'd have to smash their fancy phones."

She slanted a quick glance toward him.

"But you're wrong about material things not mattering. They do. Or at least, some material things matter." A soft exhale. "I lived in a piece of shit trailer when I was a kid. My dad was drunk or high most days, when he wasn't in jail. My mom was dead." He stared into the dark. "Growing up, I always dreamed of having a big house. So big that no one would say I was trash anymore."

"I don't think you've ever been trash." And it made her furious that anyone had ever said that about him.

He took the wine glass from her. Put it on the balcony's edge. His fingers curled with hers. "I'm not good enough for you."

How could he think that?

"I knew it the first time I saw you. You didn't belong in my bar, and you sure as hell don't belong in my bed."

Her heart shoved hard against her chest. "How about you let me decide where I belong?" Then she rose onto her tiptoes and her mouth brushed against his.

The surge hit her—that hard pulse of awareness that arched through her body every single time they kissed. She'd never get used to it. Desire danced in her blood, and she pressed her body even closer against him.

His mouth was open, so she dipped her tongue inside. His hungry growl just urged her on. He'd brought her to his home. Cooked her dinner. Served her wine. Her *favorite* wine that he'd magically had on hand.

They'd been growing closer and closer. Sharing secret kisses. Touches that went too far, but not far enough. This night—her first night at his home—she wanted more.

She knew where she belonged, and it was in his arms.

"Make love to me," Whitney whispered against his mouth.

A shudder worked over his body.

"I want you," she told him and kissed him again. Her hand had curled around the back of his neck. She could feel his arousal thrusting against her. He was as turned on as she was. Ramsey wanted her just as much as she wanted him—

"No."

Ice cold water seemed to pour over her. She jerked back. "No?"

"You're supposed to be so good at reading criminals. At understanding them and figuring out what the hell they think and what drives them." Under the moonlight, his expression appeared stark. "But you still don't understand me. I warned you. I tried to tell you...tender kisses and touches aren't my style. Making love? No, I fuck the women in my life. The sex is dirty and hard and rough, and the pleasure is enough to make you scream. But that's all it is. A fuck. Fleeting pleasure. With me, you aren't getting some kind of happily-ever-after deal. It just won't happen."

She backed up a step.

He cursed. "I'm not trying to hurt you. Hurting you is the last thing I would ever want to do, but I don't want you thinking I'm something that I am not. I'm not your prince charming."

"Who said I was looking for him?"

"You should be looking. And he should be fucking searching the world over for you."

Her hands fisted. "There you go again!" She spun away from him and took five quick steps toward the open doors that led back into his home. "One minute, you push me away. Then the next, you say something so weirdly sweet and unexpected that I want to jump you."

"I want you, Whitney. It's because I want you so much that I have to tell you the truth. You deserve better. *More* than I can give."

She threw a hard glance over her shoulder. "I decide what I deserve."

"I grew up trash. I joined a gang when I was a teenager. I ruled that gang within two years. And the stories in the news? They're not all wrong. I am not a good man."

"You're good to me."

"To one person in the world..."

"And you're not *bad*." She turned to fully face him. "You think I haven't seen *you* when I've been in your bar? I see the way you help those people who come to you. You give them money. Jobs. I also know you're paying for two of your waitresses' kids to go to college. One of the girls is in my criminal psych class." Her words were tumbling out too fast. "Just because you did bad things in the past, it doesn't make you bad. I know you're more than that. I know you've had to fight hard your entire life." The fighting had only made him stronger. "You do good things. There is so much more to you than the world thinks."

And that was why he was pushing her away. She understood him, even if he didn't understand himself. Ramsey truly did think that he didn't deserve to be with her. Maybe he even thought that he didn't deserve love.

Too bad.

Too late.

Because Whitney was sure that she was falling in love with him.

"You want me." She could smell the salt in the air as the waves kept pounding the shore.

"You know I do."

"You just don't want me badly enough. Not yet."

"What?" Ramsey shook his head. "No, trust me. I want you *plenty* badly. I'm just trying to do the—" He stopped himself.

Too late.

"Right thing?" Whitney taunted. "You need to stop that." Then her hands slid behind her, and she lowered the zipper of her dress.

Ramsey stiffened. "What are you doing?"

She let the dress fall and pool at her feet. Then she stepped out of her heels and away from the dress. "Isn't it obvious?" Now she arched her back and unhooked her bra. But before she could let it fall, Ramsey was there.

He'd lunged toward her. His hands grabbed the straps of her bra and held the material in place.

"I have to ask you," she murmured, "do you usually try to stop women from undressing in front of you? Or am I special?"

"You are *very* special." His voice had gone guttural.

"So are you." She smiled at him as her hands fluttered near her hips. "And I just dropped my panties."

"Oh, fucking hell." He looked down. His grip slackened and her bra fell to join the panties. A shudder worked over him. "I was...*trying*..."

"I get what you were doing. Mostly because I get *you*. But here's the thing." Her hand pressed to his heart. "I want you. If the sex is dirty and rough and wild, then that just sounds like a grand old time to me. We can do dirty and rough. We can do slow and tender, despite you trying to act like you magically can't. We can do everything. I just want to do it all with you."

"You need to get inside. Someone else could see you..." His voice became even more growly. "Then I'd have to rip the bastard's eyes out."

"Oh, you say the sweetest things." She rose onto her toes. "Kiss me."

He did. Whitney could tell the kiss was different. More savage. Possessive. Hungry. Demanding. As if his precious control had finally shattered, and he was giving her the real man that he'd held back.

Ramsey lifted her into his arms. Her bare legs curled around his hips as he carried her back inside. It was cute that he wanted them inside his home. He could have made love to her right there on the balcony, and she would have loved it.

Mental note...*Next time, have sex on the balcony*. With the waves pounding and the moon shining down on them.

He strode easily through the dark house. His steps never faltered, and his mouth kept coming back to hers. Her legs were tight around him, and the hard fabric of his jeans brushed over her sensitive core. His cock shoved against the front of those jeans—against her—and she just had to ride him. Her hips arched against him even as a moan rumbled from her.

He lowered her onto a bed. A massive four poster with silk sheets. The sheets felt like sweet sin beneath her. And he felt like hot temptation over her. His mouth kissed a fiery trail down her neck and had her twisting beneath him. His nimble fingers teased her nipples.

Her hands slid between them. Whitney fumbled with the button and zipper of his jeans. She managed to yank the jeans open, and his heavy cock thrust into her fingers. Her hand closed over him. Squeezed. Pumped.

"Oh, baby, not yet. You touch me much more, and I'll go crazy."

He pulled away, and she could have howled in frustration. But then he pushed apart her legs. Brought his mouth down on her. Licked her clit even as he carefully pushed two fingers into her. Her hips flew off the bed as Whitney choked out his name. He was merciless. Determined. His mouth ruthless. He kept licking and tasting even as his fingers stroked in and out of her, and Whitney's release hit her with the force of a maelstrom.

She opened her mouth to scream even as her hands flew out and fisted around the sheets. *"Ram!"*

He kept tasting her through the orgasm. Making the pleasure stronger and wilder. So good. Better than anything that had come before.

Then she felt the head of his cock against the entrance to her body.

His fingers closed around the fists she'd made as she grabbed the sheets.

"Look at me." A sensual order.

Her eyelids lifted.

"No going back."

"I don't plan to go anywhere."

He drove into her.

***

"Whitney? Baby, what's wrong?"

She felt a touch against her cheek, and Whitney's eyes flew open. She lurched upright, hauling the black silk sheets with her.

The lamp on the table had been turned on. Light spilled onto the four-poster bed. Ramsey sat on the side of the bed, and his dark, worried gaze was on her.

"You were moaning. I was afraid something was wrong. That you were in pain."

She didn't feel like anything hurt. She felt a little flushed and her heart was racing and—

Her attention shifted to the silk sheets. Then to the bed's heavy, wooden posts. Familiar posts. "I'm...not in pain."

"Were you having a nightmare?"

No, she didn't think that she had been. Bits and pieces of the dream still remained.

"You look flushed. Should I call Dr. Marshall?"

Of course, he knew the name of her OB-GYN. She wasn't even going to ask how.

Whitney could feel the heat in her cheeks, but she wasn't flushed because anything was wrong. She was blushing because she was pretty sure she'd been having a sex dream. Or, rather, a sex memory. "Bits and pieces come to me sometimes." She was still staring at the wooden post on the right. "Familiar places or things can spark them. It can be a sensory experience. Like feeling silk against my skin..." She was fisting the silk of the sheets.

I've done that before. Just like I've been in this bed, with him, before.

"Whitney, are you telling me that you remembered something?"

She drew in a bracing breath before forcing her stare back to him. "Bits and pieces. They vanish quickly when I wake. That's what happened last night. And what's happening now." Except this time, a few of the memories were lingering in a more tangible way. "I've been in this room with you before."

A nod.

"It's...your bedroom."

"Yes."

Her breath rushed out. "So you got me in your bed. You could have said something. Pointed me to another room."

"Yes, I could have. I didn't." No apology. "Have you stopped to wonder how you knew to come to this room? Because I watched you. You walked straight to it as if you'd done it dozens of times." A small hesitation. "Which, by the way, you have."

It had been automatic. She'd been tired and wanted a safe place to crash. Her feet had carried her to his bedroom. She hadn't even bothered looking too closely at the furniture or her surroundings. She'd pretty much collapsed in bed. Now her gaze did track around, and she realized there weren't any personal touches in the room. The dresser top was empty. The heavy, cherry wood chest had all of its drawers shut. A lamp and a small clock were the only things on the nearby nightstand.

He followed her gaze. "Feel like something else should be there?"

She actually did. The certainty that something was missing nagged at her.

He reached over for the nightstand. Opened the top drawer. Pulled out a framed photograph. He stared at the photo, then turned the frame toward her.

Me and Ramsey. In the photo, he had his arms wrapped around her shoulders as they stood on the beach. His eyes seemed to gleam and the smile on her own face stretched from ear to ear.

"A tourist took the photo for us one day. He wandered up the beach where we were walking, and you stopped him. I don't normally do pictures. Not at all. But this one time, with you, I wanted that memory."

We look so happy.

"Maybe this will make you feel better." He put the frame near the lamp. "You can see that once upon a time, you obviously trusted me."

Anger flashed inside of her. "You should have come to me. Told me *sooner—*"

"I have lots of regrets in this world. I learned long ago that I can't change what I've done. So I just try to alter my course going forward." He swallowed. "Consider my course altered." His nostrils flared. "Do you need anything?"

Answers. But she realized that him just *telling* her about their past wasn't the same as having the memories awaken in her mind.

"Okay, then, I'll let you get back to sleep." He shoved from the bed as if he'd been burned. "Too hard being this fucking close to you," he muttered.

Her eyes narrowed. "Why did you have the photo in the drawer?"

He looked over his shoulder. "Can't you figure that out?"

"If you wanted me out of your life, why not just throw it away?"

"Never said *I* wanted you out." He marched for the door.

"*Ram.*"

He stopped. "The photo was in the drawer because seeing it every day when I woke up hurt. I didn't have you any longer, and it gutted me."

Was that the truth?

"But I couldn't throw the photo away because I needed to see your face at night. You were the last thing I wanted to see. So I kept the photo in the drawer where it could be close to me." A shake of his head. "You think I don't get how screwed up I am when it comes to you? I do. Yet another reason why you were better off without me." He curled his fingers around the doorknob.

"I was the one to seduce you."

His body jerked.

"You said no. So I stripped. Told you that I knew what I was doing. That it was my choice." The bits and pieces seemed to grow stronger in her mind. "You carried me in here. This..." The bed she was in... "We had sex here for the first time."

"Doesn't sound like a question."

It wasn't. Whitney *knew* everything she said was the truth.

"Looks like some memories are definitely coming back." He threw another glance over his shoulder. "Wonder what caused the change?"

She knew exactly what had caused it.

You did.

"And...follow-up question, just what will you remember next?"

***

Ramsey slipped into the hallway and quietly closed the door behind him. Then he released a long breath.

Fuck.

He'd heard her moaning and hadn't realized those sounds were because she'd been having a sex dream—sex memory, whatever—and he'd gone rushing in there because he'd thought that something might be wrong.

When he'd found out the truth...

All he'd wanted was to climb into that bed with her. To have her over and over again. To feel her nails raking down his back as his cock shoved into the hot heaven that he craved so much. Her sweet smell had wrapped around him. Her gorgeous eyes had stolen his soul. And his eager cock had immediately gotten hard and ready.

He glared down at his body. "Yeah, we're trying to *woo* her, not scare the hell out of her."

Like his dick knew anything about wooing. He just knew about fucking. And he knew he loved fucking Whitney.

Ramsey stalked away from the door. Headed back into the den and back to the laptop he'd been searching moments before. Yes, he knew going through her laptop was a total invasion of privacy. So what? He was used to doing shit like that. When it came to Whitney, he was going to have to play dirty.

He'd managed to access some sort of journal or diary. She'd probably call it one of her scientific logs, but the info in it hardly all seemed scientific. Maybe she'd started with that intention when she'd first visited his bar, but things had changed.

They'd gotten personal.

Unfortunately, it seemed that most of the data was corrupted. He kept seeing lots of ones and zeroes interrupting her entries and that wasn't helping him much.

Fortunately, there was a tech guy who owed him some favors. A guy he'd already contacted previously because he'd wanted help with that prick Rudy and his freelance boss. But now, it seemed his tech buddy was about to get a second job.

Ramsey hauled out his phone and dialed as he opened up the laptop with his left hand.

"Why in the hell are you bothering me?" A growling demand.

"Hello to you, too, asshole."

"Ramsey."

He almost smiled. *"Cyrus."*

"We aren't supposed to be communicating. You know this. I told you this shit *last* time. I don't want any links between us to be found."

"Good for you, but I have another problem, and you owe me so..."

"Are you shitting me right now? Since when did I become your problem solver?"

Ramsey ignored the question. "I have a corrupted laptop. You retrieve all the data on it for me, and I'll call us even."

"What you *need* to be doing is calling your local tech repair company. Jeez, man, are you seriously hitting me up for a technical issue? Do you know the kind of jobs that I usually handle—"

"Of course, I know. We've worked together enough that I know." More secrets. Ramsey had so many of them.

"And yet you are calling me in the middle of the night to handle your tech shit?"

"Yes." He was getting annoyed. "Because the 'tech shit' on this laptop is of extreme importance. No one else can see it, understand? You share not a word about what you discover with anyone."

Silence. "Okay. Now I am vaguely curious..."

Curiosity was Cyrus's main weakness. "How wonderful for you. Arrange a pick-up at my bar tomorrow at nine in the morning. You retrieve the data, and I'll consider us done."

"And if I can't retrieve it? Because I'm not a miracle worker, you know."

"Then you'll still owe me. The next time I call in my debt, I won't be nearly as friendly."

"You are never friendly."

"Good of you to notice." No, he wasn't the friendly one. That was his brother Jinx. Ramsey was more the one who did the dirty work so that everyone else could continue living their happy lives.

Someone had to handle all the blood and pain. Some days, it felt as if Ramsey had been made for that job. "And I need that information on Rudy's boss ASAP. You told me you could find this shit."

"I *can*. And, actually, I already did, but you're not going to like what I discovered."

"What in the hell does that mean?"

"It means don't shoot the messenger, okay? It means take a breath when I tell you what I discovered and remember that I am a semi-friend to you."

"You think we're friends?"

"No, I really don't. The words felt weird when they came out."

Ramsey grunted. "Tell me the bastard's name."

"Well, now, I don't exactly have that."

His hold tightened on the phone. "So much for being the friggin' best."

"I *am* the friggin' best. The guy never used a real name. He tried to hide his location, too, but I tracked him down because I am awesome."

The man's ego was annoying.

"And when I figured out the location, I kinda thought you were testing me. Aren't we supposed to be past the testing point in our relationship?"

"What in the hell are you talking about?"

A sigh. "I'm talking about the fact that I traced those messages back to an IP address...used a basic IP geolocation lookup to do the deed. When I realized he'd been sending his messages for those flower deliveries from your bar, I thought you must be jerking me around—"

"Back up," Ramsey rasped.

"To which part?" Cyrus wanted to know.

"The prick sent the orders from *my* bar?"

"Can't exactly say if he was in your place or outside your place, but yeah, he was there in the general area. So, I take it by your tone that this was *not* a test of my skills?"

"I want his name."

"Well, look, I can't give it to you...yet. I'll keep digging. Meanwhile, though, I just let you know the mystery guy is someone who frequents your bar. Can't you do your usual routine of scaring the hell out of everyone near you and figure out who the jerk is?"

Yes, he absolutely could do that usual routine. And he planned to do it...immediately.

CHAPTER NINE

Observation notes: I'm not going to Ramsey's for observation any longer. Everything has changed. Last night, there was a chance to walk away. He gave me that chance, but I didn't want to take it. Because what I wanted most was—

***

"Why the hell does the file turn to shit when things get good?" Ramsey glared at the screen. He should close the damn thing. Wait for Cyrus and his tech crazy self to do his mojo, but instead, Ramsey kept scrolling through the semi-legible material even as he felt like some voyeur who'd gotten hold of a diary.

What had Whitney wanted most? If he didn't know, then how the hell was he supposed to give it to her?

His phone vibrated. Gave a warning peal. Instantly, his body went on alert as he grabbed the phone. A few taps on the screen showed Ramsey the uninvited visitor who was striding up the stairs of his beach house and straight toward his door.

He should have expected this.

Now Ramsey did close the laptop. He also managed to sprint across the room and yank open the door before his brother could pound on it and wake up Whitney.

"Normal people visit during the day," Ramsey pointed out to the unwelcome visitor. Or at least, he'd been told normal people visited during that period. "Not in the middle of the night." He made a shooing motion with his hand. "Come back tomorrow."

"Technically, it is tomorrow." Jinx flashed his wide grin. "So I guess I'm right on time." He moved to slide into the house.

So Ramsey side-stepped to block him. "Not really in the mood for visitors."

"I'm not a visitor. I'm family. Huge difference."

He kept blocking the entrance. "Don't you have somewhere else you need to be?"

"Yes." Sad. Long-suffering. "In bed with my gorgeous lady. That is where I would *love* to be. But then I heard on the police radio about a fire at Whitney's house..."

Suspicion filled him. "Why were you listening to the police radio?"

"Why not listen to it? I like to know what's going on in my community. Is that a bad thing?"

"*Jinx.*"

His fleeting humor vanished. "I was worried. The neighbor reported that a man fled with Whitney. When I heard the man was on a motorcycle and then the next thing I knew, the whole fire thing seemed to be magically hushed up—well, I, of course, immediately thought of you."

"The fire is not being hushed up," Ramsey clarified. "It's being thoroughly investigated."

"But I *am* a private investigator. I can help on this."

"Believe me, you've helped enough," he muttered. *You told me she was pregnant.* "Now, how about you hit the road and—"

"Ramsey? Who's here?" Whitney's soft voice. And she sounded far too close.

He whipped around. She was so damn cute in those pajamas. Blue shorts and matching top, and he could see the thrust of her nipples against the soft fabric and—

Ramsey cleared his throat. "It's just a nosey neighbor. Don't worry. He's leaving." Ramsey grabbed the coat he'd hung near the door and hurried toward her. "You should put this on." He put the coat over her. "Don't want you getting a chill."

She shoved the coat back at him. "Do you *know* how hot it is?"

He knew she was hot. *Focus.* Dammit. What was wrong with him?

Oh, not much. The woman of my dreams is pregnant with my baby, and I don't know how to win her back.

Whitney peered around him. "And that's Jinx, not some neighbor."

"I actually don't live too far away," Jinx revealed in a helpful tone. "Just a few miles. I suppose if you stretched it, you *could* call us neighbors?"

She moved around Ramsey and toward Jinx. "Why are you standing in the doorway?"

"Because I don't think my baby brother wants me inside. Hurtful."

Her lips parted as she jerked her head back toward Ramsey. "You didn't invite him in?"

No, he'd wanted to slam the door shut on Jinx, but obviously, that ship had sailed. With no other option, Ramsey grudgingly waved Jinx inside.

"So gracious," Jinx drawled. "Thank you. Truly. From the bottom of my heart."

"Fuck off."

Jinx smirked before shutting—and locking—the door. Then his stare swept between Ramsey and Whitney. "Cozy. Am I to assume that all is right in this wonderful world of—"

"No," Ramsey snapped before Jinx could say the wrong thing. "You shouldn't assume anything." He sounded too growly. Clearing his throat, he tried to sound somewhat polite and normal. "Her place isn't safe. Some dick started the fire while we were both inside." Okay, so he'd failed at being polite. When it came to Whitney's safety, polite just didn't cut it.

Jinx's expression hardened.

"I got her out and brought Whitney here so I could keep her safe." *And she'll keep staying with me.* Though he made a mental note to get clothes and toiletries for her. The stuff at her place probably smelled of smoke, so he'd get new things delivered.

They should probably start to make plans for what the baby would need, too.

His head turned as his thoughts were diverted. He calculated and tried to see just how far along she was. He didn't think she was showing. Shouldn't she be showing? Was everything all right? His feet hurried toward her, and his hand reached out to—

Her fingers curled around his wrist. "What are you doing?"

Should he admit that he'd really, really wanted to touch her stomach and *feel* to see if there was a sign of his baby?

"Oh, dude," Jinx called out with a disapproving tut-tut. "Major no-no. You do not touch a pregnant woman's belly without her permission. I was reading about that earlier and it seems they do not like that. Big invasion of personal space."

His head turned toward his brother. "An invasion of personal space." His gaze raked Jinx. "You don't say."

"Wait. Hold on." Her grip tightened on Ramsey's wrist. "Did you *both* research pregnancies when you found out about me? Is that how you spent your free time?"

Ramsey might have done some reading, yes.

Jinx shrugged. "I've never been an uncle before. I thought I should be prepared."

"Uncle." She sucked in a breath and let go of Ramsey's hand. "Right. Because you're family. And you're the one who told Ramsey about my pregnancy. Then he headed to my place after apparently reading pregnancy books—or something—and the revving car came by and my front window exploded into lots and lots of pieces of glass."

Jinx closed in on them. "I want to help on this."

"This will be a shocker," Ramsey began as he slanted a hard glance Jinx's way. "But I actually have plenty of people on hand who can cover this."

"He has cops that owe him," Whitney chimed in to say. "He called them earlier. They're going to report in soon."

Jinx rocked back onto the heels of his feet. "Cops...on the take?" His lips thinned. "Thought you were leaving that life behind."

Ramsey just stared back at him.

Jinx's jaw hardened.

"I have people," Ramsey said simply. Yes, some of those people were on the take. For the right price, Ramsey had learned he could get some very useful contacts. "I do not need the assistance of Trouble for Hire Private Investigations, but I certainly appreciate the house call—"

"*Stop it.*" An angry snap from Whitney.

He blinked. "Excuse me?" Why was she so upset?

"He is your brother. He's worried about you. *That's* why he's here in the middle of the night. You don't have to be growly and rude to him. You could try saying, 'Thanks for checking on me. Thanks for rushing all the way to my side. And, yes, I can use your help.'"

"God, I love her," Jinx muttered as he stared at Whitney with adoring eyes. "Why have you not put a ring on her finger?"

Ramsey thought about putting his fist in Jinx's—

"You're doing it again! You're *glaring* at your brother."

He was. Guilty.

"Trouble for Hire Private Investigations is the best," she said flatly.

"Aw, thanks for noticing." Jinx beamed.

"They found the people who tried to kill me. They've stopped other high profiler killers. If someone is targeting me—or you, or us both— then it makes sense to have the best in the business looking out for our interests. And, no offense, Ramsey, but I'm not completely sure I trust all of *your* people. Cops on the take and criminals looking to score may not be overly motivated to help us bring down bad guys."

"And no one is more motivated than your brother when it comes to protecting you," Jinx chimed in. He put his hand over his heart. "I swear it." His voice turned serious as his hand dropped and he gazed at Ramsey. "I want to look out for you. It's what I wanted my whole life."

Yeah, he knew that. He also knew that he wasn't a damn kid any longer, and he'd long since passed the point of needing his big brother to swoop in and clean up his messes.

But try explaining that to Jinx. Jinx had worked covert ops for Uncle Sam that were dangerous as hell because Jinx had thought that taking those jobs would result in Ramsey's crimes being erased.

Jinx still didn't know what a raw deal he'd gotten for that exchange.

Jinx offered his hand to Ramsey. "Let's make a deal. I help you, and you stop acting like you're a monster who doesn't have a heart."

He stared at the offered hand. Ramsey was surprised by just how insightful Jinx's comment actually was. He shouldn't have been, though. Jinx might flash his easy grin all the time, but the man was wicked smart. Always had been.

When they'd been thrown into the foster care system, Jinx had learned that a relaxed air and fun-loving grin reassured people. It warmed up potential families. Disarmed them.

Meanwhile, when Ramsey had been on the streets, he'd learned that showing any weakness would get your ass beat. You had to be the coldest bastard on the block if you wanted to get business handled.

But he *did* have a heart, and that was the problem. He had a very big weakness that someone had discovered, and if he wanted to keep Whitney safe, then maybe he needed to use every resource available.

He took Jinx's hand. "Am I getting the package deal? Are War and Odin going to be thrown in, too?" Oh, he could just imagine the expression on War's face...

It was *almost* enough to make him smile.

"Odin's lady is best friends with Whitney. Hell, yes, it goes without saying that you are about to get the package deal."

"Excellent!" Whitney excitedly declared before Ramsey could respond. "Then I think we should all start the investigation with *this*." And she pulled a phone out of the loose pocket of her pajama shorts.

"What's on the phone?" Jinx asked as he peered down at it.

Ramsey dropped his hold on his brother's hand.

"I installed one of those video doorbells at my place yesterday. Forgot about it in the excitement of the night. Then when I woke up and, ah—" A blush tinged her cheeks as she cut a quick, nervous glance toward Ramsey. Her throat cleared. "When I woke up," she said, voice cracking a little, "I couldn't get back to sleep and I remembered that the doorbell was supposed to constantly be recording video if it was triggered by motion. There was lots of motion happening with the fire, so I thought there could be something useful for us on the recording." She turned the phone toward Ramsey. Hit a button and a video began to play. "I was correct. There was something useful."

Ramsey watched the video fill the screen. He saw the man in the ski mask leap out of the car. Saw him throw a burning bottle toward Whitney's house. Then another.

Then he saw the SOB drive away...in a very distinct and classic ride. Ramsey had thought that growling engine sounded familiar.

"Oh, no. No way." Jinx was adamant.

He'd recognized the car, too. He should. Wasn't as if there were a ton of mint condition 67 Impalas on the roads.

"We both know he would *not* do that. No way, not any freaking day," Jinx said quickly.

"Who?" Whitney demanded.

"War," Ramsey gritted out. "Warren Channing. The owner of Trouble for Hire."

"There is no way," Jinx repeated. "He would never do anything like that."

"I'll find out," Ramsey promised, "when I have a fun one-on-one chat with War." A chat that was long overdue.

"It's *obviously* a frame job. Someone wants you to think that War is coming after you. It's not a secret that the two of you have a bit of an...antagonistic relationship."

"We don't have any relationship," he corrected. *I stay the hell out of his business, and he stays out of mine.* Or at least, that had been the case.

"Someone wants you pissed at War. Someone wants you looking the wrong way. Don't do it. Let Trouble for Hire help you. Don't turn your back on the real people who want to protect you."

***

"You realize, of course, that he's running straight to War," Whitney said as soon as Jinx left.

"Of course. Where else would he run?"

There was something about his tone...Her head tilted as Whitney studied Ramsey. "Are you...jealous?" No, surely not.

He laughed. "Of what? My estranged brother's friendship with that arrogant ass War?"

She actually thought, yes, that was exactly what he was jealous of. She'd done research on Trouble for Hire after she'd learned how instrumental they'd been after her disappearance. "War and Odin worked special ops together." She was trying to connect the dots. "Did Jinx do the same kind of work?"

"Can't really say. I hear all of that is hush-hush. Need-to-know-level spy BS."

"I will take that as a yes." She bit her lower lip. "So I don't remember a lot of specifics about your relationship with Jinx..."

"That's because there was no relationship. We got sent into the foster care system. People wanted to take Jinx into their homes—get him out of that group place where we were living, but he kept insisting that we were a package deal." He rolled back his shoulders. "It's hot in here. I'm going for some air."

He strode toward the balcony doors. Hauled them open. The thunder of the waves reached her ears.

He walked out.

Her shoulders straightened as she followed him. Whitney found him leaning up against the railing and staring out into the night.

It took her a moment to decide which of the questions rolling through her mind she should ask first. "How did a package deal become so separate?"

"Apparently, I'm a moody sonofabitch."

She raised an eyebrow.

"The social workers threw lots of labels at me back then. Said some stuff about me having attachment issues. Said I couldn't bond with families. Basically said I'd never have a family of my own again." His stare was on the darkness of the waves. "But Jinx had a chance. Everyone always likes Jinx. So I made sure he got his chance."

"You left." Certainty filled her.

"I left." A hard nod that she could just make out because of the moonlight. "He was better off without me, and—"

"You *bastard*." She rushed toward him. Grabbed his arm and spun him around. "*That's* your go-to, isn't it?"

"What?" Instantly, his voice gentled. "Sweetheart, calm down, it's not good for the—"

"You left Jinx because you thought his life would be better without you in it!"

"Uh, his life *was* better. He became a freaking international hero. Became best buds with War and Odin and he got the family he'd always deserved."

A family that didn't include you. "You tried to do the same thing to me." The wind caught her hair and tossed it against her cheeks. "You wanted to stay away because you thought my life would be better without you in it."

"It's a common refrain. The good people tend to be better without—"

"Nothing was better for me!" She wanted to shake him. "I felt like a giant chunk was missing from my heart. When I walked in that bar and finally talked to you, I could almost hear pieces sliding into place. I was suddenly angry and scared but I also—and it made *no* sense—I also finally felt safe. Right. Like I had come home."

"Whitney..." He brushed her hair behind her ear.

"Don't you dare be a martyr with me ever again, got it? That ends. Now."

Ramsey laughed. "I'm hardly a martyr. More like the one who turns everyone else's world into a nightmare. Those social workers thought I was dangerous when I was a kid. Can you imagine what they would think of me now?"

"I don't care what they would think of you! Knowing DHR as I do, I can tell you they were probably exceedingly overworked and didn't have enough time to thoroughly look at the kids. Huge strides have been taken since then, but there is always more work to do. They made a mistake with you. You have it in your head that you can't have a family, but you're wrong. The very crazy, *martyr-like* acts that you do prove that you care. So let it all go." She could feel his pain beating at her, and Whitney hated it. "Just let it go," she pleaded. "Because they were wrong."

His gaze seemed to search hers and then...

His mouth crashed onto hers.

Or maybe her mouth crashed onto his. All Whitney knew was that she was on her toes, her hands were wrapped tightly around his arms, and she was kissing him with every single bit of passion and hunger that she possessed. And it felt right. It felt familiar.

It felt like she'd finally found the part of her life that she had been missing.

CHAPTER TEN

Observation notes: I think someone followed me today. It was strange. I felt this prickle in the back of my neck, and I kept looking back, but no one was there.

I know the people at Ramsey's are dangerous. I'd be a fool not to know that. I also know that Ramsey put out an order of protection for me. No one is supposed to so much as touch me while that order is in place.

I asked him how long the order would last. He said...forever.

So why do I feel like someone is after me?

***

He lifted her against him. Her legs curled around his waist. The delicate fabric of her pajama shorts rode up, and she could feel the rough denim of his jeans against her thighs. He pulled his mouth from hers. Began to kiss a heated path down her neck as she arched against him.

We've done this before. The knowledge settled fully within her, and it made her want him all the more. Her heart raced, her body quivered, and she wanted to rip off his clothes and jump him, right there.

Considering the way that her legs were clamped around his hips, maybe she *was* jumping him and...so what? She wanted this. Wanted *him*.

He carried her back into the house. Took her to his bedroom. Lowered her carefully onto the bed. He loomed over her and braced his hand near her head. His eyes were so dark and deep, and Whitney could not look away.

"You need to be sure." His voice was guttural. "I let you go once. I can't have you and do it again."

There it was. The possessive edge in his voice. And when he kissed her once more, the possessiveness was there, too. His mouth was harder, more dominant, pulling out a response she was only too eager to give him.

His left hand slid between their bodies. Easily undid the small line of buttons on her pajama top and opened it.

But when his fingers pressed to her skin, she jolted.

"Whitney?"

"I..." Her body was different now. Breasts bigger and more swollen. Waist and stomach expanding.

"I'll be careful," he promised. "I swear, I won't hurt you."

She hadn't thought he would. Before she could say anything, he was pulling back. He stripped her with careful, tender motions. There were faint calluses on the tips of his fingers, but somehow that small bit of roughness just aroused her all the more.

He stared at her body when she was naked. He still had on his jeans and t-shirt, and she wanted those gone. A flash of vulnerability hit her as she lay spread before him, and his eyes slid over every inch of her body.

He'd see the changes from the pregnancy. No baggy clothes could hide her. No—

"You are beautiful." He leaned forward. Pressed a tender kiss to the curve of her stomach. Another.

Tears pricked her eyes. She was just emotional. Hormones. That was why she had to blink so quickly and not because...

I missed him.

His hands slid between her legs. Pushed her thighs farther apart. "I missed you." His words, but for a moment, it seemed he might be echoing her.

No, no, I didn't say my words out loud. I didn't—

His fingers teased her core. Stroked over her clit and had her breath sawing out. "Ram!"

"Love the way you say my name." He was on the bed. Between her legs. And then his head lowered and his mouth took her.

Her ankles dug into the mattress as a surge of heat flooded through her whole body. He licked and savored her. Lapped her up even as his fingers dipped inside of her. His tongue teased her clit, working her over and over again, and his fingers were ever so careful as he stretched her and pushed into—

Pleasure erupted. She shoved her hips up against him as the orgasm ripped through her. It was wave after wave of release that surged and surged, and she felt the powerful release in every inch of her body.

When she could breathe normally and when she could open the eyes she'd tightly squeezed closed, she looked at him.

He stared back at her with an expression that was absolutely savage. "Now," Ramsey demanded, "you choose."

She did what? Uh, hadn't she already made a choice? She was naked and quaking in front of him.

"I can't have you and let go again. If you give yourself to me, there is no going back."

What was she going back to? The emptiness of not knowing what the hell had happened to her life? Whitney shook her head.

His jaw locked. His lips thinned. Pain flashed in his eyes. "I understand."

He climbed from the bed.

Her hand flew out and curled around his wrist. "I don't think you do."

He stared at her hand. A shudder worked along the length of his body.

"*You* need to choose," Whitney told him. "I already made my choice. That's why I'm the naked one. Seems like I tend to get naked with you a lot while you stay all prudish and dressed."

His eyebrows flew up. "Prudish? I just had my mouth on your clit, baby. And I want to eat you up again and again."

She flushed. He wasn't going to distract her. *Okay, he is, but...* "You give yourself to me, and there is no going back." Those *had* been his words. Now they were hers. "You don't get to pull away because you think you're too dangerous or because you think you know what's best. We start over because that's what we have to do. You remember, I don't, so we just go forward, and we see what works and what doesn't." She rose to her knees. Faced him. "Maybe we'll be amazing. Maybe we'll be tragic. But we both agree to try and see how this thing ends."

He took a step away from her and broke the grip that she had on his wrist. Whitney bit her lip and waited.

Ramsey whipped his shirt over his head. His muscles flexed and tensed with the movements. His hand went to the front of his jeans. He yanked open the button and hauled down the zipper.

His dick was thick, long, and bobbing toward her. She wanted it *in* her. But...

Her gaze rose back to his chest. He closed the distance between them, and her fingers reached for one of the long scars that sliced over his skin. "From a knife?" She thought it was. That one, as well as the others she saw on him. Except for the round one near his side. That looked like a bullet wound. And he had tats on his chest. Different swirling tats. Beautiful and dark.

"Doesn't hurt me anymore, baby."

She was stroking one of his scars. Whitney leaned forward and brushed her mouth over it. "I hate someone hurt you."

He sucked in a breath. "That's exactly what you told me before."

It was?

"No one but my brother ever gave a shit if I hurt or not...until you." One hand slid under her chin and tipped her head up. "We won't be fucking tragic. No one will hurt you. I swear it. Nothing bad will ever happen to you again."

His mouth swept over hers. His tongue thrust into her mouth, and she closed her eyes because she wanted him to be right. She didn't want anything bad happening to either of them, but the truth was...

The world was full of bad things. Good things, bad things, and everything in between. Safety wasn't promised for anyone.

He released her, and she slid over in the bed to make room for him. But instead of reaching for her once more, Ramsey stretched out on the bed.

She crouched beside him as her knees pressed into the mattress.

"I want you on top." His voice was a sensual rumble. "I don't want to go too hard or deep. You show me what you want."

He kept worrying about hurting her. "My doctor said sex was fine. Normal."

A low laugh came from him. "Sex between us is never just *fine*."

No, she didn't think it was. Based on the release that still sent little aftershocks through her, Whitney thought that sex between them might just be mind-blowing.

"Come here," he ordered. He tugged her toward him.

She climbed on him. Straddled his hips. Felt the wide head of his cock push toward the entrance to her body. Her hands pressed against his rock-hard abs as she tried to brace her body.

"Take as much as you want, sweetheart," he growled. "I'm yours."

If only.

The thought was fleeting and caused a pang within her. But then she was slowly sinking onto him. He was filling her, inch by delicious inch, and there wasn't any more time for deep thoughts. There wasn't time for anything but the raw need and passion that stirred between them. More and more and more...she took. He held himself still beneath her. All heat and strength. She rocked her hips as she took ever more. Her head tipped back, and a pleasure-filled moan escaped from her because he filled her so well.

His hand moved down. His fingers pressed over her. Strummed her clit.

Whitney's movements became harder. More frantic. She took even more of him.

Her knees pushed into the mattress as she kept rocking up and down. His guttural growls urged her on, and there was no stopping or holding back. Pleasure snapped through her as a second orgasm rocked her and she choked out his name.

He erupted right after her. A long surge spilled inside of her even as she greedily clamped her inner muscles around his cock. He roared her name, and she collapsed on top of him.

Their hearts were racing together. Breaths panting. His arms closed around her, and he held her against him, and it all just felt so right.

Maybe...maybe it could be. Maybe *they* could be.

"Did I hurt you?"

She smiled but he couldn't see it. "No." Though she might have given him lots of scratches. He was still inside of her. Still, um, getting hard again?

"I missed you," he said.

She squeezed her inner muscles around him once more. "I can tell." He'd said there hadn't been anyone else since she vanished. Her head lifted. She smiled at him. "How can I miss someone that I didn't remember?"

His expression...*Ramsey?* For just a moment, there had been something else there. But when he'd realized she was looking at him, it had vanished. She could have sworn that she'd just seen—

Longing?

"Easy enough to do," he rumbled. "I missed you my whole life and we'd never even met."

She sucked in a breath. Stared into his eyes and said, "You do that."

"Do what?"

"You say sweet things that I don't expect from you."

He smiled. "Want a secret?"

I want every single one you possess.

"I'm only sweet with you. With everyone else, I'm a complete bastard." His hips pushed up.

Pleasure shot through her. "Why...why am I the lucky one?"

His eyes gleamed. "You'll figure it out. Soon enough. But for now, I want to fuck you again."

"Excellent plan." She licked her lips. "Genius."

"So glad you think so..."

***

She'd eventually fallen asleep in his arms. He'd drifted off, too. And he'd been as close to heaven as a guy like him could ever hope to get.

She didn't have any other moaning dreams. A pity. But then again, he'd had her doing plenty of moaning *before* she'd fallen back to sleep.

He had Whitney back in his bed. In his life. He didn't plan to let her go anytime soon. *Or anytime at all.* He'd started making arrangements yesterday, as soon as he'd learned about the baby. It wouldn't be easy, but in the end, Ramsey would have what he wanted.

He just had to take care of a few bloody details first.

Carefully, he slipped from the bed. The glowing clock told him it was nearing seven a.m., and they'd be having a visitor soon. He needed to go over duties and details. Then Ramsey would have to break the news to Whitney. She *would* be having a bodyguard when he wasn't around. Her safety had to come first.

After a quick shower, he dressed, and his gaze only darted to Whitney's sexy form in the bed about a dozen times. She looked as if she belonged in his bed.

Then again, she always had.

She was the only woman he'd ever brought to his house. She was also the only woman who'd ever gotten into his heart.

When Jag knocked on the door ten minutes later, Ramsey was ready for him. He waved in his right-hand guy and ignored the worried glances that Jag kept giving him.

"Got a new assignment for you today," Ramsey told him. "And I cannot stress to you just how important this job will be."

Jag straightened. "Who the hell are we taking out?" A tigerish grin slid over his face. "Is it that jerk Malles who thinks he's going to take over territory in—"

"I want you guarding Whitney Augustine."

"What?" Jag frowned at Ramsey. "Why the hell would I do that?"

"Because I'll be paying you to do that." Jag was one of the best fighters he knew. The man was brutal to enemies. A true force to be reckoned with. And he was one of the few people Ramsey trusted. Well, semi-trusted. "I want you and Darius on this. When you're not tailing her, he will be."

"We're the best two men you've got!" Jag's face mottled.

"Absolutely." That was why he was giving them the job. "Now keep your voice down."

"What? Why the hell would I keep—"

"Because Whitney is sleeping, and I don't want you waking her up."

Jag gaped. "Sleeping? *Here?*"

"Someone torched her house last night." He'd filled Darius in on the details already. Darius was currently meeting with the PD—the cops that Ramsey had an, um, working relationship with— to get the latest intel. "She was inside at the time. So was I."

"Damn." Jag plopped down on the couch. "What dumb bastard are we about to kill?"

"Darius is working on that right now."

Jag dragged a hand across his face. As always, he was completely clean shaven. "You didn't see anyone? You don't have any suspects?"

"There's someone I'll be talking with this morning." He inclined his head toward Jag. "That's why you will be staying with Whitney."

"She doesn't remember me, man. I saw that at the bar. Not a flicker of recognition on her face. I'm not thinking she'll be real comfortable with a stranger dodging her steps."

"I can deal with her lack of comfort. I can't deal with someone hurting her. Whitney will remain safe."

Jag glanced around. "So, like, are the two of you an item again?"

"Yes."

Jag's wide gaze jumped back to him. "That was fast."

"We are one hundred percent an item. You can let that word spread." This time, it would not be a secret. This time, everyone would learn he'd destroy the world for her. "You can also make sure that everyone knows that any insult to her is an insult to me."

"Uh, Ramsey..." Jag frowned. "I thought you were staying away from her. Pretty sure you told me that was the plan not even a week ago when you were slamming down shots as fast as I could line them up."

His hands went to his hips. "The plan changed."

Footsteps padded down the hallway. Shit. *Be dressed. Don't be in those sexy pajamas.* But, hell, her clothes hadn't been delivered yet and—

She came into the den. Saw him and a wide smile spread across her face. Her green eyes gleamed.

She's happy to see me.

No one was ever happy to see him. Most people *ran* when they saw him. Not Whitney.

"Hope you don't mind," she said, a little bit shyly, "but I borrowed your robe."

The robe swallowed her. And she still looked sexy as hell. "You can have anything of mine that you want." He meant it.

"Ahem." Jag cleared his throat. Twice.

Whitney's eyes flared and her gaze flew toward him.

She hadn't even realized he was there. Normally, Whitney was a whole lot more situationally aware.

"Uh, hello." She tucked her hands into the pockets of the robe even as a faint blush stained her cheeks. "You're the bartender, right? I, uh, saw you at Ramsey's."

"Jag is one hell of a lot more than just a bartender. He's been with me for years. Knows my business inside and out. And he's the dirtiest fighter you'll ever meet."

"Aw, you say the sweetest things," Jag mocked.

"I tell Ramsey that very thing, too." But Whitney wasn't mocking.

Ramsey actually *did* say sweet shit to her. When it came to Whitney, he couldn't help himself. The woman deserved to hear those kinds of things.

Jag frowned at her. "You tell him what?"

"That he says sweet things—"

Yeah, time to divert the conversation. "Jag is going to be your bodyguard when I can't be close. He and another associate of mine, Darius, will switch out so that you aren't left alone."

Anger flashed on her delicate features. "Ramsey! We talked about this." The full force of her gorgeous glare was on him. "I told you that I can't have a bodyguard trailing around while I'm working on campus. That's just not an option—"

It was the only option. "I called in Jag because he knows how to keep a low profile."

"The lowest," Jag assured her. He'd risen to his feet. He did give her a quick smile.

She didn't look reassured by it. Probably because it was still tigerish.

"Jag can blend," Ramsey tried to reassure her. "He can stay in the periphery, and if he spots trouble coming, he can step into action immediately." Just like Darius could. They'd watched his back and saved his ass plenty of times over the years. "He and Darius have been my bodyguards, and they've kept me alive."

She took three hurried steps toward him. "When were you in danger?"

"Oh, that's cute," Jag said. "He's *always* in danger."

Ramsey sent him a hard stare that clearly said *not now*. "This isn't a negotiable point," Ramsey explained as he turned back toward Whitney. "Until I find out who torched your place, you will have protection."

"And neither one of us actually believes it was War." She huffed out a breath.

"War?" Jag's shoulders straightened. "Tell me we are not talking about that jackass War Channing. Prick always thinks he's so freaking perfect."

"That would be the jackass in question," Ramsey stated flatly. Jag was right. War always did think he was perfect. Drove Ramsey up the wall.

"And we think *War* is involved in what went down at her place?" Jag made a fist and then drove it into his opposite palm. "Please let me question him. It can be my early Christmas present or something."

"I'll be questioning him." He'd already said where Jag would be heading.

"I need coffee before dealing with this," Whitney announced. She turned on her heel and marched for the kitchen. "With that really good cream you keep for me."

Wait. She *remembered* that he kept that cream for her?

Curious, he followed her and was aware of Jag trailing behind, too. "I could go for coffee," Jag muttered.

Inside the kitchen, Ramsey halted. Whitney had just opened the cabinet that contained the coffee mugs. She plucked three down, then reached for the drawer with his spoons. She pulled them out before snagging the specialty coffee grounds that he kept sealed inside—

She stopped. Swallowed. Her gaze rose to meet his. "How did I know where everything was?"

He smiled at her. "Guessing my place seems familiar, huh?"

Hope lit her gaze, and it was a beautiful thing. No, *she* was beautiful.

"My memory is coming back." She put down the coffee, ran for him, and tossed her arms around his neck. *"My memory is coming back!"*

His arms closed around her.

***

"You sure you know what you're doing?" Jag demanded as he followed Ramsey down the stairs that led to the beach.

Ramsey had a backpack slung over one shoulder. In the bag? Whitney's laptop. Her clothing and essential supplies had been delivered, and when she'd gone to shower and change, he'd slipped the laptop into his bag. He had an appointment to keep—several of them—so it was time to be on his way. "She agreed to protection." Reluctantly, she'd agreed. "When she's ready, you take her to work. You stay in the background, but if you see any danger, you rip the threatening sonofabitch apart." Seemed simple enough to him.

"No, man, I'm talking about you. The way I saw you acting in there..." The lines near his mouth deepened. "You're doing it again."

His shoulders stiffened. "It?"

"Getting all wrapped up in her. I don't get it. I mean, sure, fucking is always fun—"

He lunged forward and grabbed Jag around the shoulders. "Watch the mouth. Now."

"What? Since when is fucking a bad word—"

"You don't say anything negative about her. No one does. Thought I'd made it clear before that she was off-limits. In case you were confused, let me repeat...Whitney is mine. No one says or does anything that causes so much as a flicker of unease to come into her life, got me?"

"What the hell, Ramsey? Why are you threatening me? I'm one of your best friends!"

He didn't let Jag go.

"Fine," Jag spat. "Got it. I will use only soft words and my sweetest voice with your delicate flower, is that good enough for you?"

Ramsey smiled. "That's just fucking wonderful."

Jag's eyes narrowed.

Ramsey let him go and turned for his motorcycle. He'd be picking up a new ride before he returned to Whitney's side.

"So if she's not supposed to have even a flicker of unease, how does that measure with the shit that happened to her before?" Jag's curious voice drifted after Ramsey. "The people who hurt her are in jail, but if you're telling the world she's your lady and you *don't* go after them, you let them just sit behind bars, it's gonna make you look weak."

Now it was Ram's turn to smile. He glanced over his shoulder so that Jag could see his face— and his intent. "What makes you think I don't plan to go after them?"

"Uh, Ram..."

"Killing is easy, and it's certainly something I have considered." He'd even gotten in the jail. Stood outside their cells and thought about how simple it would be to kill the people who'd hurt her. "But you know what's worse than death? Losing everything that matters in your life. Staying behind bars until you die. Waking up each morning and knowing that the other prisoners are going to come for you and that today might be another day when they beat the hell out of you." His cold grin stretched ever more. "That's worse. That's what they deserve."

"But...how do you know...are you *sure* they'll be convicted?"

"They're not getting away." There was more than enough evidence to hold them. He knew. He'd seen every bit of it. And once they were in prison...there were plenty of people behind bars that would be happy to help Ramsey make their lives miserable.

"You are a cold bastard, you know that?"

"Thanks for noticing." He climbed onto the bike.

"Does *she* know that?'

His fingers tightened around the handlebars. Ramsey didn't answer. He drove the hell away as his motorcycle's engine snarled.

CHAPTER ELEVEN

Observation notes: Ramsey's world is made of secrets. Dangerous secrets. Sometimes, I wish that he'd tell me all of the secrets he keeps.

Other times, I think I'm better off not knowing because I suspect some of his secrets will terrify me.

***

"It's not good for us to meet up. Too many government agencies are after my ass right now. Being popular sucks." Cyrus Hendrix—former spy and current cyber gun for hire—took the backpack from Ramsey and frowned at it. "Seriously? You didn't think to use something a little less conspicuous? There's probably a cop or a Fed with a camera snapping a pic of us right now and thinking she just got herself proof of a drug deal or major crime exchange."

"No one is snapping a pic. Calm your nervous ass down."

Cyrus slung the pack over one shoulder. "I am totally calm."

Ramsey glanced toward the sky.

"So...your girlfriend had a fire at her place."

His stare jerked back to Cyrus. "What do you know about it?"

"I heard chatter. You know chatter is my thing. Cops don't seem to have many leads yet, but I'm thinking you probably have a few ideas."

He did. "Call me when the files are recovered."

Cyrus shook his head mournfully. "That's it? You don't want to know how my life is going? Don't want to thank me for the previous help I gave you? Don't want to—" He broke off. Frowned. "You look angry. Bad morning?"

"I helped *you*. When the government agency *you* worked for wanted to throw you to the wolves, I'm the one who gave you protection. I'm the one who financed your work." A reminder Cyrus shouldn't need.

"Oh, come on, you know I made you a ton of money, too—"

"I'm the one who helped you clear your name. I did all that shit from behind the scenes. No one knows that we are connected. I want it to stay that way."

Cyrus's eyebrows rose. "Then maybe you should stop asking to meet with me..."

Ramsey growled.

"Jeez, man, I am kidding. *Kidding*—"

Something heavy hit the closed door of the bar. A very loud thud.

Cyrus's eyes widened. "I swear, I was not followed. You know I watch my back."

More thudding. Heavy and hard.

"Not the cops," Ramsey murmured as he moved behind the long bar counter and reached under it for the weapon he'd put there. "They would have just stormed in by now." He jerked his head to the side. "Get your ass out the back way. Let me know what you recover, ASAP."

But Cyrus hesitated. "What about the, ah, other matter?"

"You mean the fact that some prick used *my* bar when he made those rose orders for Whitney? I'm on it." Low. Lethal.

Cyrus swallowed. "Yes, yes, I am sure you are."

More thudding. Then... "*Ramsey!*" A bellow. "I know you're in there! Don't make me break this door down."

Oh, he'd like to see the asshole try.

Cyrus gave an almost soundless whistle. "You bring out the best in people, don't you?"

"I do try. *Go.*"

Cyrus went.

Ramsey slid the gun under the back waistband of his jeans, and he pulled his shirt down to cover it. He took his time walking toward the door. The bangs and thuds continued. He also heard...

"You could help!" An annoyed snarl from the guy banging outside his place.

Ramsey unlocked the door.

War Channing stood there, with his fists raised, glaring at him.

And Jinx was just a few feet behind War.

Ramsey slowly let his gaze sweep over the two men. When War had snarled, "You could help!"— obviously, he'd been talking to Jinx.

After a tense moment, Ramsey gave them both a cold smile. "Thanks for coming to my door. Saved me the trouble of hunting your asses down."

He and War had clashed more than a few times. The guy was one of those annoyingly upright types. Freaking Captain America. Or, as Ramsey liked to think of him...Captain Asshole.

"My car was stolen," War gritted out. "My precious baby was taken, and I want the fucker who did it caught just as much as you do."

"First, you have an unhealthy attachment to your ride." Granted, the classic 67 Impala was a thing of beauty, but... "You're recently married, War. How about directing some of that feverish attention of yours to your lovely bride, hmm? Unless you have some, shall we say, performance issues—"

"Don't worry about my wife—"

Jinx stepped between them. "This is going as well as I'd hoped." His smile seemed strained. "How about we take things inside?"

Ramsey didn't move. "I don't think so."

Jinx rolled his eyes. "Stop being an ass. You obviously don't believe War is the bad guy or you would have already had him on the ground."

True.

But War sniffed. "I would like to see him try."

Ah, now that was just too tempting. Ramsey's muscles tensed as he got ready to lay out this SOB—

"No." Jinx's firm voice. "Don't do it, Ram. We are here for business, not so you can play."

Dammit. Jinx was always trying to stop his fun. But Ramsey spun and marched back into the bar because this was a conversation that should be held in private.

The door slammed shut behind the other men. Ramsey didn't bother glancing back because he knew Jinx would lock it.

"For the record," War's rumbling voice announced, "I would never do anything to hurt Whitney Augustine. I get that you don't much like me, but I'm not some hardened criminal. I don't get my kicks by going around terrorizing people and—"

Ramsey slowly turned to face War. "Oh, that's right. You're describing *me*." He held War's stare. "Because I very much get kicks from terrorizing people. Especially if those people have tried to hurt a woman who belongs to me."

Jinx hurried toward him. Worry flashed over his face. "Are you keeping your shit together? Or are you planning some bloody rampage?"

Obviously, Jinx thought option two was occurring, or else he wouldn't have been there with War.

"We found the car," War said flatly. "No way would I have let my baby be so unprotected that I didn't have a way to track her in case she was stolen. I was, ah, distracted last night when someone took her."

Ramsey could read between the lines. "You were fucking your new wife. Got it."

War's hands fisted. "*Watch it.*"

Ah, so War was protective of Rose. Good to know. Ramsey always liked to know which buttons to push with his enemies and—

Fucking hell. The realization slammed into him...Rose was War's weakness. Just as Whitney was Ramsey's. There were some things that should be off-limits. *Some people.* Always. Ramsey locked his back teeth. "My apologies. I will not be bringing up Rose again."

War blinked at him. "Are you screwing with me?"

"Trust me, that is the last thing on my agenda."

Jinx squinted and searched Ramsey's eyes, then Jinx even tried to put a hand to Ramsey's forehead. "Are you feeling all right? Should I call a doctor?"

Ramsey shoved him away. "I don't have time for this shit."

"You *apologized* to War. You don't apologize to anyone." He looked back at War. "Call an ambulance."

War was squinting at Ramsey, too. "You sick, bro?"

And *this* was why he thought they were both assholes. "Tell me about your car and then get the hell out of my place."

"Okay." Jinx exhaled heavily. "He sounds better now. Good."

"You're wasting my damn time." Time he didn't have to waste.

War held up one hand. "We got the car. Found it abandoned near the public beach."

"How great for you. Sure you're thrilled to have your *baby* back."

War's jaw hardened. "I know a few things that might help in your hunt."

Why the hell didn't War just spit out the details? Did it look as if Ramsey was in the mood to be left in suspense?

"I've got top notch security on my ride. That goes without saying. This guy was a professional. He got into my car and away from my place without making a sound. When I realized the car was gone, I tracked her movements. She went straight to Whitney's place and then he dumped the car at the beach. Choosing my ride was deliberate. This guy *wanted* you to take out your wrath on me." A pause. "The car thief wanted you at my throat. He knows you hate me, and he was hoping to set up a scene where you'd come at me with guns blazing."

Ramsey slowly removed the gun from the waistband of his jeans. He stared at the weapon.

The tension around him seemed to ratchet up.

He put the gun on a nearby table. "I'm looking for a professional car thief." Because he had no doubt that an amateur wouldn't have gotten away with War's ride. "I'm also looking for a bastard who likes playing with fire." Rage burned through him. "Whitney could have been hurt when he torched her place. Maybe he was trying to cause a battle between you and me, but he made a fatal mistake when he pulled her into the mix."

"There were no prints in my car. Already checked. Looks like everything has been wiped down."

No, a professional wouldn't leave any evidence behind.

In order to hire a professional for a job like that...well, there was really one main place in town you'd go to find the best.

Ramsey glanced around his bar.

Fucking hell.

"Yeah..." Jinx cleared his throat. "Want to tell me what's going through your head right now? Because it looks like you're ready to kill."

"Funny you should say that..." Ramsey returned. "Because I am." He pointed to the door. "Gentlemen, time for you to get the hell out. I have business that needs my attention."

***

"Deviant behavior often captures human interest because we want to know what motivates individuals to act outside of the norm. Why do these people choose to violate our social rules? What drives them? Is the behavior addictive? Thrilling?" Whitney stared into the auditorium full of students. She was far too conscious of Jag lounging in the third row, with his eyes on her. "Why are true crimes shows so popular? Why do we avidly tune in to watch fictional shows like *Dexter* when we know the bad guy is dangerous and a killer? Why are we drawn to these—"

"Why?" Jag called out.

There was a quick twitter of laughter from the group of coeds who'd picked seats close to him. The girls had been eyeing him all during class and very much not listening to Whitney.

She hadn't realized that he'd be participating in the discussion but...

Why?

"Because sometimes, we're all fascinated by darkness." A glance at the clock told her the class was due to end. "With that in mind, be sure to finish your readings on Ted Bundy. He was captured not too far from our location, and I expect you to be fully able to discuss his case when you arrive in class next week."

Everyone began to file out.

Whitney noticed that one of the blond girls stopped to slide a piece of paper toward Jag. He pocketed it without even glancing at what she'd written.

Shaking her head, Whitney packed up her gear. That had been her last class of the morning. Her afternoon was slated for prep work and test grading, but she was probably going to let all of that slide because she was dying to find Ramsey and see what he'd learned.

"You could be the topic of your own lecture." Jag had ambled toward her. His hands were shoved into the back pockets of his jeans. "You're a real-life crime story, aren't you? The big survivor."

She swallowed and fiddled with the notes at her podium. "For years, I talked about victims. It doesn't feel quite real to be one." It felt as if everything had happened to someone else. Mostly because she didn't even remember the attack. She just remembered being in the water. Choking. Drowning...

Some of the note cards flew from her fingers.

She bent to pick them up. So did Jag. His fingers brushed over hers.

Startled, her gaze jerked up to his.

"You should be real careful with the dark," he murmured. "It's not as safe as you think. *He's* not."

Her lips parted.

"What the fuck are you doing? I told you to *watch* her," Ramsey's voice snarled. "Not try to hold her damn hand."

Jag immediately sprang upright. "I was just— I was getting her cards—"

Ramsey stood a few feet behind him. He raised an eyebrow.

Whitney scooped up the cards before straightening. She tried to ignore the pang of unease that Jag's words had created within her. Why had he been warning her away from Ramsey? They were friends.

"Got all your cards?" Ramsey asked her in a silken voice.

She managed a nod.

"Good." He stalked toward her. Slid his hand under her chin and tipped back her head. Then his mouth brushed over hers.

They shouldn't be kissing in public. What if they were spotted by one of the students? Not that she minded. *Let them see.* But he'd always wanted them to be careful, to keep their physical relationship hidden while they were in public.

How did I know that?

But she let the thought slip away because his tongue had just thrust past her lips and heat was flooding through her body. He could do that so effortlessly. Just kiss her and make her want him and that was so very—

Dangerous.

You should be real careful with the dark. It's not as safe as you think. He's not.

Ramsey slowly lifted his head. Her lashes rose, and she stared up at him. Not looking away from her, he asked, "Any trouble today?"

"Ah, no. No, boss." Jag coughed. "Nothing odd so far."

"Good. I'll have her the rest of the day. You're relieved, Jag."

Her gaze darted to Jag. He didn't waste any time rushing out of the door—or getting past the very large, very intense-looking man who stood just to the right of the door.

The rest of the auditorium was empty. Just her, Ramsey, and the stranger.

Though, perhaps he wasn't a stranger. Something about him nagged at her...

I hate this! I hate feeling like I should know things when I don't! "Who is he?" Whitney asked.

Ramsey stepped back. "Darius. He's spent the morning with the cops, and I asked him to meet me here so that we could go over what he learned. Unfortunately, it wasn't a lot."

She offered the watchful man a tentative smile. "Hello, Darius. It's nice to meet you."

She could tell by the sudden tenseness of his expression that, yep, they'd met before. But instead of correcting her, he just inclined his head and said, "The pleasure is mine. Not every day you get to talk with the woman who makes Ramsey lose his mind."

"I haven't lost it," Ramsey muttered. "Yet."

Darius headed toward them. "The cops don't have jack. They did retrieve security footage from a neighbor, but the man who torched your house was wearing a ski mask. No way to ID him."

That wasn't what she'd been hoping to hear. Her gaze darted back to Ramsey. "What about the leads you were running down?"

He seemed to hesitate.

"Ramsey?" He'd better not even think of holding out on her.

"Let's just say they turned out to be dead ends."

Well, dammit.

"Are you ready to leave?" He tucked a lock of hair behind her ear. His touch was so gentle. Disarming.

"I...ah, I need to get a few things from my office, then I'll be ready." It was Friday. She'd take off early, grade the papers at home—or, not, since her home was a crime scene. *I'll grade the papers at his place.* "Maybe I can help you track down some leads," she suggested. "I'm actually quite good at understanding criminals."

Darius gave a bark of laughter. "Obviously."

Ramsey cut him a glare. "Seriously? Now you want to be a comedian?"

"I think I'll just..." Darius coughed into his hand. "I'll go see what kind of security is working at this place. Make sure the people in charge know just how important Dr. Augustine's safety is." He turned on his heel—a very brisk, almost military-like move—and marched away.

"The people in charge know safety is important," Whitney said. "They've recently beefed up all the security here, so I can assure you, I don't need bodyguards."

Ramsey leaned forward and brushed a kiss over her forehead. "Humor me?"

"Fine. But you have to agree to let me help you track down leads. I'll *humor* you, and you let me *help* you. Deal?"

His eyes gleamed. "Deal." His hand lowered. Twined with hers.

And they walked through the busy hallways like that. With their hands linked together as if they were a couple. More than a few curious students glanced their way and she could catch whispers every few moments...

"Dr. A has a hot guy."

"Wonder if Dr. A gets deviant with him? I totally would."

Her cheeks heated.

Ramsey just laughed and brought their joined hands to his lips. He pressed a kiss to her knuckles. "I'll get deviant with you all night long, sweetheart."

"Ramsey!" His voice had been loud. Way too loud.

But he...laughed.

And she stopped. Her feet rooted to the floor as her head swung toward him. She stared at him, aware that her eyes had flared and her lips had parted. She was surprised her mouth hadn't hit the floor.

A furrow appeared between his eyebrows. "What?"

"You laughed."

A shrug.

"You *never* laugh."

He leaned in close. "You remember?"

More and more. Bits and pieces. This truth...she just *felt*. "You're always so sad. Making you smile always made me feel good."

His laugh had seemed to warm something in her.

Once more, his lips took hers. This kiss was different. Sweet. Tender. "You make me feel good," he rasped.

She pretty much bolted for her office because he was making her feel far too *good* right then, too, and she wanted to get him behind closed doors and away from gaping college kids. She wanted to kiss him hard and deep and see if having him pressed tightly against her could banish some of the cold fear she'd felt all morning.

They hustled by the intern who was manning the reception desk. His eyebrows shot up as she flew past. "Hey, Dr. Augustine, you got—"

"Doc's busy right now," Ramsey growled back.

Then they were in her office. He kicked the door shut and just—pounced.

No other word for it. He reached for her, pulled her against him, and, this time, when his mouth took hers, the rest of the world seemed to fall away. The kiss was hot and frantic and intense, and her body rubbed eagerly against him as she tried to get closer and closer.

His fingers curled around her hips. He lifted her up. Carried her. And she felt the hard edge of wood beneath her when he put her on her desk. His mouth never left hers and, if anything, the kiss became even more possessive and primal. He positioned his body between her legs, and since she'd been wearing a loose, flowing dress, his movement pushed the skirt of that dress up to her thighs and gave him easy access to—

"Ramsey!" Her mouth tore from his. Her hands clutched his shoulders as her heart thundered in her chest. Holy crap, she was pretty sure they'd been about ten seconds away from having sex on her desk.

His gaze blazed down at her, dark with need.

Maybe not ten. Maybe more like five seconds...

One of his hands was on her thigh. He'd pushed up the edge of her skirt, and his callused fingertips were on her skin.

"We can't...not here," she whispered.

"We can...*anywhere,*" he corrected in a voice like rough sex.

Her body quivered. "Was it always like this?"

"Like what?"

"Like you touch me and nothing else seems to matter."

"You *are* the only thing that matters." His hand lifted from her thigh. Moved toward her stomach. Hesitated. Didn't touch her. "You and the baby." His gaze swirled with so many emotions. "Can I feel you?"

You can do anything you want with me. She pressed her lips together and managed to *not* blurt out that ever too embarrassing and revealing truth. When it came to Ramsey, she was at a serious disadvantage. Her body kept betraying her. It was obvious that while her mind had forgotten him, her body hadn't. Her body had been longing for him all along.

"Whitney?"

Her head moved in the faintest of nods.

His hand lowered over the small curve of her stomach. Her pregnancy wasn't obvious, not with the loose clothing she kept wearing. His touch was gentle, almost reverent. She had to blink quickly when the expression on his face changed. His fierce expression softened, and he leaned closer to her.

His lips brushed over her ear as he promised, "I will do whatever it takes to protect you both."

A shiver slid over her.

And her office door flew open.

A warm voice exclaimed, "Didn't Jason tell you that I was waiting to see you?" A quick rush of steps. "Come on, Whitney, I can't believe you didn't *call* me and tell me—" The voice broke off.

A familiar voice. A voice that belonged to Whitney's best friend, Maisey Bright.

Maisey...who was involved in an ever-so-hot-and-heavy way with Odin Shaw at Trouble for Hire.

Ramsey didn't jerk away at Maisey's interruption. His body tensed, but he took his time easing back. And before he moved from his position in front of Whitney, his hand snaked out to pull her skirt back down to cover her thighs.

Then he eased to the side, positioning his body near Whitney's. "Hello, Maisey," he said in a cool-as-can-be voice. As if Whitney's skirt hadn't been tossed high and they hadn't been frantic moments before. "I was wondering when I'd be seeing you again."

Shock was clear on Maisey's face. "*Ramsey.*"

He nodded. "The one and only."

Maisey glanced back and forth between them with speculation clear to see in her eyes. "You two are together again?"

Wait...Maisey had known about their involvement?

"Oh, no." Maisey put her hands on her hips. "Do not look at me that way, Whit. You kept him secret from me. I just found out bits and pieces when you went missing."

"But you *did* know I was involved with him." She couldn't have this conversation while she sat on the desk. *Awkward*. "Why didn't you say something?" Whitney hopped off the desk.

"Why didn't you tell me that your house was torched last night?" Worry filled Maisey's voice. "I had to hear it from Odin!" She bounded forward and grabbed Whitney's hands. "Are you okay?" Her gaze swept over Whitney. "You look okay, but you must have been terrified! And, of course, you can't stay at your place while the cops are investigating. You can come and stay with me and Odin and—"

"No." Ramsey's low voice cut right through her words.

Maisey jerked her head toward him. "Not your call. If I remember correctly, you were the one walking away at the hospital. As far as I'm concerned, you don't get any say in Whitney's life. She's *my* friend, and I'm going to—"

"I'm not staying with you and Odin." Whitney was amazed by how steady her own voice was. "But thank you for the offer. And the reason I didn't call to tell you about what happened..." She raked a hand through her hair. "It was late. Ramsey rushed me out of the fire and took me to his place, and..." *And we had sex. Super amazing sex. I didn't think about calling you because everything seemed to be happening at one hundred miles an hour.*

"Ramsey got you out of the fire?" Maisey's bracelets jingled as she pointed toward him. "He saved you?"

"I can do more than just be your friendly neighborhood asshole," Ramsey murmured.

Maisey slanted him a suspicious glance. "How did you happen to be at her house that late?"

Whitney's lips parted. She hadn't told Maisey about the baby.

"The usual way," Ramsey replied easily. "I went to see her because I want her."

Okay, so...

"Well, that explains the rose," Maisey's hand dropped. The bracelets jingled again. "I saw it on her desk when I was in here looking for her earlier. As soon as I spied it, I started to wonder if the two of you were a thing again."

Now she was lost. "What rose?" Whitney asked.

"Uh, the one in the middle of your desk. You were like two inches away from it a moment ago. You must have seen it."

No, she hadn't seen it because she hadn't been looking at her desk. She'd been focused on Ramsey. They'd rushed inside the office and gone right at each other. Now her head slowly turned, and she saw the single rose sitting in a clear glass vase on her desk. "Ramsey?"

"Not from me, sweetheart." She could hear the rage in his voice.

The rose had *not* been there before she'd gone to her lectures. She pushed past Ramsey and hustled into the reception area.

Jason was just slinging his laptop bag over his shoulder. He glanced up and gave her a quick smile.

She didn't smile back. "I had a flower delivery."

"Uh, yeah, you did. I was trying to tell you about it when you flew by my desk."

"*Who delivered the rose?*" Ramsey thundered.

Jason flinched. "Oh, no. Is this like...a lover's quarrel kind of thing? Because I have a rule about not getting involved in personal situations like—"

"Who. Delivered. It?"

Whitney was sure that Ramsey's voice would probably make small children—and potentially grown men—cry.

"Oh, hell." All the color drained from Jason's face. "I'm in trouble."

Ramsey grabbed for him.

Whitney caught Ramsey's arm. Hauled him close. "Give him a chance to talk, Ramsey."

"Yes, yes, let me talk." Jason's Adam's apple bobbed. "It was just—just some guy in a black coat. Tall, muscled. Shaggy blond hair that fell over his eyes. He said that he had a delivery and asked me to put it in her office. I swear, I thought it was no big deal. Everyone knew that Dr. A used to get roses delivered here all the time—"

Ramsey's body went rock hard against her.

Her head turned. "Ramsey? You know who it was?"

"Could someone please tell me what is going on?" Maisey demanded.

But...there were footsteps rushing toward them. More people coming to join their little party. When Whitney turned her head, she saw a woman in a black suit and shiny, no-nonsense, black flats storming toward them. A cop in uniform trailed her.

A badge was clipped to the woman's hip. Her gaze zeroed in on Whitney, then darted to Ramsey. Recognition filled her stare.

"Dr. Whitney Augustine?" The woman halted near her. "I'm Detective Melissa Wright. I need you to come with me to the station and answer some questions."

Ramsey immediately moved to position his body in front of Whitney. "She's not going anywhere without me."

"Wonderful...*Ramsey*. I was so hoping you'd say that." She smiled at him. And it was a chilling smile. "Because you're wanted for questioning as well." Her brow furrowed. "I'm assuming you still have your lawyer on retainer? And she'll meet us at the station, as per her usual routine?"

Whitney's temples throbbed. "What is happening? Is this about my house? Because I'm happy to answer any questions you—"

"It's not about your house, sweetheart," Ramsey rumbled. "And it would be better if we waited for my lawyer before we say anything else."

She could only shake her head.

"I should have clarified," Melissa noted with an inclination of her head. "I'm a *homicide* detective, Dr. Augustine."

Homicide? She'd talked with plenty of the cops down at the station, but Whitney didn't recall meeting Melissa Wright.

Big shocker. Maybe I met her in that six months that I can't remember...

"Do you know a Ronald Rudolph, Dr. Augustine?"

"I—"

"Wait for the lawyer," Ramsey told her. His eyes glittered. He'd fired a text to someone on his phone. Probably the lawyer.

Whitney's heart drummed faster as she shared a fearful glance with Maisey.

"Ramsey..." Melissa drawled out his name. "I can't help but notice you've got some bruises on your knuckles."

Whitney glanced down. Ramsey *did* have bruising on his knuckles. The skin was black and bluish.

"Want to tell me how that happened?" Melissa asked sweetly.

He didn't speak.

"I don't suppose," she continued in that same sweet tone, "that you got those bruises when you were beating Ronald Rudolph to death?"

OhmyGod. Whitney started to sway. Ramsey immediately wrapped his hands around her. His bruised hands.

His gaze locked on hers, and she could hear Jag's strange warning whispering through her mind.

You should be real careful with the dark. It's not as safe as you think. He's not.

CHAPTER TWELVE

Observation notes: Ramsey has a secret hobby. Though I don't know that "hobby" is the right word. I found out about the activity by accident. He had bruises on his knuckles, and I asked him what happened.

Ramsey told me that when he'd been a teen, he'd been desperate for money. He only had his fists as a way to survive on the streets. He fought, brutal fights that didn't end until his opponent was on the ground...and couldn't get up.

Even after all these years, it seems that he still fights...

***

"So, Ramsey..." The detective lifted her eyebrows. "Want to tell me what happened to your knuckles?"

"You absolutely do not have to answer that question," his lawyer interjected crisply. Aspen Gray gave the detective a cold smile. "And, seriously, Melissa, I hope this little chitchat doesn't take much longer. Because my client and I are both growing bored. We've been here forever as it is."

Aspen Gray was the best criminal defense attorney in the area. She'd only been out of law school for a few years, but she'd shot to the top of the game very easily. Mostly because she'd gotten kickass referrals.

Referrals that had come from Ramsey.

Once upon a time, her father had been one of Ramsey's bartenders—and bodyguards. When Saul had died, Ramsey had stepped in to pay for Aspen's college and her law school. And on the day she'd graduated, she'd told him that she *would* be paying off her debt.

She'd kept him out of jail, so he figured she'd been doing a stellar job.

"Your client was seen leaving the house of Ronald Rudolph this morning at shortly after ten a.m.," Melissa announced, delivering what she no doubt thought was a major bombshell.

"Seen by whom?" Aspen immediately purred back. "And, side note, isn't it such a shame the way eyewitness testimony can be so very unreliable?" She made a tut-tut sound with her tongue. Obviously, she was ready to rip apart the eyewitness.

And, about that...Aspen was about to get pissed but...keeping his eyes on the detective, Ramsey said, "We both know he was dead by then."

Melissa practically salivated. "You admit you were there."

Aspen shot him an are-you-insane glare.

But Ramsey knew the game. He also knew that Melissa wasn't as bad as she pretended to be. "I was there. I had some questions for Ronald."

"Questions that relate to Dr. Augustine?"

Whitney had been separated from him once they'd been brought to the station. Ramsey very much did *not* like that situation. It was why he was talking. The sooner he got this mess cleared up, the faster he'd get back to her. "Yes. Though you already know that, so let's cut through the BS, shall we?"

Melissa nodded. "I would love to do that."

Aspen shoved back her chair. The chair legs screeched against the floor. "My client has nothing—"

"Ronald recently delivered some flowers to Whitney," he said smoothly. "I wanted to see if he knew anything else about the person who'd hired him to make the deliveries. I went to his house, but when I arrived..." A shrug. "Ronald was dead."

"You went *inside* his house." Melissa watched him like a snake that was ready to strike.

"Um."

"How could a dead man let you *inside*? Unless you are confessing to breaking and entering?"

"The door was unlocked and open."

"Good Samaritan!" Aspen declared with a jerk of her chin. "My client was simply being a Good Samaritan who rushed to the aid of a victim."

Melissa slanted her a fast glance. "Then why didn't he call the cops when he found the dead body?"

"But I did." When she looked at him again, Ramsey offered her a slow smile. "Like any good, concerned citizen, I made a call to the police department. *That's* how you knew to go to his house." He'd been the one to give the cops the tip.

The faint lines near Melissa's eyes tightened. "If you made the call, then you should have *waited—*"

He put a hand to his chest. "With a potential killer on the loose? You wanted me to just stand there? No way. I was afraid for my life."

Melissa snorted.

"Ronald Rudolph had previously told me he was hired to deliver roses to Whitney. I'm sure you already figured that out when you found his phone and tech equipment." Ramsey knew exactly what to say and what not to say. "I've been afraid this mystery individual may have an obsession with Whitney. I'm sure you are aware her house was torched last night."

Melissa's nostrils flared. "I'm aware."

"Then when I found Ronald dead, you can understand why I immediately rushed to her side. I had to make certain she was safe."

Her glare cut to Aspen.

Aspen patted his arm. "Such a good citizen. After everything that Whitney Augustine has been through recently, isn't it wonderful that she has someone looking out for her now?"

Hell, yes, he'd be looking out for Whitney.

"But..." Aspen winced. "I must tell you, detective, it doesn't look very good for you to have hauled Whitney in the way you did. Everyone loves her and her story of survival, but here you are...treating her like she's some sort of common criminal." She glanced around the small room and wrinkled her nose. "I bet you have her just sitting in one of these unfortunate interrogation rooms."

"I have questions for her," Melissa snapped.

About that...Ramsey straightened in his chair. "Seeing as how Aspen is Whitney's lawyer, too, you won't be asking those questions without her being in the room."

Melissa's gaze sharpened on Aspen. "You're her lawyer, too?"

"Did I not mention that?" A vague flutter of Aspen's hand in the air.

"No, you did not."

Probably because Aspen hadn't realized she would be representing Whitney, not until that very moment.

"Ramsey, I want to know how you got the bruises on your knuckles." Melissa redirected with tireless energy. "And, yes, my ME is telling me that the vic was dead for hours, so I know you didn't kill him at ten a.m."

"Good of you to proclaim my client's innocence," Aspen declared brightly.

Melissa kept focusing on Ramsey. "He was killed last night. Probably between midnight and three a.m. My ME will narrow it down more for me, but I have to ask, do you have an alibi for that time?" Her cold grin said she didn't think he would.

But Ramsey nodded. "Of course."

"And...?"

"You don't have to say anything more," Aspen declared flatly.

This was important. He wanted to say this. He wanted word to spread. "I was with Whitney Augustine. She can verify my alibi."

Melissa's stare glinted. "What sort of game are you playing with that woman?"

"I'm not playing." He never had been. "And I'm done with the interrogation. Take me to Whitney."

"What happened to your knuckles?"

He hadn't used them to beat Ronald Rudolph to death. He stared down at the bruising.

"Ramsey..." Aspen warned.

He looked up at the detective. "I punched a wall."

"And why would you do that?" Melissa wanted to know.

"Because the wall had it fucking coming." He rose. Pressed his hands onto the table. "Where is Whitney?"

***

She'd been in plenty of police stations. She'd interviewed cops. Sat in on interrogations. Whitney knew how the scene was played. The unnecessary waiting. The uncomfortable chair. The too many cups of coffee that were supposed to make her squirm because she needed to use the bathroom and if she answered the right questions, then maybe she'd get out...

Oh, yes, she knew all the tricks. So she didn't fall for them.

She didn't touch her coffee.

She didn't take the wobbly chair. Instead, she sat on the table and swung her legs to stretch them out as time ticked past. She focused on breathing—nice, deep breaths. And she tried not to think about the fact that Ronald Rudolph had been beaten to death.

When did the bruises first appear on Ramsey's hands? She tried to remember. She pictured the events of the previous night. His hands had been all over her. He'd touched her so carefully. She'd felt the faint calluses on his fingertips. She'd reached for his hand—

He had bruises last night. The image popped into her mind.

Her breath whooshed out just as the door opened.

Detective Melissa Wright paused. She took in Whitney's position on top of the table. "Guess you made yourself comfortable?"

She swung her legs. "Ramsey did not kill Rudy."

Melissa made a face at the familiar name.

Crap. Should I have called him Ronald?

"How do you know?" Melissa asked.

"Because Ramsey—"

Melissa's laughter cut her off. "Please. Spare us both. Do not say that Ramsey isn't a killer. We both know he is. Just as we both know that the man is very, very good when it comes to covering his tracks."

Whitney pressed her lips together.

"What is the nature of your relationship with Ramsey Hyde?" Melissa put her hands on her hips.

The door had been left open behind the detective, and a woman dressed in an elegant suit, with pearls wrapped around her neck, walked inside. Her high heels tapped across the floor. "Do not answer that question, Dr. Augustine."

Whitney lifted her brows.

"As Dr. Augustine's attorney," the dark-haired woman continued as her heels tapped, "you should know that I don't want anyone talking to my client unless I am present."

This woman was her attorney? Since when?

But then Ramsey appeared behind the lawyer.

Ah, okay. That explained it. The sharply dressed woman was there because of him.

"It's not like I'm asking for any sort of state secret." Melissa released a brief laugh. "I merely inquired about the nature of her relationship with Ramsey Hyde. Considering the alibi that he gave to me, I thought it was an important note." Her head tilted as she studied Whitney. "But perhaps his alibi was a lie, and that's why you don't want to tell me about the nature of your relationship with—"

"I don't have anything to hide." Whitney lifted her chin. "Ask me your questions. I'll answer them."

The lawyer pinched the bridge of her nose. "I should have stayed in bed today."

Grim satisfaction flashed on Melissa's face before she demanded, "What is the nature of your relationship with—"

"We're sleeping together," Ramsey growled before Whitney could answer.

Melissa didn't look his way. "I was asking her."

Whitney swallowed. Her dress was so loose and flowing that it completely hid the growing curve of her stomach. She didn't think that Melissa realized she was pregnant. "Ramsey and I are personally involved."

"Are you now." Not a question, more of a statement.

But Ramsey said, "Yes, we are."

Melissa's eyes remained on Whitney. "Since when?"

"Oh, for goodness' sake..." The lawyer marched forward. "The detective is trying to see if you can confirm Ramsey's alibi. Will you please just state for the record where you were last night and what you were doing?" She sniffed and shot an annoyed glance toward Melissa. "Happy?"

Melissa waited. She did not look particularly happy.

Whitney released the breath she'd been holding. "I was at Ramsey's house. He took me there after my home was torched."

Melissa nodded. "And you were there all night?"

"Yes."

"Could you see Ramsey during the night? Could you verify—"

Her fingers curled around the edge of the table. "I slept with him, so, yes, I can verify that he was there. Ramsey didn't leave the house all night."

Over Melissa's shoulder, she saw Ramsey frown.

Why was he frowning? She'd just alibied him.

Ramsey crossed to her. His fingers curled around her waist. He carefully lifted her off the table and lowered Whitney to her feet. His warmth seemed to wrap around her.

"Aren't you curious about what happened to his fingers?" Melissa asked softly.

"He had the marks on his knuckles before he even came to my house." She was pleased with the confident sound of her voice.

"Just what time did he arrive at your home?"

She tried to remember. "Nine-thirty. Maybe ten." Around then. Whitney glanced over at Melissa.

The detective's expression had tightened. "And you didn't ask him *how* he got the bruises?"

"He's a fighter. He's been involved in boxing since he was a teen. I figured he'd just gone and done a bare-knuckle bout at the gym." Whitney forced a shrug. "Isn't that what happened?"

A gleam lit the detective's eyes. "No, that's not what happened. According to your *boyfriend,* he hit a wall."

What? Whitney's stare jumped back to him. Why would Ramsey be punching walls? Why would—

He found out I was pregnant. She knew he'd been upset. So upset that he'd started punching walls?

"Well, I think we've cleared up quite a bit of information." The lawyer—Whitney still hadn't learned her name—brought her hands together in a quick clap. "Dr. Augustine has verified both that Ramsey was with her last night and that he'd sustained the injuries to his hands before your victim was killed. I believe we are now done." Her smile flashed, but it was icy. "If you have more questions, you will, of course, make certain I am present before you interview my clients."

"Come on, sweetheart," Ramsey murmured to Whitney, "we're done here."

They began walking for the door.

But Melissa rushed to step in their path. "You were given a second chance," she gritted out as her stare raked Whitney. "And you're going to throw it away on someone like him?"

Anger burned through Whitney as she stared back at the other woman. "You don't know Ramsey. You don't know me. How about you focus on doing your job and finding the man who actually killed Rudy? Leave innocent people alone." She curled her fingers with Ramsey's and tugged him toward the door.

"There is nothing innocent about Ramsey!" Melissa called after them.

Whitney hesitated in the doorway. Then she glanced over her shoulder. "There's nothing guilty, either, or he would have been locked up years ago."

"You're making a mistake," Melissa seethed.

"No, you are because you're focused on the wrong man. But then, I guess if you can't find Rudy's killer, Ramsey and I will just have to do the job for you."

"What?" Shock.

But Whitney was done. She kept her grip on Ramsey and she marched through the station with him. He was silent and so was she as they made their way to the station's main entrance. As they passed the bullpen, she could feel stares on her. She could also hear the tap, tap, tap of the lawyer's high heels.

Then they were outside. The sun shone down on them, but it did nothing to chase the chill from Whitney's body.

"That was...interesting." The lawyer swept an assessing stare over her. "Hate to tell you, but I think you went from being the celebrated victim...to becoming a new target on Detective Wright's hit list. You just made yourself an unfortunate enemy." She held out her hand. "I'm Aspen, by the way. Aspen Gray. And I make enemies every single day."

Whitney let go of Ramsey's hand and curled her fingers around Aspen's. "I wasn't looking to make an enemy."

"No, you were just looking to protect him." Her head inclined toward Ramsey. "And that is not something I see often. Most people would rather throw him under the bus and let him pay for every sin in the world."

Whitney pulled her hand back. "Ramsey doesn't need to pay for my sins."

"You don't have sins." His rumble.

"Maybe she didn't," Aspen murmured. "Until she stepped into your world." Her phone pealed and she hauled it out of her bag. "Got to take this. Look, I'll check in with you both later, okay? Do *not* talk to any annoying detectives without me." She turned away and brought the phone to her ear as she hurried down the street.

A limo pulled to the curb near Ramsey and Whitney. She frowned at it—and at the man who'd just hurried out of the driver's side and around to open one of the rear doors. He looked familiar...as in...she'd seen him just a few nights ago.

He was the bouncer who'd been outside of Ramsey's bar.

"I was waiting for you, boss. Just like you said."

"Thanks, Jimmy." Ramsey tugged her toward the limo. "Take us to my place, would you?"

"Absolutely." Jimmy winked at her.

She stopped by the limo's open door. "Why are we taking a limo?"

Ramsey's lips brushed over her ear. "Because I haven't had the chance to pick out a new car yet, and this is safer for you than the motorcycle."

Safer. Her head turned. Their mouths were so close.

"It's bullet-proof, baby. Until I find out who we're dealing with, no chances will be taken with your safety."

He thought she was in danger of getting shot?

"The detective is watching us." His mouth pressed lightly over hers. "So if you're about to argue with me, how about you save it for the car?"

Oh, she had plenty to say. But he was right. They were being watched. Whitney decided to give the detective a show. She curled one hand behind Ramsey's head and locked her lips to his. Her tongue thrust into his mouth. She teased and savored and she let the kiss linger because she wanted to make sure the detective got the message.

I'm with Ramsey. He's with me.

"Get in the car," Ramsey rasped against her lips. "Because I want to fuck you right here."

Okay, *that* wasn't something she wanted others to watch.

Whitney slid into the car.

CHAPTER THIRTEEN

Observation notes: I know where he goes. When he thinks that the darkness is getting too strong, Ramsey sneaks away. He comes back with his hands bruised and bloody. He told me he had a violence burning inside of him, but he's never been violent with me. If anything, he treats me like I might break.

I'll have to prove to him that I won't.

***

Cyrus sat back and stared at the screen before him. Recovering Whitney's files had been child's play for him. Mostly because the virus that had been used on her system was basic tech. He'd had the little beast gone in moments.

He could have called Ramsey. Told him the news.

But he'd been curious...curiosity had always been one of his weaknesses. So he'd started reading through a few of the recovered files. Perhaps Dr. Whitney Augustine had begun her work at the bar as some sort of field research project, but after a few weeks, that had certainly changed. She still called her entries "observation notes" but they read more like diary entries. And the more time that passed, the deeper her relationship with Ramsey had become.

So deep that she'd discovered his secrets.

Ramsey would not be pleased.

Then again, was the bastard *ever* pleased?

Time to stop reading. Before he went way too far.

A knock sounded at his door. Considering that he was using an assumed name and he'd taken plenty of ever-so-careful steps to hide his location, the knock had him jerking to attention. No one should be paying a visit to him.

No one.

But...

He hid the laptop and crept toward the door. Peered through the peephole. And swore when he saw the woman standing on the other side.

Imari Caddel. Government agent. His reluctant partner in crime. The woman who should have been very, very far away from him. The woman he was trying to stay far away *from*. His shoulders straightened as Cyrus opened the door.

She smiled at him.

"How'd you find me?" It was the only thing he could think to say.

"I'm a super spy agent. I can find almost anyone."

He wasn't almost anyone. He'd covered his tracks well.

"Or..." Imari amended with a roll of one delicate shoulder. "I *was* a super spy agent. I recently left my post."

Shock cut through him. "Why the hell did you do that?"

"Because when you work for people who turn out to be asshole liars, it makes you think you need a life change." She tucked her hands into the back pockets of her jeans. "Also, since I'm no longer a government agent and you're not the bad guy I'm supposed to track down, I thought this might be a good time to ask...do you want me?"

Holy fuck.

He opened the door wider.

"I hope that's a yes," Imari murmured.

***

The limo's door shut. Ramsey stretched out on the leather seat and kept his eyes locked on Whitney. His hands were clenched into fists— mostly because he was trying not to touch her. She'd kissed him so passionately moments before, and his dick had surged toward her. He wanted *in* her. Wanted her moaning and arching against him.

But there were things they needed to cover first.

She licked her lips. The limo had lights in the back, a soft glow that came from the floorboard, so he could see her perfectly. The privacy screen was up, and he knew that Jimmy couldn't see or hear them.

He had Whitney all to himself.

The way I always want her.

"I didn't kill Ronald." He thought it was best to get that out of the way first.

"I-I never thought you did."

"Why the hell not?" The question tore from him. Angry. Rough. He didn't want to be rough with her, dammit. Not her. Never her.

"Because I trust you."

She might as well have gutted him. Ramsey sucked in a sharp breath. "Don't."

"Don't?" She moved closer to him. Her dress hiked up.

I want to fuck her.

"Why not?" Whitney pushed. "Are you lying to me?"

"No."

"Are you planning to hurt me?"

"Fucking never."

Her hand pressed to the stubble on his cheek. "Do you trust me?"

"I trust you more than I've ever trusted anyone." Truth.

"Then why shouldn't I trust you?"

Her mouth was close again. He wanted it. She tasted so sweet, and the light scent of raspberries that clung to her was driving him crazy.

"Is it because you're so bad?" Her fingers stroked him. Teased him. "Because the world thinks you're a monster?"

"Be...careful," he gritted out.

"I don't think I need to be. I may not remember everything we did, but I remember how it feels to be with you." She licked her lips. "And it feels *safe*. So don't tell me I can't trust you. Instead, tell me why I am *right* to put my trust in you."

He did not deserve her. But he would never, ever give her up again. No matter what he had to do.

"Why did you hit a wall?"

His fingers were still fisted. "Because I was furious."

"At?"

"My damn self. I had just found out about you and the baby. I'd been pushing you away to keep you safe, but all I was doing was putting you at risk. I was so fucking furious with myself that I wanted to pound and pound that wall until my knuckles were bloody."

Until he could hurt himself...as much as he had unknowingly hurt her.

Screwed up? Yeah. That was him. The social workers hadn't been completely wrong...

I don't belong. I don't fit in. I don't connect the way other people do.

Except...with her. He'd sworn he belonged to her moments after they'd met. He'd felt the connection in his bones.

She sucked in a sharp breath, and Whitney moved quickly—but not away from him. Not away as if she'd been frightened by what he'd said. Instead, she moved to straddle him. Her knees pressed into the leather on either side of his body. Her dress hiked up. Her hands clasped his shoulders as she balanced herself.

"Sweetheart?"

She kissed him.

Something broke apart inside of Ramsey. He knew this wasn't the time. He shouldn't be fucking his Whitney in the back of a limo. He should be showing her every single care in the world. Wining and dining her and treating her like the princess she was.

But he had to take her. Fucking her was as necessary as breathing. His hand snaked between their bodies. He ripped her panties out of his way and touched her warm, wet sex. Wet...but not wet enough. Not yet. He stroked her. Rubbed her clit. Greedily swallowed her quick moans. Strummed her and thrust two fingers into her core.

She rode his fingers. Tightened her sex around him.

And then her hands shoved between their bodies, too. She yanked open his jeans. His cock shoved toward her.

Be careful. It's her. It's—

His cock pushed at the entrance of her body. She sank down on him. Took every single bit of his cock into her, and she was so tight that he was sure he'd lost his mind. Tight. Hot. Perfect. His mouth pressed to her neck. He licked and sucked and wanted to mark her so that the whole world would know she belonged to him.

Have to put a ring on her finger. Have to make her mine. Have to have her...always.

She lifted her body up. Eased back down. Her rhythm was slow and careful, and he wanted to slam into her but—

Pregnant. My baby. My Whitney.

Sweat beaded his brow, but his thrusts were controlled. Over and over again, he sank into her until she was twisting and arching and sobbing his name as she pushed faster and faster toward her release.

He kept thrusting. Relentlessly sinking into the heaven that was his and his alone. The paradise he'd gladly kill to possess. Whitney thought he was some misunderstood bad boy? She was wrong... so wrong.

"Ram!"

Her sex squeezed around him. The ripples of her climax stroked over his cock.

He watched the pleasure sweep over her face.

Then he let go. He drove into her once more and his release tore through him.

Yes, Whitney could trust him. He would never, ever hurt her. But the rest of the world? Hell, no, they should never make the mistake of thinking he was anything less than a monster at his core. He would steal, fight, freaking slaughter and burn the world down around any enemies who ever thought to hurt her.

And actually...that was exactly what was on his agenda for the night.

***

"You are not seriously leaving me here." Whitney glared at Ramsey and tried to ignore the fact that her thighs were still trembling. The climax in the limo had left her more than a little shaken. And wanting so much more...

But they'd reached his beach house. He'd rearranged her clothes, pocketed her torn panties, and taken her in as he carefully held her arm—all gentleman-like. And before the door had even shut behind them, he'd announced his plan to ditch her.

Unacceptable. "No."

"Yes." He lifted his eyebrows. "But don't worry, you won't be alone..."

And Darius walked out of the kitchen, eating a slice of pizza. "Took you longer to get here than I expected."

"Watch her. Don't let her leave your sight."

Darius inclined his head. "On it."

So she had a babysitter—okay, fine, correction, she had one very large bodyguard for the night...That had *not* been on the schedule. "I thought we were going to figure out who killed Rudy by working together."

Ramsey smiled at her. "Loved it when you told that to the detective." He pressed a kiss to her forehead. "Also loved the way you stood up for me. That doesn't happen a lot." He took a step back.

She grabbed his hand. "It doesn't happen because you deliberately try to make everyone think you are the biggest, baddest bastard in the world."

He winked. "That's because I am." Ramsey gave her another kiss.

One that had her body humming again. Dammit, was this her pregnancy hormones? Or was she just hyper tuned to Ramsey and always wanted to jump him?

Her grip tightened on him. "If you're hunting for the man who killed Rudy, I want to be with you!"

He glanced over at Darius. "Go outside, would you? We need a moment."

Darius took his pizza and headed outside. The door closed quietly behind him. For such a big guy, he could sure move quietly when he wanted.

Ramsey stared down at her. "I'm not hunting tonight."

"No?"

"No. I don't intend to go out and look for prey."

His word choice felt very deliberate to her. "Then what are you doing?"

"Tying up loose ends. Knocking items off my to-do list."

Like that wasn't suspicious. At all. "And why can't I come with you?"

He pulled his hand from her grip—and put his fingers tenderly over her stomach. "Because I go to dangerous places."

Damn him. "I thought I was safe with you."

"You are."

"Ramsey..."

"I'll be back before you can miss me."

Doubtful. She'd missed him when she hadn't even known who he was.

He let her go. Turned away. Stopped. "Am I supposed to apologize?"

"For ditching me? Uh, yes, absolutely—"

He glanced over his shoulder. "For fucking you in the car."

"Oh. That."

A nod. "Yes. That."

"I wanted to be fucked in the car, so I don't think an apology is necessary." Her hands twisted in front of her.

"I want to fuck you everywhere, but I'll try to keep better control."

She considered the matter. "Am I supposed to make the same promise? To keep control?"

His gaze sharpened.

"Because I don't think I can. When it comes to you, my normal self-control seems to evaporate."

A slow half-smile curved his lips. "Good."

Good?

"Because you can absolutely, one hundred percent...fuck me anytime you want."

***

Ramsey pulled the door shut as he stepped onto the porch. Darius stood in the shadows, a big, hulking form.

"You finish up that private chat?" Darius asked, all casual-like.

She'd been blushing beautifully when he left. "I did."

"And did the doc agree to stay here while you go off tonight?"

He thought about it...and realized she hadn't. Hell. "Don't let her leave your sight."

"Already told you, I'm on it."

Ramsey grunted as he marched forward.

But Darius stepped out of the shadows. "You know what the hell you're doing?"

"Don't I always?"

"No, hell, no, you don't. But somehow, things *usually* work out because you get lucky."

"That's just insulting. Luck has nothing to do with it." Jinx was the one who believed in luck, not him. Ramsey tended to rely more on brute strength and an inability to give up even when he was bloody and broken. He'd learned early on that showing weakness was a fatal flaw...

But I still tipped my hand with Whitney.

That was why he had to take care of this business tonight. "You arranged things as I ordered?"

"The fighter was already on the list for tonight."

"Excellent. And his competitor?"

"He'll make sure not to show. You can step in." Darius crossed his massive arms over his chest. "Why don't you just let me handle this for you?"

"Because there are some jobs that a man likes to do himself." And taking care of *this* job was a high priority.

Detective Melissa Wright could search for Ronald's killer. She could collect her evidence and follow through with her whole due-diligence routine.

But Ramsey didn't have to hunt. He knew exactly where his target would be...

There were several important things Ramsey knew about the man he was after.

Point one...the bastard had arranged for the rose deliveries *from* Ramsey's bar—that meant the jerk was someone Ramsey had seen before. Someone in his world.

Point two...the prick was a pro at hot-wiring rides and getting past security.

Point three...he was a pyro. One who had used an old school Molotov cocktail on Whitney's house. Using that particular method was a clear signature.

Then, of course, there was the final point. The nail in the man's coffin.

Point four...

Ramsey *had* gone to Ronald Rudolph's house. The door had been open, and, yeah, he'd let himself inside. He'd seen Ronald's body. Had noticed all the tell-tale breaks. He'd seen exactly where the killer had focused his attack. Again, talk about a clear signature.

When he put all the stuff he knew together, Ramsey had come up with one man in particular who matched up with that—well, Whitney would have called it a profile.

He had learned a few things from her when she'd been doing her "research" at his place so long ago. He'd made a profile of the man he wanted to find. And now he knew exactly who matched up with this deadly skill set...

So it was time for Ramsey to have a meeting with him. Only this wasn't going to be some polite, sit-down chat. No, that wasn't the way things worked in Ramsey's world.

When you struck out at him...

Ramsey struck back, harder.

That was exactly what he intended to do that night.

CHAPTER FOURTEEN

Observation notes: Even when he's in a bar surrounded by people, Ramsey seems alone. When he's approached, it's with caution. Others eye him like he's some kind of wild beast who will attack with the least provocation.

He sits alone. Except...when I'm there. I stay with him.

I think...I think I always want to stay with him. I don't worry that he'll attack me. When I'm with Ramsey, I feel safer than I've ever been at any other point in my life.

***

"So...do you know where the town's favorite villain, Ramsey, is tonight?" Imari asked as she stared down into her wine glass and stood on the balcony of Cyrus's rented condo.

At her question, a sad sigh slipped from him. "Disappointing."

Her head snapped up. "Excuse me?"

"You come here." He motioned toward the slinky black dress she wore. "Looking all sexy. Asking me if I want you when the answer to that question would be obvious to *anyone*..."

"Uh, you never actually answered me," Imari pointed out, voice careful.

"Oh, that's an affirmative. I definitely do want you. You're freaking gorgeous and you make me want to do some extremely bad and dirty things with you all night long."

She brought the wine glass to her lips. Took a long gulp. "Okay."

"And then...then you just had to go and prove what I suspected. Talk about ruining the moment."

"I don't follow." Her grip on the stem of the wine glass tightened.

He stalked toward her.

Her shoulders stiffened. "Cyrus?"

"You don't trust me." Not overly surprising, but still disappointing. "You never trusted me, not completely. I came to you, I laid out the case against your boss—"

"My *former* boss."

"And I tried to prove to you that I wasn't the evil villain." Despite evidence to the contrary.

She licked her luscious lips. "And I worked with you. We got my *former* boss taken out of power."

"Yes, but you haven't stopped being a super spy, have you?"

"I—"

"You came to me tonight for a very specific reason."

"Yes. Yes, I did." Once more, she lifted the wine glass. Took another long gulp—

"You came for a reason," Cyrus repeated, "and it wasn't to fuck me."

She spat out the wine.

He offered her a napkin.

"Are you serious right now?" Imari demanded as she snatched the napkin from him.

"Dead serious."

She was cursing and cleaning away the wine.

"So, I don't know which government agency you're currently working for...I always suspected you had a few allegiances, but partnering with you—on a superficial basis—worked for me at the time, so I let things go."

She put down the wine glass. Fisted the napkin.

"You could be FBI," Cyrus mused. "You could be DEA. You could be working some kind of task force with the local authorities. I don't know. What I do know is that I'm not going to help you."

"What is it that you think I need help with?"

"Bringing down Ramsey Hyde."

Her nostrils flared.

"And you're not going to seduce me into giving you intel on him. Though..." His gaze swept over her. "You are welcome to try." *You can try all night long, if you'd like.*

The wine-soaked napkin hit him in the face. "You are an ass."

"Been told that before." The napkin fell to land near his feet.

"I'm not trying to seduce you for info!"

"No?"

She lunged forward. Stood toe-to-toe with him. "No."

His hand lifted. Slid over the silky skin of her shoulder. She truly was sexy as hell. His fingers eased under the small strap of her dress. "Then why are you wearing a wire?" He turned over the strap. Touched the small wire.

"Dammit," she whispered.

Dammit, indeed.

***

Imari hurried out of the high rise. Her ankle nearly twisted in the ridiculous heels she was wearing. Her face felt too flushed. Her heart raced too quickly. And she kept seeing the rage glittering in Cyrus's eyes...

He'd been well and truly pissed.

He'd also been...aroused. So had she. And she had the sinking feeling that she might have just screwed up something very, very important.

Imari jumped in her car. Nearly screeched out of the parking lot in her haste. She flew down the road, zipping between lanes, and all too soon, she was at her destination. Imari leapt out of the vehicle and stormed into the packed building. After shoving her way through the crowd, she made her way upstairs. Stalked to her boss's office.

At the closed door, she didn't stop. She threw it open. "Your plan was shit."

The three men in the office turned toward her.

She ignored War and Odin and focused on the mastermind of tonight's scheme...Jinx. Imari pointed at him. "Cyrus knew I was wearing a wire. He told me *nothing* useful."

Jinx had one hip propped against the edge of his desk. "Not true. We learned several useful things."

She'd learned that Cyrus now hated her. That didn't count as being useful. It was rather depressing, truth be told.

"One, I was right. He is totally into you," Jinx said.

She flipped him off. *He's not into me any longer*.

"And, two, he definitely has a relationship with Ramsey. Those two are tight. So whatever Ramsey is involved with..."

"A murder," Odin's deep voice rumbled. "He's involved with a murder. I told you about that. You knew I started digging as soon as Maisey called me and informed me about the scene at the college."

Jinx pointed toward him. "A murder. Yes. Ramsey is involved with a murder, and obviously, he needs the help of Trouble for Hire to get him out of this desperate situation."

War glanced toward the ceiling. "He has not hired us to help him. I told you this like four times already."

Jinx merely shrugged. "He wants help. I'm sure of it. He just doesn't know how to *ask* for help. Never picked that bit up as a kid."

Imari put her hands on her hips. "Cyrus is going to run to Ramsey and tell him that I'm trying to bring him down again. It's not going to take either one of those men long to find out who my new employers are." And she was staring at them...because she'd recently joined Trouble for Hire as a new operative. From what she could see, the pay was shit but she actually trusted these crazy men. She liked them, too.

Well, except for Jinx. He could be a pain in the ass.

"Now that we know Cyrus is working either with or for Ramsey, that gives us an advantage." Jinx pushed away from the desk. "I'll take over the case for tonight. Hopefully, I'll have more to report in the morning."

She remained standing in front of the door. "How do we have an advantage?"

"Ramsey doesn't know that Cyrus didn't spill all to you. I can play that card. Act like I know one hell of a lot more than I do."

Now War rose from the seat behind the desk. "You're going to lie to Ramsey? You think that's a good idea?"

Jinx's body tensed. "I think I'll do anything necessary to make sure he doesn't get thrown in jail for a murder he didn't commit. Now, like I said, I'll report more in the morning." He skirted around Imari and strode out of the office.

The other two men looked worried. Not a good sign. "I should be concerned, shouldn't I?" Imari could feel a headache forming behind her left eye.

"Yes," Odin replied.

War nodded. "Very concerned."

***

"Where is my laptop?" Whitney paused near the couch and let her gaze sweep around the room. "I know it was here last night. I made sure to take it from my house when we were escaping."

Darius lifted his hands. "Don't have it."

She tapped her foot. She was wearing canvas shoes, some jeans with an awesome stretch waist, and a flowing top. Ramsey had stocked about a million clothes at the place for her. "I searched everywhere. It has to be—"

An alarm was beeping. In a flash, Darius was off the couch and at the door—and he had a gun in his hand.

He'd sure moved helluva fast for someone so big.

"Go to the bedroom. Lock the door. Don't come out unless *I* come for you!" Darius thundered

But...

The front door was already opening. And *Jinx* stood there.

Darius had his gun pointed straight at him. "You shouldn't be here," Darius snarled.

"No?" Jinx appeared puzzled. "But I have a key. That's how I got the door open. And I will tell you, if you happen to shoot me, Ramsey will be extremely pissed off."

"I don't think so," Darius snapped back. "He keeps telling you to stay away—"

"Whitney? A little help," Jinx prompted. "Help *before* I start sporting bullet holes."

Whitney hurriedly said, "Don't shoot him, Darius. He's right. Ramsey will be pissed if you do."

"Get the hell out, and you won't get shot," Darius blasted at Jinx.

Jinx glanced over at Whitney. "Ramsey left you?"

"Not like I wanted to be left. He told me he had to tie up loose ends." And yes, she was still bitter.

"Fuck." From Jinx.

Exactly how she felt. And the stupid alarm was still beeping. She marched toward it and typed in the code to turn it off. Even as she typed in the code...

How do I remember this? But she did remember it. Because once upon a time, Ramsey must have shared the code to his security system with her. Just as he had apparently shared so much else. Swallowing, she returned to find Jinx and Darius still facing off.

Jinx tapped his chin. "Ramsey knows who killed Ronald Rudolph, doesn't he?"

Instead of answering the question, Darius told him, "You're still here when you should be gone."

"He knows, and he left you here to protect her while he went out to—what? Kill the guy?" Jinx shook his head. Tension poured off him. "We can't let that shit happen. The cops are watching him too closely. He makes a move like that, and we will lose him."

She crept toward Jinx.

Darius saw her and swore—he also immediately put down his gun.

"Is it true?" Whitney asked Darius. "Does Ramsey know who killed Rudy?"

Darius's gaze jerked away from her. He glared at Jinx. "You're a pain in the ass, and—"

"And you've been with Ramsey long enough to know who I am to him. So you know that I want to protect him. He is in trouble. This is a line he cannot cross tonight." Jinx's bright blue eyes glittered. "Just tell me where he is. Let me help him, dammit!"

But Darius's chin jerked into the air. "It's not going down like you think. Not like he's attacking an unarmed man. If there's going to be a battle, it will be old school."

Old school. The words seemed to echo in her mind, and a surge of pictures flooded through her head. More memories pushing to the surface. As those pictures tumbled through, she *knew.* Whitney surged for the door. "I know where he is. Come on, Jinx."

"How do you know?" Jinx's voice was all suspicious.

She stopped at the door and looked back. "Because I remember—" More and more. "I know where he'd go for an old school battle."

"You *can't* leave." Flat and fierce from Darius. "He wants you safe. He wants—"

"If I've got you and Jinx with me, I will be safe. You two can be human shields around me, but we are getting to Ramsey right now." Was this a setup? Were the cops closing in and...dear God, was he really about to kill a man?

I can't let that happen.

"You get so much as a bruise," Darius pointed out with a hard edge in his voice, "and Ramsey will kill me."

She flinched. "I'm trying to stop him from killing anyone tonight, okay? That's the plan. Now let's *go.*"

No wonder he'd left her alone. He'd been so careful with his words. Tricky, tricky. He hadn't needed to hunt Rudy's killer. Ramsey knew exactly where the guy was.

And Darius still wasn't moving. Face grim, he told her, "It's the same guy who torched your house. The guy who sent the flowers to you. Ramsey needs to handle this shit. He's protecting *you.*"

She'd feared the man would be one and the same. "By protecting me, Ramsey could throw away his whole life." That wasn't happening. It was her turn to protect *him.*

Darius swore, but he finally got moving. So did Jinx. They hurried out of the beach house with Whitney. The wind whipped at her, and the waves crashed against the shore.

"We're taking my ride," Darius ordered. He lifted his hand, and the lights of the nearby black SUV flashed.

"How do you know where to go?" Jinx asked as they approached the vehicle.

The vivid memory pushed through her mind. Shoved through the darkness as if it needed to come into the light. "Because I followed him once before."

"Where? Where did you follow him?"

The wind tossed her hair around her face. "Into Hell."

CHAPTER FIFTEEN

Observation notes: It was...brutal. Savage. Terrifying.

I could feel Ramsey slipping away all week. A darkness seemed to grow in him, and when he left me at my house, I had to follow.

He taught me how to trail someone and not be seen. I used the tricks he showed me. I went to the warehouse. I heard the shouts even before I slipped inside. And when I got inside, I smelled the blood.

Fists were swinging. Bones crunching. I had to put my hand over my mouth because I wanted to cry out and beg for it all to stop.

Ramsey was there. He was bloody. He was—

***

Ramsey smiled as he stepped into the cage. Did he think the cage was annoying as fuck? Yeah, he did. But it kept the opponents trapped inside until the match was over. The match only ended when one fighter couldn't get up.

"You're not supposed to be here!" The muscled man across from him took a quick step back. His shaggy, blond hair hung over his left eye.

"No?"

Ramsey's opponent had stripped off his shirt. The tattoos on his chest flexed with every movement.

"I'm going against Enzo tonight, not you, not—"

"Enzo has other plans." Ramsey noted the bruising and cuts on the guy's knuckles. "So I volunteered to take his place."

Axel Porter's beady eyes jerked to the left, as if seeking escape.

Cute. There was no escape. Ramsey rolled back his shoulders. "You've made some big fucking mistakes lately..."

Ramsey and Axel began to circle each other as the crowd started to roar. Ramsey hadn't participated in one of the fights in a while, and he suspected a shit-ton of money was being exchanged as bets were placed.

"You don't know what you're talking about!" Spittle flew from Axel's mouth.

"You came after me."

"No, no, man, I have *not*—"

"Lying just pisses me off more." He didn't strike. Not yet. "Before you leave this cage, you will tell me everything I want to know."

"I'm not sayin' nothin'!"

Ramsey smiled. "You will. You'll bleed *and* you'll talk."

Axel bellowed in rage and launched his massive body straight at Ramsey.

***

"Why are there so many cars in the lot of a closed-down warehouse?" Jinx asked in a careful tone.

"Because it's not closed down," Whitney replied. "It's used for matches."

Jinx stood beside the SUV and made no move to approach the warehouse. "Matches..."

"Bleed and beg fights," Darius explained as he crossed his arms over his chest. "You bleed and you don't stop, not even when your opponent begs."

The moonlight revealed the tenseness of Jinx's expression. "Just how long has Ramsey been running these fights?"

A shrug from Darius. Whitney took that shrug to mean...*a very long time.*

Tired of just standing there, Whitney began heading for the door—and for the guards who were blocking the door.

Darius closed a hand over her shoulder. "Forgetting someone? I'm the human shield, remember? I go first and that SOB..." He jerked his thumb over his shoulder to indicate Jinx. "He covers your back."

"Fine, let's just *go*." Because she had a terrible feeling growing in her heart. The kind of feeling that told her something very, very bad was going down inside of that place.

The shouts were nearly deafening once they stepped inside. Men and women were yelling and shaking their fists as they tried to hype up the fighters. The two men in the cage.

Two men who were beating each other with powerful blows.

Whitney sucked in a breath when she got a look at Ramsey's enraged face.

"Oh, fuck," Jinx breathed from behind her. "He's not going to stop."

Ramsey drew back his fist and plowed it into his opponent's face. Blood flew into the air.

***

Ramsey didn't feel pain. Axel had managed to get in some strong hits, but who the hell cared? He had the bastard on the floor now, and Axel wasn't swinging any longer.

"You sent her roses," Ramsey snarled as he leaned over his prey. "You torched her *house*."

"I-I..."

He pounded his fist into Axel's stomach. "Don't lie to me! I can make this so much worse..."

No one else was close enough to hear their words.

Axel shuddered. "Don't...don't know what you're talking..."

"You stole War Channing's ride!"

Axel smiled. His mouth was bloody. "Liked that...did you? Know you...h-hate him..."

"You used that freaking car when you torched *my* lady's place...with *me* inside. You came at me." It was all he could do not to rip the bastard apart right then and there. "Tell me *why*."

Axel's eyes widened in what looked like horror. "You...there? She...she's with you?"

Axel had been in jail when Ramsey first hooked up with Whitney. He wouldn't know about their past, not unless someone had told him about it. "She's fucking *mine*."

"Oh, God." Fear flashed on Axel's face, as if he finally realized just how serious shit was getting for him.

Hell, yes, it was serious. This was Whitney's life.

Ramsey pulled back his fist, ready to pound—

"Ramsey!" A roar of his name. The shout stuck out from all the others because it was a voice Ramsey knew too well—his brother's voice. But Jinx damn well shouldn't be in that warehouse.

His head turned to the right. Through the wire of the cage, he saw Jinx staring back at him. But Jinx wasn't alone...

Whitney was at his side.

*No, no, Whitney cannot be here. It's not safe for Whitney to be here...*The scene was too wild. The people too dangerous.

He'd given orders. Darius should have her back at home where she would be *safe*. He surged away from Axel and rushed toward her. "Get her out of here!" Ramsey thundered at Darius. He ignored the blood dripping from a cut in his brow. "Get her—"

Whitney's eyes flared wide. "Behind you!" she yelled.

Axel had been on the floor. Beaten. Weak.

Or had he been pretending?

Instinct had Ramsey jerking to the side as he whirled back around, and that side movement—those few precious inches—saved him from getting a knife shoved in his gut.

There were rules about the matches.

Rule one...The only weapon was your body. Axel *never* should have come into that match with a knife. And the fact that he'd been lunging for Ramsey with it...

You want me dead, don't you, you sonofabitch?

Too bad. Ramsey wasn't going to be the one dying.

Rule two. Bleed and beg fights mean begging doesn't help. You take your enemy down.

He swept his leg out and had Axel slamming into the floor. Before the jerk could get back up, Ramsey pounded his foot into Axel's wrist over and over again, making sure the bones broke and that Axel had no choice but to let go of the weapon.

Then Ramsey scooped it up. He surged at his prey and shoved the knife to Axel's throat.

The crowd roared, urging him on. Someone had probably bet on death that night.

The blade sliced across Axel's throat. Blood trickled down his neck. Fear poured from the bastard, filling the air like thick smoke.

"You thought you were taking *me* out?" Ramsey snarled.

"Please..."

Now he was begging.

Too late. Begging never helped.

Ramsey let the knife slice deeper. "Why'd you go after her?"

"J-just a job! I was s-supposed to s-scare—"

"She's mine." The rage burned through him and blasted past his control. It would be so easy to slice the bastard's throat wide open. "You don't scare her. You don't *touch* her. You don't—"

The crowd was roaring even louder. They wanted him to end Axel. Axel was known as a brutal bastard in the cage and to see him getting taken down was driving the crowd crazy. They were pushing toward the cage—

Whitney is in that crowd.

What if she was getting pushed? His head snapped up, and his gaze searched for her.

She was staring right at him, and there was horror on her face. Her eyes were wide and desperate.

"Don't."

He couldn't hear her say that one word. Everyone else was too loud, but he saw her lips move.

She thought he was about to kill Axel. She was asking him to stop.

But I want to kill the bastard.

"I-I was paid for the jobs!" Axel's words rushed out. "Got texts telling me what to do. That I had to order the roses from your bar. That I had to use War's car. Didn't know I was crossing you, I-I f-fucking *swear* it!"

But when he had learned the truth...Axel had come at Ramsey with the knife. *Because he knows what I'll do to him for targeting what belongs to me.*

Some men grabbed the cage and shook it. One shouted, "Kill him! Slice his throat open!"

Ramsey's gaze snapped to Jinx. "Get her out!" he ordered.

Jinx jerked his head in agreement and immediately put his hands around Whitney's shoulders. But as he turned her to leave—

Someone bumped into them. A big bear of a guy who'd been jumping toward the cage. Jinx curled his body protectively over Whitney, and Ramsey—

He didn't quite remember knocking out Axel. He just saw the man's eyes roll back into his head before he slumped. And Ramsey didn't quite know how he was able to fly up and scale the cage's side so fast, but he did it.

He just knew—

He was suddenly beside Whitney. He scooped her into his arms and bellowed for everyone to get the fuck out of his way.

And everyone got the fuck out of his way.

He could feel her trembling in his arms. She was afraid—of the crowd? Of the violence? Of him?

"Boss!" Darius shouted after him. "What do you want me to do with Axel?"

He wasn't done with Axel. Not even close. "Lock him up." He'd deal with him soon enough. But even as Ramsey gave that order, the wail of sirens cut through the night.

Cops.

Closing in.

And if the crowd had been wild before, they became frantic when they heard the sirens.

He pulled Whitney closer, held her tighter, as men and women ran for the doors. *Have to get her to safety.* This was his warehouse. He knew the best way to escape. Curving his body over her, he took her toward the side door. Slipped away from the fleeing throng and eased into a long corridor that would take them out a private exit.

The door clanged shut behind them.

But Ramsey realized he wasn't alone in that corridor with Whitney. He heard the heaving breaths behind him and glanced back to see Jinx.

"That was close," Jinx muttered.

"Put me down," Whitney said, voice husky.

The hell he'd put her down. She was in his arms—safe and warm and he wasn't letting go. "You brought her here," he snapped at Jinx. "She should be at home where she can be protected, and you brought—"

"I was afraid of what you'd do!" Jinx jumped toward him. "You're not thinking straight! I was afraid you'd cross the line and kill!"

"Who said I don't still plan to kill him?" Ramsey taunted.

"*Ramsey.*" Whitney.

He looked down at her. Felt his chest tighten. She'd seen him at his worst. At his absolute fucking worst. He hated that Jinx had brought her there. Now there would be no pretending he was anything but the monster everyone said. He'd been beating Axel in front of her. He'd had a knife at the jerk's throat.

"He was the one who sent you the roses," Ramsey rasped. "He stole War's car. He set your place on fire. He did all that shit. I got him to confess." That had been the point of the fight. Wasn't like people in his world sat down for a friendly little chat.

Hell, no, that didn't happen.

Her hand rose, and her fingers slid over his cheek. "You're hurt. Put me down so I can help you."

No. He marched down the corridor, aware that Jinx trailed them. "We need to get you out of here. Someone called the cops." He suspected that *someone* was his brother. "They'll be arresting anyone they can find. They *won't* find you." No way was Whitney spending even a moment in a cell.

He kicked open the back door. Never let her go. He rushed toward the limo that was idling back there—and toward a pacing Jimmy.

"We need to *go!*" Jimmy cried out. He ran a shaking hand through his hair. "The cops are out front!"

Ramsey wasn't leaving. He was going back inside, and he would be getting Axel to tell him *everything.* "Take Whitney back to my place. You stay with her until I return."

Jimmy bobbed his head in agreement.

Ramsey eased Whitney into the car. When he started to retreat, she grabbed his hand. "Come with me."

Axel came after her. "I can't."

"You can. Get in this car and let's drive away."

Fleeing wouldn't protect her. The threats to Whitney and their baby had to be eliminated. "You shouldn't have come here. It wasn't safe. You put yourself and the baby at risk—"

"*You* were at risk. I had both Darius and Jinx acting as human shields for me!" Whitney threw back immediately. "You were the one trapped in a cage and doing some insane death match! Don't expect me to sit on the sidelines while you risk yourself like that. I *can't*. When I saw you fighting before, it scared the hell out of me! I couldn't just stand back while you did this again!"

Before?

"I remember Hell," she whispered.

Hell. The nickname he'd given the warehouse. If she remembered that...if she remembered seeing him fight before...

She knows I'm a monster. "Take her home," he ordered woodenly. The sirens screamed. "*Now.*"

"Dammit, Ramsey, don't do this!" Whitney cried.

He had to do it. He had to keep her safe. "You were never here, understand? Whatever goes down...*you were never here.*" The cops would not touch her.

"Ram!"

He slammed the door. Jimmy floored the limo and got them the hell out of there.

"What kind of self-destructive bullshit was that?" Jinx asked flatly.

Ramsey shot past him. "Get the hell out of here while you can. I don't think you want to get caught up in an illegal betting scene." Like that was the only crime going down...

Jinx grabbed his arm and swung him back around. "*You* don't want to get caught here, either! Let's *go*."

"Got something else to handle first—now get your damn hand off me."

Jinx's grip hardened, but then he let go. Ramsey didn't waste any more time. He ran back into the warehouse and flew through that corridor. When he shoved open the door that would take him to the fight zone—the place was empty. Correction, mostly empty. Darius stood near the cage.

Everyone else was gone. The crowd could sure as hell move fast.

Ramsey heard voices outside. Shouts. Barked orders. He realized the cops were stopping people in the parking lot. That gave him a little more time...

He rushed toward the cage.

Darius whirled toward him. "I...I only left for a minute. Wanted to make sure you had Whitney out okay..."

What?

"Don't know who got to him. Sorry..."

Sorry? He peered around Darius and saw that Axel was still sprawled in the cage. They'd need to get that guy out, quickly. There were only moments left before the cops stormed inside.

That's one hell of a lot of blood.

And...wait...

Ramsey stepped forward. The knife was near Axel's body.

That was *too* much blood. Too much...because someone had stabbed Axel in the chest.

"Your prints are gonna be on everything," Darius muttered. "Your prints, your DNA. Boss, they will pin this on you. You have to get the hell out of—"

The cage door had been unlocked. Ramsey rushed inside.

"What in the hell are you doing?" Darius yelled. "Get out of there. We need to go! We need—"

"He's not dead." He'd seen the bastard's chest rise.

"What?"

Ramsey dropped to his knees beside Axel. "You're still alive," he snarled. "And you're staying that way." Because someone had hired Axel. Someone had sent the SOB after Whitney. Axel didn't get to go into the great pit of hell that was waiting for him, not yet. Not until Ramsey had his answers.

He shoved his hands over the wound. Tried to stop the pouring blood with pressure. "Get an ambulance!" Ramsey bellowed.

Footsteps thundered toward him. He looked up and over...

And saw Detective Melissa Wright pointing a gun at him. "Get your hands up!" she barked.

"I would," he snapped back, "but I'm kinda busy trying to stop this bastard from bleeding out."

**

"Stop this car right now!" Whitney blasted as she glared at the back of Jimmy's head. She'd lowered the privacy screen as soon as he'd started driving. "Take me back to Ramsey!"

"I can't do that." He sounded miserable. "He'd freak out! You don't make Ramsey freak out."

"I'm going to freak out if you don't turn us around! We can't just leave him!"

"He wants you safe. Told me to take you home." His grip was tight on the wheel. "That's what I'm doing. I don't want Ramsey as an enemy."

This couldn't be happening. "The cops will lock him up!"

"He'll get out. He always gets out."

His words weren't quite confident.

Whitney wanted to *scream*. "I can't leave him!"

"Sorry, but you don't have a choice."

Yes, she did. Whitney was not about to let Ramsey be sent to jail. If she couldn't get to him and protect him, then she'd hire someone else to take care of the job. She pulled out her phone. Dialed with shaking fingers. When her call was answered...

"You have to help Ramsey. I'll pay anything."

CHAPTER SIXTEEN

Observation notes: The cops have never been able to make any cases stick against Ramsey. There are plenty of suspicions about him...stories to make him into a legend. But as far as I can tell, he's never spent more than a handful of nights in jail before being released.

Does that mean the stories are wrong? And he's a good guy after all? Or...does it just mean that Ramsey is very, very good at hiding his sins?

***

"So you want to explain to me why a man was nearly murdered on your property tonight?"

Ramsey glanced up at the detective. "What do you mean, my property?" He frowned. "Are you talking about the warehouse? If so, I don't own that place. You must be mistaken."

"I received a tip—"

"Oh, wait, is that like one of those anonymous things? You know, the calls that turn out to be bullshit?" Ramsey smiled at her. "You can't believe those."

Melissa straightened her shoulders. "The PD received a tip tonight that an illegal fight was happening at a warehouse owned by Ramsey Hyde."

"Not my warehouse. You should check the property records on that place. See who really owns it." He knew with one hundred percent certainty that his name couldn't be officially tied to the warehouse.

"The tipster said one of the fighters involved was the man who'd recently torched the home of Whitney Augustine."

His fingers tapped against the side of the table. "What a helpful anonymous tipster you have."

Her eyelashes flickered. "We rushed to the scene. Caught half the crowd leaving..."

"Yes, but can you charge those people with anything? I think most of them believe they were at a rave of some sort. That is actually what *I* thought I was doing..."

Her eyes burned with fury as she leaned forward in the interrogation room. "Excuse me?"

"Heard it was a hot party scene. You know, one of those trendy spots where cool parties pop up randomly in abandoned buildings. I went there because I do like to party."

Beside him, Aspen let out a slow exhale.

"You went to the warehouse to party," Melissa said flatly.

"Um." Hadn't he just said so? "Imagine my surprise when I realized there was much more happening at the scene than just the good time I expected. It was chaos I tell you, chaos."

Her nostrils flared. "When we found you, you were in a cage and the man with you had been stabbed."

He nodded. "I was bravely trying to save his life. Because, as you discovered in our last chat—in this very room—I am a Good Samaritan. When I saw him in that terrible condition, what else could I have done?"

"You mean you *weren't* the one to stab him?"

Aspen touched his arm before he could speak. "Did any of those people at the scene *say* that Ramsey stabbed him?" she inquired ever so sweetly.

Ramsey knew there had been no recordings of his fight with Axel. No quick pics on a camera. One of the rules for admission—no phones or cameras were ever allowed. You violated that policy, and you'd be paying in blood. Attendees were searched before they went inside.

Just as the fighters were searched before they entered the cage. Yet, somehow, Axel had gotten a knife.

Instead of answering Aspen's question, Melissa lifted one eyebrow. "When we check the knife, are we going to find your fingerprints on the weapon?"

"Yes," he answered immediately.

Aspen's nails dug into his arm.

"I shoved the knife out of my way in my desperation to help the victim," he explained.

"You're bullshitting me," Melissa snapped.

Was he? Oh, yes, he was. Ramsey shrugged.

"Your knuckles are bruised and bloody, you've got bruises all over you—it's obvious you just went several rounds in that cage nightmare crap. You are the one who beat Axel Porter until he was flat on the mat."

He stared back at her. "I think I hit another wall."

Her lips thinned.

"Though, of course, you will find my DNA all over the scene because I was trying—"

"So desperately to save Axel. Yeah, yeah, I got it the first time." Her gaze cut to Aspen. "Does your client understand the seriousness of this situation?"

"I think my client understands pretty much everything."

He did. "When your victim wakes up, he can tell you that I wasn't the one who stabbed him. Thanks to my quick intervention, he gets to live another day."

Confusion flew over Melissa's face. "You really want him to be okay?"

"That man torched Whitney's house. He stole War Channing's car. I also believe he is the individual who murdered Ronald Rudolph."

"*What?*" Melissa's voice notched up several octaves. She caught herself and cleared her throat. "How do you know all that?"

"Because I know Axel Porter's MO. I'm sure you've pulled his rap sheets by now, so you realize that his past crimes make him fit the bill nicely for this situation. But the guy isn't what I'd call an idea man. I think he was hired for the jobs, and I intend to find out exactly who was pulling his strings."

Melissa pointed at him. "You're lucky."

Why did people keep saying—

"You have a war hero backing up your account. Actually, you have a few of them."

What in the hell was she talking about?

But Melissa motioned toward the one-way mirror on the right. Like he hadn't realized he was being watched by people behind that glass. A few moments later, the door to the interrogation room opened.

Jinx walked in.

He was followed by Odin.

Then War.

"What in the hell is this?" Ramsey demanded as he straightened in his chair. "A parade?"

War lifted his hand and scratched his right cheek...with his middle finger.

Yeah, fuck you, too, buddy.

"They are here to alibi you," Melissa said, and it sounded as if she choked on the words.

"Absolutely, we are." Jinx nodded. "I was with Ramsey when that Axel guy was being stabbed. We were outside together. I'd just seen him leave Axel—very much *alive*—even after the creep tried to stab him. Ramsey defended himself and left the guy behind."

So that was the truth. And Ramsey was glad that Jinx had exhibited the good sense to leave Whitney *out* of the story. But what BS were Odin and War about to share?

"I tracked down the man who stole my ride. It was Axel Porter," War announced. "I got word that he was at the warehouse, so Odin and I snuck in to see what was happening."

Odin nodded.

"When the cops arrived, everyone fled. Ramsey and Jinx left, and we figured that we needed to go out front and see if the cops wanted any help. That was when *you* ran into us," he added with a nod toward Melissa.

"You were on your damn phone," she snapped. "Didn't see you *helping* much."

"I'm the one who called with the tip about the warehouse," War drawled. "Figured that was *helping* plenty."

Of course, the sonofabitch would have been the one to rat him out.

Jinx shifted his stance. "Ramsey didn't stab that man. You've got the three of us telling you he didn't do it. I also know that Darius Addams told you he found the vic and that Ramsey arrived back to the scene *after* he did."

Aspen rose. "This has been such incredibly helpful information. I'm so glad that you are here to stand up for my client. He tries to help others and in return, he's just treated like a common criminal by the authorities."

Melissa laughed. A mocking sound. "We all know there is nothing common about him."

Ramsey had to smile at her. "Good of you to think I'm special."

A rap sounded at the door. A uniformed officer poked his head inside. "Chief wants to see you, Detective Wright."

Her expression tightened. "No one leaves this room until I get back." She jabbed her hand toward the uniform. "Guard the door."

He gulped and nodded—and side-eyed Ramsey.

Ramsey fought the urge to say, "Boo."

The uniform stayed in the room with them. Melissa marched out.

The silence and tension grew thick.

Aspen cleared her throat. "Don't think we've been formally introduced." She stood and offered her hand to War. "I'm Aspen Gray."

"I know who you are." He shook her hand. "War."

She pulled her hand back. Offered it to Odin.

The big blond's grip seemed to swallow her hand as he introduced himself.

Then she glanced at Jinx. Then back at Ramsey. There was a whole lot of speculation in her eyes. Before she'd turned to law, Aspen had been an artist. The woman always saw things a little too deeply for Ramsey's liking. He had the uncomfortable feeling she was studying bone structure or some shit like that and reaching some telling conclusions.

He tuned her and Jinx out as they made BS small talk. He was trying to hold onto his control, but he needed a phone. He needed to call and make absolutely certain that Whitney was—

"Relax." War sidled closer and offered him a smile. "We stopped to talk with the police chief on our way inside."

Great. So he was supposed to owe War for this scene? The guy thought he was saving the day?

"Took on a new client," War continued as if they were besties and Ramsey gave a fuck about what he had to say. "Though, technically, we were already involved with this particular client, so when we got her phone call, we sprang into action."

"More like leapt," Odin corrected. He'd closed in, too.

Ramsey's eyelids flickered. He got the message they were delivering. "Your client is doing well?" *Tell me she's safe. Tell me that she got home and—*

"Fantastic. Even now, our client is enjoying a quiet night at home."

Some of the tension left his body. "Thank you."

War inclined his head.

Shit. I will owe the bastard now.

The door swung open again. "What in the hell do you have on the chief?" Melissa demanded.

Ramsey shook his head. "I have no idea what you're talking about."

"Bull." She strode right up to him. "You must have some porn video of him with a dozen prostitutes."

Jinx whistled. "That is a lot of—"

Ramsey cut him a glance.

Jinx stopped talking.

"Or you must know where he buried bodies because this is some bullshit. *Bullshit*. He tells me I'm supposed to let you walk?"

Aspen cleared her throat. "The chief—a man well-respected in this town—probably just realizes that my client is a hero tonight. Not some thug. He saved a life. He didn't take one."

Ramsey flexed his fingers and felt the tightness near his knuckles. "It appears that our time together has ended again, hmm, detective?"

She motioned toward War, Odin, and Jinx. "I don't care how many new friends you get."

"We are *not* friends," War corrected. "More like acquaintances."

"You can't hide behind them forever," Melissa snarled.

"I don't hide from anyone." He was done with this place. "If your *chief* said to release me, then I'll be on my way. Have a lovely night, Detective." He stood and took his time heading for the door. Aspen was at his side. "Oh," he called back just before he exited. "When Axel wakes, and he tells you who hired him to commit those jobs..." Ramsey glanced over his shoulder. "I will be very interested in learning that information."

"Why? So you can kill the guy?"

Yes. He feigned shock. "Is that what a hero would do?"

Her glare would have burned a lesser man.

No, it's not what a hero would do. But it is exactly what I plan to do.

CHAPTER SEVENTEEN

*Observation notes: I can't shake the feeling
that something is wrong. I found myself jumping
today when a door slammed in the hallway on
campus. I could swear someone is watching me.*

*Ramsey won't like it if I'm afraid. He's never
wanted me to be afraid of him. And I haven't
been. But...*

*I am afraid of what he'd do...if someone tried
to hurt me.*

***

The door opened at four a.m. Whitney
jumped up from her position on the couch and
hurtled toward Ramsey as he crossed the
threshold.

She was vaguely aware of Jimmy and Jag
rising from their seats, too. She hadn't just gotten
one bodyguard. Jag had appeared at the beach
house shortly after she and Jimmy had arrived.
They'd refused to leave her side.

Ramsey's hands closed around her shoulders
before she could hug him. "No."

The one word seemed to pour like ice water
over her.

"Baby, I've still got blood on me. I can't let it touch you. *I* shouldn't touch you." He let go of her shoulders. "I need to shower. Change."

She wanted to hold him.

He looked over at Jag and Jimmy. "I'll be with her. Go get some rest."

They filed out. She watched as he locked the door after them. Set the alarm.

Her hands twisted in front of her. She wanted to hold him so badly.

But he was walking past her. "You should be in bed." Ramsey's gaze raked over her. Took in the sweats and loose t-shirt and her bare feet. "It's late. You and the baby need rest."

He stripped as he passed her. She realized that shirt wasn't even his. Had the cops taken his clothing as evidence and given him whatever the heck he was wearing?

He headed into the bathroom. She followed slowly and heard the thunder of the shower as the spray of water rushed out. He'd seemed...cold when he came inside. His eyes had been too dark. Too hard. His whole expression had been locked down.

And he didn't want to touch me.

She stood near the bathroom door. Waited. Waited and—

Screw this.

Whitney threw open the door and marched inside. Barely glanced at what had to be an insanely expensive bathroom set up. Ramsey had multiple shower heads pouring water down his super muscled, super hot body. And he was standing there with his hands slammed against the shower walls, with his head bowed, and that sexy ass of his toward her.

"I am pissed at you."

His head shot up. He turned to look at her.

There was no shower door. Just a massive open structure. She stomped toward him. The steam from the water wrapped around her. "What were you thinking tonight?"

"Go to bed, Whitney."

"Stop tossing out orders! You might be the big, tough guy that all the criminals fear, but in case you missed it, *I am not a criminal!* I'm not scared of you!"

"No." He turned off the sprays. Moved toward her as water dripped down his naked body. "You're not. Even when you should be."

He was sporting a massive erection. *Now?* She grabbed a towel and threw it at him.

He caught it in one fist. One bruised fist.

"He could have killed you." Her voice had gone husky.

Ramsey didn't dry off. He did knot the towel around his hips. He stepped out of the shower and onto the lush mat. He towered over her, but Whitney didn't back up.

"The plan wasn't for me to die," Ramsey told her.

"Oh, I get that your plan was to force a confession out of him. You knew he was behind the attacks, but instead of turning him over to the cops, you set up that whole scene so you could go at him."

He shrugged. "The cops have their methods of interrogation, and I have mine."

She could see a darkening bruise along his ribs. "He came at you with a knife!"

"And I took it away easily enough."

"Dammit! Stop being so calm!" Whitney felt like she was about to break apart. "You could have died. Right in front of me."

"Or worse...I could have killed...right in front of you."

Her chin jerked up. "There is nothing worse than you dying in front of me!"

"You sure about that? Because I saw your face tonight, *and* the first time you walked into Hell. You looked at me and you were terrified."

"Not *of* you!" Was that what he thought? "I didn't want something happening to you! The fights are brutal and savage, and yes, they scare the hell out of me. I study violence, and I know that it can lurk inside of anyone, but in that cage, it's different. There are no constraints. There is no control. And I *don't want anything happening to you!*"

His eyes glittered. "Why not?"

Why not? "Are you serious right now?"

"Why does it matter so much to you that I stay safe?"

"Because—" She stopped.

"Say it," he urged.

Whitney sucked in a breath. She didn't speak.

"You remember going to Hell with me before."

"I didn't go with you," she corrected. "I followed you."

"You remember."

A nod. Yes, yes, she did.

"How much more?"

"Bits and pieces. The more time I spend with you, the more the memories come back." Like water dripping out of a crack in a dam. Only she had the feeling that dam might be close to bursting...

"You need to take some breaths. Getting upset isn't good for the baby."

"Like I don't know that!" She spun on her heel and strode away from him. She also tried to pull in deep breaths. Lots of deep breaths. "You know what else isn't good for the baby? Having his father hurt!" More deep breaths. More steadying breaths. More—

"When I went back inside Hell after you left...Axel Porter—he's the bastard I was fighting—had been stabbed."

She spun back around.

"Deep breath," Ramsey reminded her.

"Do not piss me off more than I already am!"

"Someone hired him to pull the jobs he did. They had to pay him well. Crossing me isn't something he would have done lightly. I'm not even sure he knew that he *had* crossed me until we were in the cage. That was why he pulled the knife. He knew if he didn't kill me..." His words trailed off.

She swallowed. "You *wouldn't* have killed him."

His lashes flickered. "Sweetheart, he tried to burn down your house, with you inside. There is very little I would not do to him, so don't pretend otherwise."

She stared into his eyes and saw the truth.

"The person who hired him was in Hell tonight. There is no security footage. No phones are allowed there. The place was packed, but I will find him. Until then..."

She knew how his sentence would end. "Until then, my guard duty continues."

He shook his head.

No? He was letting her go?

"I want to stay with you. I want you at my side because when it comes to your safety, I have to be there." He closed the distance between them. Stared down at her. "I know I'm wrong for you."

She couldn't look away from him.

"But I need you. If you're honest, you feel the same way. An attraction that's not quite sane. A craving that never truly fades."

It wasn't about a craving. It wasn't some basic need she couldn't control. Yes, she wanted him. Yes, that desire was unlike anything she'd felt before, but there was so much more at play than just a need.

His hand curled under her chin. "I'm bad for you."

"No."

"We both know that I am. But you are the only good thing I have in my world. I will do whatever it takes to protect you." His gaze dropped down her body. "Both of you."

"While you're doing that, who protects you?"

His stare lifted. "You did, tonight."

"You shut me out. You wanted to keep me locked away—"

"Yes." No denial. "You want the brutal truth? If I could, I'd lock you away from the rest of the world and keep you all to myself."

Her brow furrowed.

"I want you to be mine. I need you to be. And I don't want you hurt." He drew in a ragged breath. And...

He sank to his knees before her.

Whitney's hands fluttered around his shoulders. "Ramsey?"

His arms curled around her waist. His head pressed gently to her stomach. "When I thought you were dead before, my whole world went dark. *I* went dark. I didn't care about anything. Without you, nothing could touch me. I felt *nothing*." His head turned. His lips brushed tenderly against her belly. "I am not a good man, not on my own. The only time I'm good is when you are with me."

She had to blink away tears. "That's not true."

He looked up at her. "Yes, it is. You saw me tonight when I didn't think you were there. And if *you* hadn't called out to me, I wouldn't have stopped."

She tugged on his arms, pulling him up toward her. "I know who you are."

"Do you? Bit and pieces, that's what you have. Not the full picture."

Whitney shook her head. "I feel it. Inside. I know that you're meant for me. I know that I—" She stopped. Just as she'd stopped making her confession before.

"What?"

Her lips pressed together as her lashes swept down to conceal her gaze. It was late. Her emotions were all over the place. They should go to bed. Cool down. Regroup and talk in the morning but...

"What were you going to say?"

Her lashes lifted. She stared into his eyes. "I love you."

He took a step back. "Whitney..."

"Don't tell me how I can't know that I love you. Don't tell me all the reasons that this is crazy. Believe me, I get that. A few days ago, you weren't in my life. A few days ago, you seemed like a stranger." She lifted her hand and touched her heart. "But I feel it. It's like part of me knew all along and was just waiting to have you back with me again. I love you, and I wouldn't love some twisted bastard who was a monster. I would love a man who was strong and fierce and who protected those who mattered to him. That's who you are. That's who I—"

His mouth took hers. His lips crashed onto hers and the kiss was burning with desire and a fierce intensity that demanded a response from her—a response that Whitney was only too happy to give him.

She loved Ramsey. Complicated, maddening, and confusing—she loved him.

"I have always loved you," he growled against her mouth. "*Always*."

What? He—

He lifted her into his arms. Her legs automatically locked around his hips. His towel had fallen, and the thick length of his cock pushed against her. She had on loose sweatpants—and the thin fabric was just in the way because she wanted Ramsey inside of her. She wanted him thrusting deep and holding her and saying that he loved her over and over again.

His tongue slid into her mouth. His hands were so careful on her body. He walked across the bedroom and lowered her onto the bed. He stripped her—and his fingers were shaking. She stared at him and knew there was no way she could ever want anyone more than she wanted him.

Ramsey didn't scare her, but the way she felt about him? The emotions that wanted to consume her? Their intensity did. Because Whitney wasn't sure what she'd do if something ever happened to him...

He wasn't in my life days ago. How can I be this deep into him already?

He tossed away her clothes. His hands worshipped her body, only to be followed by his mouth. Lips and tongue. He had her twisting against the bedding and grabbing tightly for the covers, and when his mouth slipped between her legs...

Her head pushed back against the pillow. "Ramsey!"

He licked and stroked and had her going wild beneath him. He knew exactly what she liked. Every move was designed to drive her closer and closer to the edge. And just when Whitney was sure that she couldn't handle more...

The climax swept over her. The release quaked through her body, and he lapped it up.

Her breath heaved in and out. Her eyes were on him, and she saw the savage smile of satisfaction that curled his sensual lips as his head lifted.

"You're delicious."

His words sent a shiver over her.

Ramsey stretched out on the bed beside her. "Get on top, baby. Tell me how deep to go."

She was still trying to catch her breath. But she knew exactly how deep she wanted him to go—and *where* she wanted him. Whitney rose to her knees. Inched toward him. Her fingers slid over his chest. Over the bruising on his ribs. Her head bent and she pressed a tender kiss to his skin.

His breath hissed out.

But she was just getting started. Her mouth trailed carefully over him. Kissing his bruises. Whitney wished she could take his pain away. Ramsey had known so much pain in his life. Nothing had ever been easy for him. He'd had to fight for everything that he possessed.

Her fingers slid around his cock.

His powerful body jerked. "Whitney..."

"Let's see how deep you can go..." Her mouth closed around him. At first, she just took the tip of his cock into her mouth. Then she pulled him in deeper. Her tongue licked and she sucked and his rough growls just drove her on. He'd given her so much pleasure. She wanted to do the same for him.

His cock was long and thick and wide in her mouth. With every movement of her mouth, arousal pulsed through her. She wanted him to lose his control and—

His hands were on her. "Up." Guttural.

She gave him another lick, then lifted her head.

"In. You."

He had been...*in* her mouth.

But he was lifting her, making her straddle him, and the heavy head of his cock pushed at the wet entrance to her body. She was so ready that he slid right inside of her. His fingers rubbed over her clit.

"Ride," he ordered.

She pushed up. Down...

And was lost. But he was, too. She knew it. They pushed toward release. Their bodies heaved together, and there was no stopping. She couldn't take her eyes off Ramsey, and when she came, she was staring straight into the darkness of his eyes.

He shoved upward. Wrapped his arms around her. Pulled her against him.

When *he* came, he was kissing her.

***

A phone was ringing. Ramsey opened his eyes and stared up at the darkness. Whitney snuggled closer to him.

I love you.

The phone rang again.

He didn't want her waking up. She needed her sleep. Carefully, he eased from beneath her and made his way to his study. The phone that was ringing was one of his backups. Only a select few had the number.

"Do you know how late it is?" Ramsey asked when he answered.

"Yes, well, if you weren't out pulling some cage fighting bullshit and getting hauled in for chats with the cops, I could have talked to you earlier. As it is, I had to wait until you were back home..."

Cyrus. "You fixed the laptop?"

"Yeah, yeah, I did. But you got more worries than that." A rough exhale of air. "You remember a while back when you got that lovely visit from the Feds, and a woman named Imari Caddel burst in your bar?"

"I thought she was working with you."

"She was...then. Now she's some kind of free agent, and the woman tried to seduce me."

His lips curled. "Well, good for you."

"No, not fucking good for me. She was *using* me. She wanted intel on *you*."

His shoulders stiffened. "Now you have my attention."

"Well, I certainly hope so. Look, I screwed up, okay? She realized I was trying to protect you. She gets that we're working together. I don't know who sent her, but you need to be alert."

He was always alert. "I'm assuming you're on the hunt for her boss?"

"Damn straight. Just because she is the sexiest woman I've met in years doesn't mean I'll overlook this BS. No one plays me."

Ramsey glanced over his shoulder. "I want the laptop."

"Good to know. Because I'm so helpful, I'm putting it on your doorstep right now. You're welcome."

The guy was outside? No alarms had been triggered on the property.

"You get that she loves you, right?" Gruff, from Cyrus.

He could hear Whitney's voice in his mind. *I love you.* "Yeah."

"Excellent. And, no, I didn't read all the entries she had on you. When things started to get juicy, I stopped."

"Cyrus."

"What? You know I'm a curious bastard. At least, I stopped." A pause. "And you'll do what you need to do?"

Tear apart the town to protect her? Destroy everyone in his path? "Absolutely."

CHAPTER EIGHTEEN

Observation notes: Ramsey asked me to leave with him. Even as he asked, I could tell by his expression that he thought I would say no.

But how could I? I love him so much that sometimes it scares me.

We will leave everything else behind and start new.

***

"You found my laptop!"

Ramsey swallowed as he glanced up from the laptop. It was close to ten a.m. He'd woken an hour before, and he'd had the laptop sitting in the kitchen, waiting for her. "It wasn't lost."

"But I couldn't find it yesterday. I searched everywhere." She had on his robe. It swallowed her but still somehow made her look achingly sexy. Then again, he always thought she was sexy.

"I gave it to an...acquaintance to repair."

She inched into the kitchen. "Why didn't you tell me?"

Why, indeed? *Be honest with her.* "Because I thought that if he recovered the files, I'd read them."

Whitney tip-toed closer. Her gaze cut to the laptop, then back to him. "You read all the recovered files?"

"No." He'd been fucking tempted. So very tempted but... "I couldn't."

"You couldn't?" A pause. "Why?"

"Because if I did that, then I'd just be back to playing the bastard, and I don't want to be that person with you."

She sucked in a breath.

"If you hated me, if you feared me...if at the end you thought you would be better without me...that is for you to know." Her choices. He pushed the laptop toward her. "What you don't yet remember...maybe you can find the answers in there."

"I don't need to remember everything." Anger tightened her voice. "And I know already that I didn't hate you. Not then. Not now. I told you, I love you."

He loved her so much it consumed him. "I asked you to run away with me."

"What?"

"Haven't remembered that yet, have you?" He scraped his hand over his jaw. Damn, he needed to shave soon. If he wasn't careful, he'd hurt her delicate skin. "Before you disappeared, I asked you to start a life with me. In this town, I'm the criminal. I've got enemies always gunning for me. I wanted something more. I wanted it with you."

Once more, she eyed the laptop, then him. "When I came to you at the bar a few days ago, you...you were denying that we were involved. You said something like, um, like it wasn't as if we were planning a future and we were going to run away from everyone.'" She sucked in a sharp breath. "But...we *were?*"

He nodded. "And when you didn't show to meet me, I thought you'd changed your mind. I thought you'd realized that you shouldn't give up everything else for me." He squared his shoulders. "Because it's what I realized, too."

Pain flashed on her face. "You think...after last night, what you said—what *we* said—you think we shouldn't be together?"

He shot to his feet. The chair screeched back behind him. "*No.* I think you shouldn't have to give up a damn thing for me." He intended to be the one who left a life behind. Ramsey reached for her hand. Lifted it and placed it over his heart. "It fucking beats for you, baby." She had to get that. "But you aren't sacrificing anything for me."

She'd loved him months ago.

By some miracle, she loved him *now.*

"I won't be reading your entries. Your secrets are—"

"I don't care if you read the entries! I want you to know me, all of me, just as I want to know you. There is no part of me that needs to be kept secret from you." Her hand still pressed to his heart. "Just as you can't keep any part of *you* secret from me. Do you think I can't handle whatever is in your life? Your past? Because if that is the case, think again. I handled you before, and I will handle you always." Fierce determination.

God, she *owned* him, and she didn't even seem to realize her power. It went far beyond need, or even love. He would wreck the world and rebuild it again for her.

That was precisely what he intended to do.

"Oh, no." Alarm flared in her eyes. "Is that the time?" Her attention dipped over his shoulder. "I have to go!"

"What?" He kept holding her hand. "What's happening?" They were kind of in the middle of something vital.

"I have an appointment with my counselor. He's—he's a friend who was trying to help me recover my lost memories. I go see him every Saturday, and I'm late."

Fuck the friend. But he couldn't say that. His jaw locked as he slowly let her hand go. "I'm coming with you. You know I want you protected until—"

"Of course, you're coming with me." Her eyebrows lifted, and she smiled. "I just told you that I want you knowing all of my secrets just as I want to know yours. This is going to be my last visit with Edward. I don't need him any longer. I have you."

Damn straight, she did.

She rose onto her toes and pressed her lips to his.

***

Jag was waiting outside when Ramsey and Whitney hurried down the steps of the beach house. He'd been leaning against the side of the limo, but when he saw them, Jag straightened. "Guess it's my turn for guard duty, huh? When I got the text that you needed a driver, I came right over." He offered Whitney a smile. "Where am I taking you today? And are there going to be hot coeds around?"

"You're taking *us*," Ramsey told him flatly. "Whitney has an appointment with the guy who's been helping her recover her memory."

"My *last* appointment," Whitney pointed out. The memories were coming faster and faster now. She could look at the beach and see them jogging together. The photo of them that he kept in his nightstand? She remembered the day that photo had been taken. How happy she'd felt. He'd chased her back to the house and they'd made love on the couch. She cleared her throat. "Between the memories that are coming back and the files that were recovered on my laptop, I know what happened back then." Not that she'd read the files yet. She would. After her appointment with Edward.

Jag smiled. "Hey, that's great news!"

Ramsey didn't speak.

Jag's smile dimmed. "Isn't it, boss?"

"There are some plans that need to be put in place." Ramsey opened the back door of the limo. "I want to meet you and Darius at the bar this evening, five p.m. Make sure the place is locked down except for us."

"Sure, whatever you want."

Whitney slid into the back of the limo. "I'll be there, too, right?" she prompted.

"Where I go, you go. Especially until we can get Axel talking." He slanted a fast glance at Jag. "Any updates on him?"

"The bastard is still dead to the world."

Ramsey climbed into the back of the limo. Whitney hurriedly rattled off the address to Jag.

"Maybe Axel should stay that way," Jag growled as he peered inside the limo at them. "I hate he tried to hurt you, Whitney, and Ramsey, if I'd been there when he came at you..." Rage flashed on his face. "Darius told me he pulled a knife and tried to drive it into your back! I would have killed the bastard myself if he'd pulled that move around me!" His breath huffed out.

Whitney realized that Jag's loyalty to Ramsey went very, very deep. So deep that he'd be willing to kill.

"If Axel is dead, then he can't tell me who hired him." Ramsey's voice was easy. Casual. "He can't die until I know his employer's identity."

Jag gave a jerky nod. He moved back. Slammed the door shut.

When the car began to move a few moments later, Whitney carefully asked, "Do you always inspire people to kill for you?"

"Jag has been at my side for years. We met when we were both kids on the streets." His fingers drummed on the seat. "He has it in his head that I saved his life."

"Did you?" The privacy screen was up.

"We've been over this, sweetheart. I'm not the hero. I'm not—"

He wasn't looking at her. So she curled her fingers under his chin and made him look. "Did you save him?"

"Jag was getting his ass beat by three guys. I helped. Not like I had anything else to do that night."

"Of course. Nothing better to do." She would not smile at him. "And after you jumped in the fight? What did you do after that?"

"What do you mean?"

"With Jag. What did you do?"

"I cleaned him up. He was bleeding all over the place."

"That was nice of you."

He growled.

She wasn't done. "Have there been others like Jag?"

"There's nobody quite like Jag. That guy is vicious in a fight. He made sure he could never be taken down again—"

"How did you and Darius meet?"

"Why?" Suddenly suspicious.

Her fingers stroked along his hard jaw. "Because I told you, I want to know all your secrets."

"We fought."

She waited. Her hand stayed pressed to his cheek.

"When I needed cash, I bare-knuckle boxed. He was my opponent. We tried to destroy each other."

Hardly a heart-warming start to a friendship.

"He wouldn't give up. No matter how many times I knocked him down, he would shove himself back up. Everyone was screaming for me to finish him. But I knew that to stop him, I might have to kill him." He swallowed. "He was just trying to earn money, too. That money let us eat back in those days. Was I supposed to kill a man because he wanted to eat?"

No.

"So I stopped fighting him. Just turned my back on him. And I charged for the man who'd organized the match. The prick who was counting his money and yelling the loudest for me to end Darius. And Darius—when he realized what I was doing—he had my back. He's had it since then."

"He's not the only one," she whispered.

Ramsey frowned.

"I have your back, too. Know that. I will always watch out for you. I will always trust you."

His head turned and his lips brushed over her palm.

***

"Whitney!" Edward hurried across the small reception area toward her. They'd just entered his office on the third floor of the downtown building. His hands lifted toward her. "I was starting to get worried that you'd forgotten our—"

Ramsey stepped into his path. "Hi, there."

Edward stopped. Frowned.

"I did almost forget, Edward," Whitney inserted smoothly, "and I do apologize for being late." She squared her shoulders. "There have been some developments recently that have changed my situation."

His eyes widened. "You've remembered your missing time?"

She couldn't help but smile. "I've started to recall, yes."

"Wonderful!" He beamed at her. "Come into my office, and we'll get started talking." A quick glance toward the wall that was Ramsey. "Your...ah, friend, can remain here in the waiting area. We have a lovely selection of reading materials—"

"Why isn't a receptionist here?" Ramsey asked. He pointed toward the empty desk on the right. "Shouldn't someone else be here to welcome the clients?"

"I, ah, I only see special clients on the weekend. There's no need to bring in my assistant."

Ramsey's gaze slid to Whitney. Then back to Edward. "Special. Got it." His lips curved into a shark's grin. "I'm actually going to be coming in with her. Consider this meeting a couple's therapy session."

"What?" Edward took a step back.

Jag opened the lobby door. "Building seems secure. You want me to stay close?" he asked Ramsey.

"I've been told there is quite the selection of reading material here in the lobby. Take a seat, Jag. We'll be back soon." His fingers threaded with Whitney's, and he advanced toward the open door of Edward's office.

Edward stared at him with wide eyes. She should probably introduce the two men. As soon as they were inside of Edward's private office, she did just that. "Edward Wilson, this is Ramsey Hyde."

"*Dr.* Edward Wilson," he corrected as he inclined his head.

Ramsey's smile stretched a little bit more. No amusement gleamed in his eyes. "You like roses, doc?"

"Excuse me?"

"Can't help but notice you've got a vase of red roses on your desk. You must really like them."

Edward's gaze darted to the roses, then over to Whitney. "They're for her."

"Are they now." Ramsey's voice became a little flatter. He wasn't asking a question.

"How freely can I speak with him here?" Edward asked Whitney. "Because I think it would be better if your friend returned to the lobby—"

"You can speak as freely as you'd like. Ramsey knows everything about me. And he's staying in here with us." Because she wanted him there. Seeing those flowers had caused a shiver of unease to dart down her spine.

Ramsey let go of her hand, and he walked toward Edward's desk. His hand lifted, and he carefully touched one of the rose petals. "Why do you have these for Whitney?"

"She likes roses. They're her favorite flower."

"Tell me something I don't know."

Edward frowned at him. "We were using a sensory technique to help restore her lost memories. By putting her into contact with familiar objects, scents, tastes, sights...the goal was to stir up the memories she lost during her dark time."

"Dark time," Ramsey repeated. "That's what you call those six months?"

The six months she'd spent with him. "They're not dark any longer." Her chin lifted, and her hair slid over her shoulders. "The sensory technique worked pretty well for me, actually." Her gaze was on Ramsey's fingers as he carefully touched the rose petals. "I found a familiar environment, and the memories began to resurface."

"You're going to bruise those petals," Edward snapped at Ramsey.

"I doubt it. I know how to hold precious things." He smoothed his finger over one more petal. "When did you realize roses were her favorite?"

"I've known Whitney for a very long time," Edward replied stiffly. "We were in grad school together. I am quite familiar with her tastes."

Ramsey glanced over at Whitney. His fingers fell away from the roses. "You never mentioned him to me."

There was something about his tone...

Wait, was Ramsey jealous?

"Why would she have mentioned me to you?" Edward huffed. "I'm sorry but exactly *who* are you to Whitney and why—"

"I'm the guy who took her into the dark," Ramsey cut in to bluntly say. "And I'm the one who's pulling her back out."

CHAPTER NINETEEN

Observation notes: Ramsey doesn't trust easily. He only lets a few people into his inner circle. Jag and Darius are close to him. They have his confidence. And I do. But I'm not so sure he trusts anyone else.

He told me once that people who betray him pay a very high price. When I asked how high, he didn't answer.

But then, I think perhaps that was an answer.

***

"The patient isn't doing well, detective," the doctor told Melissa Wright as he heaved out a breath. "This is not the time for you to go in and interrogate him!"

"Actually, if he's dying, this is the only chance I've got."

The doctor stared at her as if she was insane. Fine. Maybe her words sounded heartless, but she didn't have a choice. "Axel Porter saw the man who stabbed him."

"Look—"

"I need to know who did this to him! Give me two minutes—just two—with him. If Axel dies without talking to me, then his killer might never be caught. I get that you're concerned with keeping him alive, but I'm concerned with justice. I want to stop the attacker before he goes after someone else." After pleading her case, Melissa held her breath.

The doctor—a young guy who she *would* have thought of as attractive if he hadn't been glaring so hard at her—gave a disgusted shake of his head. "One minute, and that's it. You do not upset him. You do not stress him. You do not—"

"Settle down," she told him. "The man isn't some delicate flower. He's suspected of committing a murder himself, and if you saw his rap sheet, your knees would shake every time you went near him."

"I help patients no matter what they've done. I don't judge them," he gritted out. Behind the lenses of his glasses, his dark eyes glinted.

"I'm afraid that I do, Dr. Abadi. I spend a great deal of time judging people. Now, how about stepping out of my way so that I can talk to my vic?"

He stepped out of her way. Reluctantly. She hurried forward. Machines hissed and beeped around her as she closed in on Axel.

"Axel Porter," she said his name deliberately. Loudly.

His lashes flickered. His head turned toward the sound of her voice.

"We need to talk," Melissa added. "Tell me who stabbed you with that knife."

***

"I truly feel that we should speak alone," Edward said. He pulled at the collar of his Polo shirt. "There are some things that must be kept confidential."

"I waive my confidentiality. Told you that already." He was acting oddly. "You can discuss my case freely with Ramsey."

Edward rushed closer to her. "Do you know who he is?" His voice was low.

"Uh, yes, Ramsey—"

"*I've* heard of Ramsey Hyde! He's dangerous!" Even lower. "You need to get away from him!"

"And you need to step back from my lady," Ramsey drawled, "because you are crowding her, and I don't like it."

Edward gulped and jerked back.

"Better," Ramsey praised. His gaze assessed Edward. Edward was several inches shorter and at least twenty pounds lighter than Ramsey. "You're the one who told her to go looking for me?"

"I absolutely did *not*—"

"Actually, you did." In a roundabout way, at least. Whitney continued, "You told me to keep working sensory memories, and that's precisely what I did. When I'm around Ramsey, I remember." He seemed to ignite all of her senses. "So I won't be coming back for more sessions. I appreciate you working me into your schedule, but with the time during my lost six months returning, I don't think that I will need to meet with you any longer."

"But you do! You need me!"

Ramsey's shoulders rolled back. "You should take some breaths and lower that voice, *Dr. Wilson.*"

Edward's lips thinned as he focused on Whitney. "You're my client. More than that, you are my friend, Whitney. I care about you." He reached out to wrap his hand around her shoulder.

A little warning rumble came from Ramsey. "You should *not* get all touchy with your clients. I am sure that breaks some kind of rule."

Edward's hand immediately fell back to his side. "I was going to give her a comforting touch. There is nothing inappropriate about that! Nothing at all!" he sputtered. His wide stare flew between Ramsey and Whitney. "Whitney, what are you doing? You have never mentioned this man in any of our sessions, yet you bring him in here and let him act as if—as if he has some sort of right to—"

"To be annoyed that a guy who *should* be helping Whitney has his office set up like some sort of date scene?" Ramsey finished in a voice of silky menace. "There are roses on your desk and scented candles near the couch. Were those candles supposed to help with her sensory recall, too?"

"Yes!" Edward's cheeks reddened.

"And the fact that your assistant isn't here? That it is just you and Whitney? That's all part of the setup, too?"

"Like I said, Whitney is a friend. I wanted to give her privacy."

Ramsey's laugh was mocking. "I think you wanted to get in her pants."

Whitney's jaw dropped. "Ramsey!"

"Sorry." He didn't sound it. "Was that not tactful? Should I have said...I think you want to be romantically involved with her, and that shit is just not gonna happen because she is with me?"

Edward straightened his shoulders. "She doesn't know you."

"Sure, she does. I told you, I was part of her *dark* time."

This was unbelievable. Whitney looked between the two men, and then she looked around the office...Hold up. Was that soft music playing in the background?

"You were part of a time she wanted to forget, obviously," Edward snapped back. "And I can see why. After just a few moments with you, I realize why Whitney was so traumatized that she blocked those memories. You were a mistake she wanted to put behind her, and I am happy to assist Whitney in any way that she needs."

"I'll be taking care of her needs, thanks," Ramsey replied.

Whitney glanced up at the ceiling. Seriously?

"After all," Ramsey added ever-so-smoothly, "that's my baby she's carrying and—"

"*You're pregnant?*" Edward was shocked.

He would be. Considering she hadn't told him about the baby. Her hand automatically dropped to her stomach as she glanced toward him.

Her response must have been confirmation because Edward's mouth opened wide, only to snap closed a moment later. After a moment, he managed, "You became pregnant during your lost time? No wonder you were so frantic to rediscover your past!" He stepped toward her.

Ramsey shook his head. "Is she some kind of magnet for you? Because I don't get why you keep sliding back when you need to stay away."

"How do you even know he's the father, Whitney?" Edward wanted to know. "Have you done a DNA test?"

She wet her lips. "No, we haven't gotten around to that yet."

"The baby is mine," Ramsey said flatly.

Edward didn't look convinced. "We must talk alone, Whitney. *Now.*"

"Nope," Ramsey's fast refusal. "That's not happening—"

"Ramsey, I want you to step outside for a moment." Her voice was crisp.

His jaw immediately locked.

"You'll be just beyond the door. I'll be fine. I need a moment with Edward."

Oh, Ramsey's expression said he did not like this plan. She thought he would argue. Instead, he moved closer to her. His hand slid over her cheek. "I don't like this." He kissed her. "You need me, I'll break the door down."

"Hardly necessary!" Edward cried as he wrenched the door open. "You may be used to such uncivilized practices in *your* world, but that sort of action is completely unnecessary here!"

Ramsey sauntered by him but stopped before exiting. "Keep your hands off her. That's the only warning you'll get."

When he walked over the threshold, Edward slammed the door. And locked it.

Whitney frowned at the lock. "Why did you do that?"

Edward hurried toward her. "What have you done?"

"I don't follow."

"You can't be involved with someone like him!"

Really? "I am."

"Whitney!" He reached out for her.

She stepped back.

His nostrils flared. "I have *heard* of Ramsey Hyde."

So he'd said before.

"You can't trust him. If he told you that the two of you were involved during your lost time, the man is obviously lying. You would never get personally involved with someone like him. If anything, he would have been a research subject for you, nothing more."

"You don't know Ramsey."

"I know *you*. You wouldn't fall for someone like him. You wouldn't sleep with him. Listen to me, please! I know why you first got involved in studying criminal behavior! Your parents were gunned down by a man who'd been let out of prison *seven* times before. You wanted to know why he couldn't stop committing such violent crimes. Why he wasn't reformed. Why—"

"Stop," she whispered. She hadn't forgotten her parents.

"You would never sleep with someone like Ramsey."

She had. Over and over again.

"He's lying to you." His focus shifted to her body. "If you're pregnant, I don't think it's his. He's playing some sort of game with you."

"No, he's not. He loves me."

Edward shook his head. "What I know about Ramsey Hyde—he *can't* love anyone. He's not capable of that emotion."

"I told you." Anger hummed through her. "You don't know Ramsey. He loves me."

"Get a DNA test," he urged her. "Until you get that back, stay with me. I can keep you away from him. I have an extra room at my place. You won't have to see him. And when you find out the truth, when you realize he's been lying to you, I can help you pick up the pieces."

Pick up the pieces?

"Doesn't matter who the father is. I can help you. I can help you both."

And there was something in his expression...

Her gaze darted to the flowers. To the candle. The soft music continued to play. And she realized the assistant *had* usually been there. Not that day, though. Her spine straightened. "I'm not broken. I don't need you picking up my pieces and putting them back together again." She turned for the door.

"Whitney!" His hand closed around her shoulder.

"Ramsey told you not to touch me."

"Because he's crazy and obviously possessive as hell about you! Fuck what he says—"

"*I'm* telling you. Don't touch me. You were my therapist, but you're crossing a line."

His fingers slowly uncurled. "You just need to calm down for a moment. If you're pregnant, you're no doubt experiencing hormone surges. They will make you emotional. You are vulnerable, and he's trying to capitalize off that vulnerability."

"No, he's not the one trying to capitalize off it." *You are.* Why hadn't she seen this sooner? "I won't be coming back to see you again. Your services are no longer needed."

"Whitney!"

She strode straight to the door. Flipped the lock. Yanked the door open.

And nearly rammed into Ramsey because he was standing right there. Just as he'd promised—on the other side of the door.

His gaze swept over her, and he nodded. He reached out, carefully slid his fingers around her shoulders, and pulled her out of the doorway. "Jag?" he called.

Jag was flipping through a magazine. "This thing lists the ten best sex positions for you."

"Keep an eye on Whitney. I'll be back in one minute."

He'd be—

Ramsey slipped into the office and shut the door.

***

"You upset Whitney."

Edward backed away. "There was a misunderstanding!"

"Yes, the misunderstanding was that you thought you could use your position to help get close to her. You were supposed to help her, but you just wanted to fuck her."

"Like you know—"

"I know a predator when I see one. I've gotten really good at spotting them over the years. You had the scene set for seduction..."

"Sensory stimulation."

Ramsey laughed. "Sensory stimulation, my ass. You made sure the office was empty, and you had her flowers and candles ready to go." He crossed his arms over his chest. "And I saw the way you looked at her in the lobby, before you realized I was there."

"You—you should go."

"Oh, I will be going. But I have a few questions first." Questions that would be answered. "Have you been stalking Whitney?"

"What? Of course, not!"

"You didn't arrange for anyone to deliver roses to her house?"

"I—*no!* I did not!"

"You've been to my bar." It was that point that had tipped him over the edge. The minute he'd spotted the guy, Ramsey had felt a nagging sensation. It had taken him a few moments to place exactly how he knew the not-so-good doctor. "I know you have. You came to my place *after* Whitney came back from her miraculous rise from the dead."

Edward swallowed. "She—she had found some old notes on a laptop. She told me that they mentioned your bar. You. So I just went to check things out."

Do not rip him apart. Not yet. "And while you were there, you didn't decide to hire a bastard named Axel to terrorize Whitney? Didn't get him to torch her house?"

"*No!*" He was sweating. "I would *never!*"

"Little hard for me to believe you. See, I know that you've been lying to Whitney. You kept your visit to my bar quiet. Because I'm thinking you didn't really want her to remember, did you?"

The man was shriveling before Ramsey's eyes. "I didn't hire anyone! I would *never* hurt Whitney! I-I—"

Rage nearly choked Ramsey as he cut through the jackass's words. "If you tell me that you love her, I will beat the hell out of you."

Edward scooted back. "I didn't hire anyone! I swear it!"

"You'd better be telling the truth. Because I am not someone you want to play—"

A shrill screech of an alarm cut through his words. The alarm didn't stop. It kept screeching and screeching.

"Fire!" Edward yelled. "That's the fire alarm!"

Ramsey was already running for the door. He yanked it open, and Whitney spun toward him with wide eyes.

"Ramsey?"

He didn't slow down. He scooped her up into his arms and raced out of that office. They were on the third floor, and he rushed for the stairwell. Jag and that prick Edward were yelling behind him, but Ramsey didn't stop. Getting Whitney and the baby to safety trumped everything else.

He could smell smoke. Saw it drifting from the open stairwell door when he hit the second floor. *Fucking hell.* Like he believed some fire had just randomly broken out in the building that he and Whitney were inside. No damn way. "Jag!" he bellowed. "Get in front of us!" They were rushing down to the first floor, and he damn well didn't want any surprises waiting for them.

They burst onto the first floor—and Ramsey surged toward the doors that would take them out. When the sunshine hit him, he took a deep gulp of air before frantically glancing down at Whitney.

She's fine. She's safe.

Her terrified gaze stared back at him.

"You're okay," he told her. He rushed toward the limo. Jag was ahead of him. Jag yanked open the door.

Edward was screaming something. Screw him.

Ramsey put Whitney inside the limo. The glass was bulletproof. She'd be safe there. She'd be—

"People are inside!" Edward yelled.

Ramsey had been halfway in the back of the limo. At the yell from Edward, he jerked back and spun around.

"That's what I was trying to tell you!" Edward cried. "There's a yoga group that meets on the floor above me on Saturdays. They didn't come down. I know they heard the alarm, but they didn't come out!"

"Why the fuck didn't you go up and get them?" Ramsey snapped at him.

"I—I..." Edward looked back toward the building. "I saw the smoke on the second floor. We...we had to get out."

"Fucking hell."

"I'll call for help," Edward said. "Who has a phone?"

Was the guy shitting him? Ramsey looked up at the building and...*holy fuck, someone is banging on the glass up there.*

Ramsey grabbed Jag's shirtfront. "You stay with Whitney, understand? Keep her in the car. *Stay with her.*"

"Ramsey?" Whitney's worried voice. "What are you doing?"

Something he never fucking expected.

Playing the damn hero.

"I love you," he told her, cutting her a glance. "And I'll be right back."

Her eyes widened. "Ramsey!"

He ran back to the building.

CHAPTER TWENTY

Observation notes: The "research" is over. It's been over for some time. I just used it as an excuse to keep coming back.

But neither of us will be coming back to the old bar much longer. A new life is waiting. Ramsey is working to tie up loose ends. He will tell his confidants, and then we will just...disappear.

I'm excited. And terrified.

I know I'll love him in ten years. I'll love him in twenty. I will love him always.

But will he feel the same? His life has been danger and adventure. Everything will change. Will he still love me in ten years when the excitement has faded? Will the life I offer be enough?

***

"Ramsey!" She shot out of the limo.

Jag immediately grabbed her. "No. *No, no, no.* You are not going in there. You stay here, you heard him!"

She struggled against his hold. "There is a fire! Ramsey is going in there alone!"

"The building's fire alarm would have sent an instant alert to the fire department," Edward said as he rubbed a hand over his face. "I don't even need to call for help. I was...flustered. I forgot. I'm sure the firefighters are already on their way here."

She looked up. She could see one of the windows opening on the top level of the building. *The fourth floor.*

"Help!" A woman's head leaned out of the window. "The elevator shaft is filled with smoke, and the door to the stairwell is jammed! We can't get out!"

Oh, God. No wonder Ramsey had run back inside. Whitney realized he must have seen the women up there.

But he needed help. "Jag, let me go!"

"I can't, you heard him. I—"

"He needs help!" she snarled. "So do they!" Those trapped women. "Go after him. Jag, dammit, *go!*" Her furious stare shot to Edward. He was just standing there.

"I can't leave you," Jag rasped. "He'll rip me apart."

"And we can't let him die!" She had to get out of his grip. "What if the smoke is too thick? What if he passes out? What if we lose Ramsey?"

Jag's hold loosened.

The women weren't in the window any longer. Where were they?

***

Ramsey covered his mouth with his shirt and ran up the stairwell as fast as he could. The fire seemed to be contained to the second floor—it hadn't spread through the building. Not yet. On the second floor, he kicked the open stairwell door shut in an effort to contain the smoke, then he kept rushing up the stairs.

Hurry. Get the hell out of here. Hurry!

He reached the top floor and came to a jerking halt.

There was a chair jammed under the door on this level. If anyone had tried to open it from the other side, the chair would have stopped them. Those women—they'd been trapped. He jerked the chair out of the way and yanked the door open.

Screams reached him.

***

Whitney could hear screams over the fire.

Edward swore and took off running, heading for the building.

Jag's grip eased even more on her. "You get in the limo and you lock the doors, got it?"

Yes, yes, she got it.

He let her go. Her breath heaved in and out. In the distance, she could hear sirens. Edward had been right. The firefighters were coming. Her fingers fluttered over her stomach.

It's okay. Your dad is okay. We're all going to be fine.

She understood an ambush attack could be waiting. She *was* going to get in the damn car.

Ramsey, get your ass back to me!

She turned for the vehicle.

And felt something slam into the back of her head.

***

Ramsey rushed out of the building and nearly ran straight into Jag. He shoved the other man back. "What the fuck?"

"You're okay!"

Ramsey coughed. He reeked of smoke, and the three women he'd led out were gasping. He pushed them forward even as he saw a fire truck flying toward the scene.

Someone had set that fire, he was sure of it. And the bastard had done it because...*he wants me*.

"So glad you're all right, man." Jag clapped a hand on his back. "How about you promise me that you will *never* run into a burning building again? Can you do that? Seriously?"

Ramsey's gaze darted around the area. "Where's Whitney?"

"In the back of the limo. She's safe and sound."

He immediately began double-timing it for the limo. "Where's that prick Edward?"

"He ran in after you. Didn't you see him in the stairwell?"

What? "No." And it wasn't like he could have missed him.

"Fuck. Do you think he's back in the fire?"

Ramsey stilled. He looked over his shoulder at the building. Unease pulsed through him. *Something feels wrong*. Instead of running back for the building...he ran for the limo. He wrenched on the door's handle.

Locked.

"Open up, baby!" Ramsey yelled to Whitney.

She...didn't.

"Whitney?"

Jag hurried toward him. "I told her to lock up. She's just being safe."

No, she wasn't. Because this was him, and she'd always open the door for him.

Jag unlocked the door with the remote. "Don't worry. I know she was getting inside—"

The interior of the limo was empty. No Whitney.

Ramsey spun around. "*Whitney!*" he bellowed.

Jag tried to peer around him. "She's not in there?" Horror filled his voice. "I swear, she was getting in the back! She promised. That's why I was coming after you. She was freaking out, worried that you would inhale too much smoke and pass out, and she got in the car and I came after you—"

"*Did you see her get in the car?*"

"I..." A shake of his head. "She was walking toward it." Fear flashed on Jag's face.

The fire truck's siren shrieked louder.

"Where is Edward Wilson?" Ramsey's mind was spinning. No, spiraling. Because he'd left Whitney. Left her side, and she was gone.

"I don't know. I thought he ran after you."

I didn't see him in the stairwell.

The fire truck braked at the curb.

"Where the fuck is Whitney?" Ramsey roared.

***

"There has to be security footage."

Ramsey glanced over at those words. The fire had been put out, but the firefighters were still running in and out of the building. They'd had to physically hold him back because he'd tried to get inside, too. He'd been terrified that Whitney was in there.

Burning.

But she hadn't been. A search had been conducted on every floor in the office building. No sign of her.

He'd tried calling her phone, thinking that maybe she still had it on her, but the damn thing had rung from the back of the limo. Another very bad sign.

Jag and Darius had helped him search the nearby area. They'd turned up nothing.

Then the Trouble for Hire assholes had arrived. And he hadn't even pretended not to be glad to see them.

"We can pull footage from every security camera in all the nearby buildings," War was saying.

"And the street cams, too," Jinx added.

War nodded. "We'll check them and see what the hell happened. Whitney didn't just disappear."

No, he knew that. She'd had help. "The bastard who set the fire took her." The fire had been a distraction. The trapped women? They'd been the bait to pull him away from Whitney.

"The guy would have needed to know the layout of this building." Thoughtful, from War. "He would have needed to know those women were up there. He had to trap them while you were occupied—"

"The damn psychologist is missing. Edward Wilson." When Ramsey got his hands on that jerk... "Jag thought he ran into the building to help, but he didn't. He's gone. Whitney's gone..." *Whitney!* He fisted his hands. "Whitney said she saw him every Saturday. He knew her routine. He could have jammed the stairwell door on the top floor before she arrived. He could have set the fire to start with some kind of trigger—"

"Yeah, but why do all of that if he thought she was coming alone?" It was the first time Odin had spoken. He'd been quiet while Ramsey explained what the hell was happening. "I mean, did he have any idea that you'd be showing up with her?"

"If he's the bastard who sent Axel after her, then yes, he knew. He would have known that I was sticking close to her." So Edward's whole response in the office had been an act. "He's gone. Whitney's gone. Pretty easy to connect those pieces."

The limo sat there. Empty. Abandoned. No Whitney. "I shouldn't have gone inside." He should have stayed with her. Fuck. *Fucking hell.*

"Hey." Jinx grabbed him. "I heard those women talking. You helped them. You saved—"

"*I left her.* Whitney matters to me more than any damn thing else, and I left her. Now she's gone. My baby's gone. And I—"

"We're getting her back. You hear me? You will get her back. Just take a minute and think," Jinx urged him. "Who would do this to you? Who would target her to get to you?"

"Everybody! She's my weakness! My only damn one!" No, not totally true. As he stared into Jinx's eyes, Ramsey knew that his words were a lie. Jinx was a weakness, too. The big brother he'd always tried to protect. He'd left Jinx's life so that his brother could have a chance at a good future. *One that didn't include me.*

"I didn't give Whitney a chance," Ramsey muttered. "I'm a selfish bastard, and I wanted her, and I took her." But she was gone.

I will get her back.

He jerked from Jinx's hold. Brought his phone to his ear. After the search of the nearby area had turned up jack, he'd sent Jag and Darius to start tearing through the town. To rip into every dark hole and all the hideouts that the worst of the freaking worst criminals used in that area. But now he wanted more.

Darius answered on the second ring. "Tell me you have her."

He had to swallow twice. "Offer a bounty."

"To get her back?"

"Yes." He felt the other men staring at him.

"How much?" Darius asked quietly.

"Anything. *Everything.* You spread the word that I want her. I will pay whoever brings her back to me, and I will pay *anything.*"

Darius whistled. "Boss, you're gonna start a war in this town. The people in our world will be ripping the place apart looking for her."

Yes, they would. That was exactly what he wanted. "Spread the word." Then he made another call.

"This had better not be another tech request call..." Cyrus began.

"I want you to access every single street cam or security video around this address." He spat out the location.

"Dude, I am not your personal—"

"*Cyrus.*"

"What's wrong?" No more humor. Just worry.

"Whitney is missing. I think someone took her. *Find* her for me." He choked down the lump in his throat. "Please."

"I will call you back in five minutes."

Ramsey was starting to think more clearly. When he'd first found the empty limo, rage and fear had blasted through him. He'd been terrified that Whitney was in the burning building.

Five firefighters had to tackle me to stop me from going back in.

But she hadn't been inside. And that meant...

Someone is going to die today. I will find the person who took her. He will die.

Ramsey lowered his phone. "I should have thought of the security footage instantly, but I wasn't...quite in my right mind."

The other men stared at him. Sympathy was on their faces. Dammit. He didn't want sympathy or pity. He just wanted Whitney.

"I will need you to bring Imari in on this, too," Ramsey directed. His voice sounded funny. Too flat. And his body felt icy. "The more people we have working it, the faster we can find Whitney."

War and Odin shared a glance. "Imari?" War repeated.

"Don't waste my time with BS. The minute Cyrus told me that she'd showed up at his door, I realized she was working with you. I already knew she'd left her previous position."

"How did you know that?' Jinx asked, voice soft.

Ramsey spared him a brief glance. "Did you really think you were the only one who ever did favors for the government?"

"*What?*"

"I knew when she left the government's employ. I also knew she was staying in this area. And it didn't take long to figure out where she'd turn for a new job." He nodded. "Bring her in. She has useful connections with the cops, and we could use those in the hunt." He started to say more, but stopped because...

Speaking of cops...

Behind Jinx, he could see Detective Melissa Wright striding determinedly toward him. Her face was set in tense lines, and her shoulders were stiff. "Ramsey!" she called.

He shook his head. "Not now, detective. I do *not* have time for you—"

She elbowed Jinx out of the way. "Oh, you're going to make time for me." Her breath huffed out. "Axel Porter is dead."

"He didn't kill him!" Jinx immediately declared. "I will testify before any court anywhere, anytime! Ramsey did *not* stab that guy in the chest."

"Yes, settle down. I know he didn't do it. Because before Axel took his last breath, he told me who did."

Every muscle in Ramsey's body tightened.

"Want to know who it was?" Melissa asked.

Was she fucking kidding?

But then she squinted around the area. "Heard on the radio that there was a fire. Everyone okay?"

"No," Ramsey snarled. "Everyone is not fucking okay. Whitney is missing, and if you have something useful to say, tell me, now."

Her stare jumped back to him. "I have something useful." She wet her lips.

His phone began to ring.

"But you're not going to like it," she added.

***

Her head *hurt*. Whitney opened her eyes as the back of her head throbbed in pounding bursts. She tried to lift a hand to touch her head, but she felt something around her wrists.

Rope. Thick rope was tied around her wrists—wrists that had been pulled behind the chair she was sitting in.

What chair? Where am I?

Dazed, she shook her head and tried to focus on her surroundings.

A groan came from beside her. Whitney's head immediately jerked to the left—sending more pain pulsing through her—and she saw Edward. He was tied up, too. But he had also had a gag in his mouth, and blood was pouring from his nose and a gash in his temple. His eyes were closed.

"You're awake."

Whitney stiffened at that voice. She didn't want to look at the speaker. If she looked at the speaker, then she'd have to admit what was happening, and she didn't want to do that. She wanted this to be just some nightmare. She wanted to close her eyes and wake up back in Ramsey's bed.

"I didn't want to hurt you, but I didn't have a choice."

There were always choices to be made in this world.

She still didn't look at the speaker, but her gaze drifted around the bar. *Ramsey's bar*. She was inside of Ramsey's bar, tied up, and sitting in one of the chairs. The bar seemed cavernous without the usual patrons inside.

"I wish..." His voice turned ragged. "I wish you'd just stayed dead."

Her lower lip trembled. Her head turned and she finally looked at the man who'd attacked her.

Jag stared back at her with glittering eyes. "Because now, I'm going to have to kill you myself."

CHAPTER TWENTY-ONE

Observation notes: I started packing today. There are things I want to take with me, and other things that I want to leave behind when I start my new life with Ramsey.

Is it the same for him? Is he trying to decide what to leave behind?

Jag came to me today and told me this was a mistake. He said that a man like Ramsey would never be happy living an ordinary life.

I actually hope that our life together...maybe it can be extraordinary.

***

"Did you hear me, Ramsey?" Melissa demanded. "Before he died, Axel Porter said one name. Jagger Dunton. I know he's one of your guys, but I'm betting you *didn't* know he was gunning for your lady."

The phone was still ringing. The chill in Ramsey's body was growing worse. So cold that he could barely feel anything.

He swiped his finger over the screen and lifted the phone to his ear.

"*Got video footage.* The guy had a van waiting at the back of the building. He dragged both Whitney and some tall, blond man back there and tossed them inside. You're not going to like this, but I swear, neither of them were conscious. Then he left them there and it seems like he—"

"He ran back around the building to meet me. To act surprised when Whitney wasn't in the limo." Each word was bitten off.

"You...you already know who did it?"

"Jag."

"Yeah, yeah," Cyrus replied quickly, worriedly. "I recognized him from the few times that I'd seen the two of you together—"

"Where did the van go?"

Everyone had their eyes on him.

"He snuck back for it a while later."

When I thought he'd left to hunt for Whitney.

"I tried to track the van via traffic cams, but I lost it after about five minutes. I'll keep searching. I'm sorry, man. I won't give up. I'm sure he took her to some place isolated and that's why I lost him on the traffic footage. But we *will* find that van again."

"Call Ali and get her to help you." *Allison Carter. Jinx's lady.* A woman as good at tech as Cyrus was.

"He's not going to get away," Cyrus rushed to assure him.

"It's not about getting away." Because it all made sick sense to Ramsey. "It's about killing her." *Fuck.* "And that will not happen." He ended the call. *I'm sure he took her to some place isolated and that's why I lost him on the traffic footage.*

The detective was in his path. Ramsey stepped around her.

Only to find Jinx right in front of him. "Where are you going?" Jinx demanded.

"To search. Now get out of my way."

"Do you *know* where she is?"

"I said to search." He had to unclench his back teeth. "You heard the phone call. Did it *sound* like I knew?"

"Who were you talking to?" War asked.

"Cyrus." Like they hadn't known. But Jinx was still in his path. "Move."

Jinx's whole body was tense. "I'll come with you."

"No, but you'll give me your motorcycle." They both had always fucking loved bikes. And he could sure use a fast ride at the moment. "Then you'll go with your special ops buddies and you guys will tear this town apart. We can cover more ground if we divide and conquer." He slanted a glance back at Melissa. "Guessing you already have an APB out for Jag?"

She nodded. "And I'll get the cops to search as hard as they can for Whitney."

"Thank you."

"I'm...I'm sorry, Ramsey."

Sorry. Because she thought he wasn't going to find Whitney alive. He let his head sink forward.

Jinx put his keys in Ramsey's hand. "Don't you give up."

He fisted the keys. Kept his head down as he strode away. *Oh, don't you worry, I'm not giving up.* He jumped onto Jinx's ride.

His head lifted. Grim determination filled him. No, he hadn't intended to give up at all. He'd just needed to ditch the others. Because Ramsey believed he knew exactly where Jag had gone with Whitney.

Ramsey just hadn't wanted the others with him when he confronted Jag. There was no need for an audience to watch him kill one of his closest friends.

***

Jinx watched Ramsey drive away. The guy didn't just slowly pull off. He raced away with a scream of the motorcycle's engine.

The detective had already hurried to talk with more cops. War was speaking to Imari on the phone, and Odin was sidling closer to Jinx.

"You buy that scene?"

Jinx glanced over at Odin.

"You know your brother pretty damn well. You think he's the type to put his head down and look defeated?"

Hell, no. "Not on any fucking day of the week."

"That's what I thought." Odin crossed his arms over his chest. "So why'd you let him go off on his own?"

"He's not going alone." War wasn't the only one who had a tracker in his ride. Jinx pulled out his phone and pulled up the app. He could see exactly where his brother was heading. "Ramsey will be getting backup whether he wants it or not."

***

"You're not good for him. I warned him to stay away from you over and over again." Jag was pacing—he'd been pacing in silence for what seemed like forever, but he was finally speaking again...and he had a gun gripped in his hand. "Did he listen? No. The first time you walked into the bar, he got hooked. Never touched a drug in his life until *you*."

"I'm not a drug." Her head *hurt*. Nausea rose in her throat, and she had to choke it down.

"He built an empire, and he was going to throw it away." He stalked behind the bar. Put the gun down.

Her breath heaved out. *Good. Good. He put the gun down.*

But then he started reaching for the bottles of alcohol. He opened them. Began pouring them all over the place. Smashing them.

"He told me he was going to run away with you!" Jag smashed another bottle. Glass flew into the air. "I told him that was crazy. I told *you* it would never work."

And she could suddenly remember that. Remember him telling her that Ramsey couldn't live an ordinary life.

"You were so fucking confident. Lifted your chin at me. Said you loved him. That he loved you. That you could have something special. *Extraordinary*. Bullshit! *Bullshit!*" He threw a bottle of whiskey against the wall.

Her hands twisted behind her as she fought to get out of the ropes. The hemp bit into her wrist. Beside her, Edward still appeared to be unconscious. Blood dripped from his temple.

"Then you disappeared." Jag strode toward her. Towered over her and smiled. "And I thought I didn't have to worry any longer. You were out of the picture. Ramsey was exactly where he was supposed to be." His smile slowly faded. "But then you came back from the damn dead." He lifted his hand. He had a bottle of tequila gripped in his fist. He began to pour it on her.

"Don't! Stop!" Whitney screamed.

"You'll stay dead this time."

"Don't do this!"

He emptied the bottle on her, soaking her hair and clothes. "Do you think I want to do this?" And he threw that bottle, too. It shattered into a million pieces. "I don't want this! I just wanted you to stay away! But you came back from the dead, and he...he couldn't keep his distance. I knew he was sneaking by your place at night. He lied and told me he was just checking up on you, but I knew the truth. He was obsessed, just like before. *Had* to see you. And then you walked back through the door again..." His breath shuddered out. "Why did you walk back through the door? Why didn't you stay away?"

"I wanted my past back." Tequila was sliding down her face. So were tears.

He glared at her. "Did you remember what I said in our last conversation?"

Last conversation? Seriously? Her wrists strained against the ropes.

"You were always writing things down. Ramsey told me about that. I was afraid that you'd written something down about me. When you vanished, I got one of Ramsey's cop informants to upload a virus in your computer. Told him it was to protect Ramsey in case any incriminating evidence was on the machine, but it was really—"

"To protect you," she finished.

"On the last night, right before you vanished..." He squinted at her. "You don't remember it, do you? If you'd remembered, you would've had Ramsey come after me."

No, she didn't remember the last night.

"But you got the files recovered. You said that when we left the beach house today. And I knew there was no more time to waste. You'd either remember on your own or maybe you'd put enough in those stupid files that you'd recall..."

"Recall what?" she whispered. Whitney was just trying to keep him talking. The longer he talked, the longer she had to escape. The tequila had dripped onto the ropes behind her, and her wrists were slick either from blood—where she'd cut herself on the ropes—or the tequila. Either way, the slickness was giving her room to move, and she'd almost worked one wrist free.

"Recall that I tried to buy you off. Recall that I offered you fifty grand to stay away from him." Jag shook his head. "You told me you'd never stay away. I...got mad at you. I've got a temper."

"You don't say," she muttered. Her left wrist was free, and with one wrist out, the ropes had slackened enough that she could work the other hand loose, too. She just had to figure out her plan for escape. Jag was way bigger and stronger than she was, and Whitney didn't have a weapon.

But there is plenty of broken glass on the floor.

"I shoved you. You fell and stared up at me like I was some kind of monster."

Newsflash. You are.

"I just wanted things to stay the way they were! Ramsey and I had nothing when we started. We built a freaking empire, and he was going to wreck it for you! A bitch who was just playing in his world!"

"*Don't call her a bitch.*" Ramsey's lethal voice.

Her head whipped toward the bar. Ramsey stood there. He must have entered via the back door and snuck to the long, gleaming bar. His hands were on the bar top. His fingers inches from the gun that Jag had left behind.

"Ramsey?" Jag spun to face him. "What—how—"

"What am I doing here? Coming to get my lady, obviously." His fingers drummed on the counter. His expression was absolutely savage. "How did I know where to find you? Well, easy. I figured you'd want to go someplace that would be deserted. I'd ordered the bar closed down, so it was the most obvious, deserted spot. Especially if you wanted to send a fuck-you message to me. You'd take my lady, and you'd kill her in my bar."

Her fingers began to twist the rope. She had an idea...

"I-I didn't...I'm not going to kill her!" Jag snapped. "I *found* her. That jackass Edward—he brought her here—"

"The jackass who is tied up?"

"Yes! I knocked him out and just tied him up." Jag advanced toward Ramsey. "Look, you misheard the conversation." His hand began to inch toward the back of his jeans.

He has another weapon hidden there. Either a gun or a knife or something.

"Edward poured alcohol all over this place," Jag added. "I think he was going to burn the bar down—with Whitney inside."

Whitney hadn't spoken. Deliberately. She'd wanted Jag's focus to shift off her. And it had. He was closing in on Ramsey. Jag's back was to her.

So she attacked. She leapt out of her chair and she went straight for his back. She jumped up, and she looped the rope around his neck. "*Liar!*" Whitney screamed. She jerked back on the rope, tightening it around his neck.

Jag slammed his head back, trying to head butt her, and her feet slipped on the wet floor. She tumbled down, landing on her hip, and her hands flew out to steady herself.

Her fingers touched a broken shard of glass.

Jag wrenched her up to her feet. She realized he had pulled something out of his jeans—out of his pocket. Not the knife or gun she'd feared. No, he'd yanked out a lighter.

Oh, God.

"She's soaking wet with booze. If I light her, she'll get burns on her body before you can put out the flames." Jag's voice was musing, "Actually, I don't even know how fast she'll burn. Axel used to talk to me about fire. The man loved his flames. He'd know exactly how long it would take before second or third-degree burns appeared on her body." The hand with the lighter was near her waist while his left hand had locked around her neck. "All I have to do is set her shirt on fire."

"You'll burn, too!" Ramsey snarled.

"Am I supposed to believe that you were going to let me walk out of here? If you'd let my plan work, I would have been okay. But when you know it's me...when you know what *I* did..." His body shuddered against Whitney. His grip on her neck was so tight she could barely breathe. "We both know you won't let me go."

Jag was thinking about killing them both. Whitney knew she had to stop him. Her frantic gaze met Ramsey's.

And she saw the terror in his stare. *"Don't,"* Ramsey rasped. "I will give you whatever you want, but don't do this. Move that damn lighter. *Move it.* And get your arm off her neck."

Because Jag could break her neck. Whitney knew it. Ramsey did, too. One hard jerk and a guy with Jag's power and fighting skills could kill her. It wasn't just about the fire—no, the fire was more of a taunt, more of a way to torture Ramsey.

Jag could kill her anytime that he wanted.

"Give me what I want? *What I want*?" Jag's voice rose. "I *want* things back the way they were! I want the empire we built. You think I don't know you've been changing things? I saw the messages you sent to Aspen. You've been transitioning to legit businesses ever since the first moment you saw Whitney! And when she came *back,* you told Aspen to shift things immediately."

"You want things back the way they were?" Ramsey nodded. "Fine. Let her go. She can walk out of the door right now, and everything will go back to what we had before."

"You're lying." Jag's voice was thick. "You won't forgive me."

Ramsey's gaze said...*No, I fucking won't.*

"I was going to make it look like Edward had done everything. I knew about her appointments with him. Even knew that the dick was sweet on her."

"That's why you got the roses sent to Whitney? All part of your frame job on Edward?" Ramsey pushed.

"Yeah. Yeah, had to give her a stalker. Had to give *you* an enemy."

"A pretend enemy, you mean. The real enemy was one of my best friends."

"If you'd let it all play out, you could have been happy!"

"There is no way I am ever happy without her."

Okay, Ramsey's words were beautiful, and if she hadn't been terrified, Whitney would have been able to appreciate them more.

The flame from the lighter was dancing. "She went to see old Edward every Saturday," Jag muttered. "So when I found out about the recovered files on that damn laptop, I just had to set the scene."

"Set the fire, you mean?" Whitney gasped out.

"It was a distraction. I needed you away from Ramsey!" His breath heaved. "I never meant to hurt you, Ramsey. I was going to leave her and that Edward asshole both here. Let them burn. We would have been free of her."

Her right hand had fisted.

Ramsey's eyes were on her.

"But you don't want to be free of her, do you?" Jag's voice thickened. "All you want...*is her*."

"Let her go," Ramsey said again.

"You'll kill me..."

A groan came from behind them. Edward.

But Jag jerked at the sound, and his hold on her neck loosened. She yanked up her right hand—and the broken glass that she'd hidden in her palm. She sliced it over his cheek.

He screamed and let her go.

"*Run, Whitney!*" Ramsey bellowed. "*Run!*"

She did. She rushed for the door.

And heard the thud of bodies hitting behind her. Whitney glanced back. Ramsey had tackled Jag. But...flames.

Flames. Flames were spreading with a terrible *whoosh* of sound. Jag must have used his lighter because flames were rushing around the room, eating at the line of liquor he'd spilled on the floor.

Frantic cries came from behind Edward's gag.

"Get out!" Ramsey shouted to her. "I'll get him! *Go!*"

"*You* come with me!" Whitney cried.

The flames were so greedy. Running so fast.

Jag swung at Ramsey and plowed his fist into Ramsey's jaw.

"*Get her the fuck out!*" Ramsey bellowed. "Get her and the baby *out!*"

Who was he talking to? She—

Arms closed around her. Lifted her up. And hauled her out of the bar. "*Ramsey!*" Whitney screamed.

***

Smoke. Fire. Hell.

Ramsey saw the figures moving behind the wall of flames. Jinx had just carried Whitney to safety. *She's going to be all right.*

War and Odin were hauling Edward out of the bar.

That just leaves me and Jag.

"Why couldn't you have stayed away from her?" Jag panted. "We had the world at our damn feet!"

"She is my world. My fucking heart." A broken bottle was near his shoe. His favorite whiskey. "And you tried to take her." He crouched on the floor and stared up at his *friend*.

Jag screamed and ran at him.

Ramsey grabbed the broken bottle and surged to his feet. He shoved the sharp edges of the glass into Jag's chest. He stared into Jag's eyes as they went wide, and Ramsey smiled. "So now...I'm taking *your* heart." He twisted that broken bottle and blood spilled down Jag's chest.

***

"Let me go! Dammit, Jinx!"

"Oh, yeah, right. Because I'm really going to let you run into a burning bar. Like Ramsey would forgive that shit if I did—"

"Then go after Ramsey!" Whitney snapped. "He needs help! He needs—" She stopped.

Because Ramsey was walking out of the bar. Flames flickered in his wake. His face was cold and hard. His eyes glittered.

And the bar burned behind him.

His steps were slow and certain.

"I don't think we want to ask where Jag is," War muttered.

"He's dead," Ramsey said. "He tripped and fell on a broken bottle."

"Uh, sure..." War inclined his head. "Totally sure that is what happened."

Jinx let go of Whitney. She ran to Ramsey and threw her arms around him. Her eyes squeezed shut, and she held him as tightly as she could.

His arms curled carefully around her. "Are you hurt?"

"My head...it still hurts. He hit me with—"

He lifted her into his arms. "Hospital!" Ramsey shouted. "We're getting her to a hospital right now!"

"Ramsey, the bar. It's burning. We should call the fire department." She tried to reason with him.

His gaze flew to hers. "Fuck the bar. I always planned to burn down that world."

What? But he'd raced across the lot. He had her at a Jeep. She didn't even know who owned the Jeep. He was tucking her inside and hooking the seatbelt, and her hand rose to press to his cheek. "I love you."

He shuddered. His eyes closed. "He was going to kill you."

"He didn't."

His eyes opened. "I'm getting you to the hospital. I have to know you and the baby are okay."

She felt pressure in her stomach. A fast push, like something had rolled inside of her. Her hand flew to her stomach.

"What is it? What's happening?" His voice broke.

"I think...I felt the baby move."

"*Fuck, fuck, fuck.*" He flew back. Raced around the front of the vehicle. Jumped in the driver seat. Odin was there—and he tossed keys to Ramsey. Ramsey caught them. Fisted them.

Jinx was shouting at him.

"Not a bad movement," she rushed to say. "I don't feel any pain in my stomach. I just—I think I felt the baby move. I've never felt her move before."

He cranked the vehicle. "Hospital."

"Ramsey?"

"Hospital."

And as they drove away, she looked back to see the flames rushing up the side of his bar.

CHAPTER TWENTY-TWO

Observation notes: Jag tried to buy me off today. As if any amount of money would ever make me leave Ramsey. But then...Jag got physical. He pushed me. His face was horrified, as if he couldn't believe he'd done such a thing.

He ran away.

I have to tell Ramsey. Jag doesn't like me, and I'm scared of him. I'm afraid of what he might do.

But whatever he plans, it won't work. I won't leave Ramsey. No one will keep us apart.

***

Ramsey looked up from the laptop. He was in the hospital exam room. Darius had brought the laptop to him. He'd needed to see it. If he'd just read the fucking recovered files earlier...

"Stop it." Jinx's order. "Whatever the hell is spinning through your mind, just stop."

Ramsey glanced over at him.

Jinx stared steadily back at him. "This isn't on you."

"He was my friend." Or, Ramsey had thought Jag was his friend. "He was in my world. At my side for years."

"You think you're the only one who has ever trusted the wrong person? Hell, no. I can make you a whole list of the times I screwed up, if you want."

"This screwup almost cost Whitney's life," he replied.

"She's going to be all right." The soft words came from Maisey as she sat at Odin's side. The small waiting room was packed. War, Odin, Jinx...and all their ladies. Rose, War's wife and a local star reporter, sat tensely, with her hand gripped with his. This was a major news story, but she hadn't asked Ramsey even a single question. She'd just sat with them all. Been a warm, steady presence.

Odin had his arm around Maisey's shoulders, and even though her words had been confident, Jinx could see the fear in her eyes.

Whitney has to be all right.

Ali Carter stood near Jinx. She would pace every few moments. Tension seemed to roll off her.

He felt the same damn tension. Like it was gonna rip him apart.

"Next time, I'm reading all the fucking files." The words burst from Cyrus. Because, yeah, he was there, too. He'd arrived just as Whitney had been taken back. Ramsey didn't even know how the guy had known they were at the hospital, but he'd just appeared. "I should have done that *this* time," Cyrus continued grimly. "But, oh, no, I was trying to prove that I could contain my curiosity. That shit ends. *I* could have stopped him. If the info was in her files all along—"

"You both have to stop blaming yourselves!" Ali let out a long exhale. She and Cyrus were old friends, and her gaze cut to him. "You know who we blame? We blame Jag. He's the one who did this. No one else gets to choke on the guilt. He did it, and he's been stopped."

Yes, he had been stopped. Permanently.

That prick Edward had been taken to the hospital, too. He was being checked out in the back, but Ramsey wasn't particularly concerned about him. *Or concerned at all.* His only focus was Whitney.

Detective Melissa Wright had been there, too, but she'd left to go supervise the scene at his bar. Not that there should be much to supervise. *I hope it burned to the ground.*

The door to the waiting room opened. Ramsey jumped up, but it was just Darius. Darius's face appeared haggard, and as he crossed to Ramsey, Darius raked a hand over his jaw. "The cops are already tossing Jag's place." His stare dipped to Rose, then back to Ramsey. "I received a tip," he explained carefully, "that they found more evidence to tie him to Axel." His nostrils flared. "Can't believe he did this shit," he mumbled. "He was like family..."

And Ramsey had still killed him. If he had it to do all over again, he would...only he'd make the death even more painful. When Ramsey thought of Jag, he felt rage surge within him. *He wanted to take Whitney*.

Because of the stupid fucking empire they'd built? Seriously? Ramsey would have given him control of the damn thing. Hell, he'd planned to pass along as much power as he could to both Jag and Darius. Ramsey had turned as many businesses legit as he could. And as for the rest...

"I don't want it," Darius rasped.

Ramsey's jaw locked. "We'll talk later."

"No, we're talking now."

Uh, yeah, with a roomful of avid people watching and listening?

"You need to know that I didn't stay at your side for power. Fuck that shit. I stayed because you were the one person who was always there for me. You want out? Then I'm out, too. And I would *never* do anything to hurt the woman you love. Know that shit. Don't go lumping me in with Jag because that's not me. That's not what I—"

"Stop," Ramsey ordered flatly.

Darius's jaw jerked up.

"I know," Ramsey told him. Darius didn't have to say or do anything else.

Darius nodded quickly. "Good. Good." He looked away. "Who the hell do I have to scare in order to get some news on Whitney? Your ass has been sitting in here far too long."

Excellent question. Ramsey was done waiting. The last bit of his patience was gone. He needed Whitney.

As if on cue, the door opened again. A young nurse with dark hair poked her head inside, "Mr. Hyde?"

His heart stopped. Darius shoved him toward the nurse.

"Come with me, please," she directed.

What the fuck? Why couldn't she tell him what was happening right then and there? "Whitney's okay?"

A quick smile from her. Was that smile supposed to be reassuring? "The doctor wants to talk with you."

As they left the waiting room, he nearly slammed right into Imari. She'd been lurking in the hallway.

"Um, Ramsey, I..."

He jerked his thumb toward the door. "Cyrus is in there, too. Better get ready to apologize to him." They could work out all of their drama without him. Ramsey had something more important waiting.

The nurse seemed to take extra slow steps as she led him down the hallway. Antiseptic burned his nose. The lights seemed too bright, and his heartbeat was far too loud in his ears. He wanted to break into a run and find Whitney. "Could we move any faster?"

She stopped in front of a doorway. "We're here." She opened the door.

It was oddly dim in that room after the brightness of the hallway, but he had no trouble seeing Whitney. She was in a bed, a sheet was pulled up to her chest, and a big, flat-screen monitor was to the right of the bed. A redheaded woman in a lab coat stood near the monitor, and another woman perched on a stool near the bed.

The lab-coat-wearing redhead turned toward him with a warm smile. "Ramsey, I presume?"

He looked at her name tag. *Dr. Marshall*. Whitney's OB-GYN. He'd done plenty of digging on her and knew she was supposed to be the best in the area. "Yes." The word came out sounding hoarse.

He cut a fearful glance toward Whitney.

She smiled at him. "I'm fine."

"A concussion is hardly fine," Dr. Marshall admonished sternly. "And that's why you are staying in the hospital overnight."

"I'm staying with her." Ramsey's fast response.

Dr. Marshall inclined her head. "She told me you'd say that. She also told me that you would very much want to be present for what's happening next."

What was happening? He hurried to Whitney's side. Clasped her hand in his.

"The baby's heartbeat is good. There is no sign of bleeding or distress. And Whitney—*after* her twenty-four-hour period of observation is complete—should be able to return home."

He brought Whitney's fingers to his mouth. Kissed the back of her hand. He was being told things were good, so why the hell did his body suddenly feel weak?

The woman sitting on the other side of Whitney's bed lifted the sheet. She had some sort of device in her hand.

"You'll want to look at the screen," Dr. Marshall advised him.

He would? Why? But he looked.

And saw gray shapes emerge on the screen. The shapes twisted. Stretched. "Uh, what the hell am I looking at?"

Dr. Marshall laughed. *Laughed?* When he was close to losing his mind? This was not the time to be laughing. Maybe she wasn't the best, after all. Maybe she was crazy.

She walked closer to the monitor and pointed. "You're looking at your baby."

His hold tightened on Whitney's fingers.

"I wanted you to see this ultrasound," Whitney whispered.

His lips parted.

"There is the head." Dr. Marshall waved her hand.

He could see it. Ramsey could swear he saw eyes staring back at him. A little nose.

"Fingers. Oh, look." Dr. Marshall beamed. "It looks like the baby is waving."

He could see a tiny hand.

A strange sound filled the air. *Woo, woo, woo, woo.* Wind. Gasping?

"That's the heartbeat," the woman on the stool informed him. "Thought you might want to hear it."

His breath came too fast. His heart seemed to beat in time with that precious *woo, woo, woo.*

"As I said," Dr. Marshall peered at the monitor, "the heartbeat is good. There is no reason to believe the baby is in any sort of distress. This child is very, very strong."

He had to blink. The screen had gone blurry on him.

"Do you want to know the sex?" Dr. Marshall inclined her head toward them. "I told Whitney that usually around eighteen weeks, the baby's sex can be determined on the ultrasound. We're a little early on that timeline, but I feel confident we can tell." A pause. "Do you want to know?" she asked again.

"Yes," Whitney said immediately. Then she pulled on his hand. "Wait, do we? Or do you want to be surprised?"

His gaze focused on her. His beautiful Whitney. She'd surprised him from the very first night. He'd never expected to love someone the way that he loved her. She'd walked into his life and changed everything.

There had been pain and fear and rage...Ramsey would never get over Jag's betrayal, but...there had also been hope. Passion. The promise of a life that wasn't just about darkness.

Love.

Whitney had given him so much.

"Do you want to know?" Whitney stared up at him with her beautiful eyes.

He bent and pressed a kiss to her lips. Sweet, sweet Whitney. "What do you want?" he murmured.

She laughed.

Laughed after the nightmare they'd been through.

"I want to know!" she kissed him again.

God, I love her. So much. So much that she made his heart seem bigger. He'd been so cold and alone for so long, but now everything was changing. Everything was different.

"Well," the woman on the stool began. "You're going to have..."

***

Ramsey burst into the waiting room. His ragged breath heaved from his chest, and he gripped the door in a hold that threatened to shatter the wood.

Jinx immediately ran toward him. Darius was right behind him.

"What happened?" Jinx grabbed Ramsey's shoulders. "Tell me. Whatever it is, it's going to be fine. I will be with you every step of the way. We can handle this. *Look* at me, brother. We can handle—"

"We're having a little girl." A wide, ridiculously happy grin spread across his face.

Jinx gaped. Shook his head. And the same grin slid over his face. "Uncle Jinxy is getting a niece?"

Before Ramsey could say anything else, Jinx hauled him close in a crushing hug.

A girl. A precious girl that I will love forever.

Just as he would love her mom.

Jinx eased back. "Everything is okay?" The others had crowded in behind them.

"The doctor said the baby is strong. I saw her. My baby. I saw her." He couldn't stop smiling. When the hell had he ever smiled so much? But the image of that dark screen with the gray form that shifted and moved and waved flashed through his mind. "She's fucking beautiful." Beautiful. And...

Vulnerable. So tiny and precious.

He inhaled. "We'll protect her."

"Damn straight, we will." This response came from War. He rolled back his shoulders. "Always."

Maybe the guy wasn't such a prick, after all. Ramsey pulled out the precious piece of paper in his pocket. "They gave me a picture of her. Want to see?"

Darius grabbed the paper first as the others swarmed.

***

"No more concussions." His voice was flat. His hold tender. "No more attacks. No more fires. No more terrifying years and years off my life."

Whitney stared out at the pounding waves. The sun was setting, and the view from the balcony was spectacular. She'd stayed in the hospital for far too long. Mostly because Ramsey had insisted that every test under the sun be run on her. She'd assured him over and over again that she was fine.

But she knew he still worried.

He'd barely been more than two feet from her the entire time. Except for when he'd rushed to tell the others about the baby...

She gave a little gasp.

"What is it? Oh, dammit, I knew we should have stayed at the hospital longer. You're in pain, aren't you? You—"

She caught his right hand. Brought it to her stomach. Pressed. "Wait for it."

And there it was. A little roll. A push. Maybe a hand or a foot or a shoulder but *something* of the baby's thrust against him.

"Is that a kick?" he choked out.

"Or a high five. Or something." She turned toward him.

His expression was absolutely priceless. So much joy and love. Her big, bad Ramsey. He was so very different now than he'd appeared the first time that she'd seen him. And, yes, she remembered that time. Did she remember everything? No. Maybe she never would. That was all right.

She didn't need every single memory. Whitney knew she loved him, just as she knew with utter certainty that Ramsey loved her.

"I'm sorry about your bar." She'd heard Darius tell him it had been a total loss.

"I'm not. I was done with that place, anyway." His hand smoothed over her stomach.

"I'm sorry about Jag."

His expression hardened. "I'm—"

"Don't say you're not sorry. Because then you'd be lying, and I don't want lies between us."

His gaze lifted.

"You were close to him, and it hurts. He's dead."

"He tried to hurt *you*. He was dead to me the minute he did that shit." His gaze blazed. "He didn't fall on the broken bottle."

"I know," she whispered. She'd heard the story. Known the truth.

"I couldn't let him come after you. Not ever. And his death sent a damn message to anyone else who might ever think they could use you."

She didn't look away. "Is that supposed to scare me?"

"Baby, you're the only one who never seems scared of me."

"Because I'm not. You think I wouldn't kill to protect you? To protect our family? I would do it and never hesitate." She'd been ready to kill as the fire spread through his bar. "You matter. If someone comes after you, I will be ready to do whatever it takes to protect you."

"I love you so much."

"Good. Because I love you even more."

His lips brushed hers. "Not possible."

He shouldn't be too sure. "I loved you even when I couldn't remember you." Because some things—some people—just could not be erased. Her heart belonged to Ramsey.

It always would.

"I've made mistakes in the past." His voice was gruff and dark and sexy. "Done things that crossed the line. I swear, I will not cross a line again. I want to be someone you can be proud of being with."

"You were never my dirty secret, Ramsey." She wanted everyone to know about them.

"My business interests are legitimate. Everything else is gone. And I have contacts in the government who are going to help make sure any problems vanish from my past." A shake of his head. "My brother wasn't the only one who knew how to make deals over the years."

His past was dark and twisted, and she hated the pain he'd experienced. But the past was over. They were focusing on the future. "Do you have a name picked out?"

His lashes fluttered. "A name?"

"For our daughter. Because I've got some ideas..." One idea in particular.

"Like what?"

"Like Hope. I think that might be really nice..."

Ramsey swallowed. "I think it's perfect."

He kissed her again.

Perfect. The life she had with Ramsey—the future that waited—Whitney knew it would be better than any memory could ever possibly be...

EPILOGUE

"It's weird watching the mighty fall..." Imari turned to the man beside her. The man who'd been ignoring her for the last five minutes while he sat at the bar in Armageddon. "Never would have expected someone like Ramsey to fall in love."

"Anyone can love."

"Ah, finally, he speaks." She tried a smile as Cyrus glanced toward her.

He didn't smile back.

"How long are you going to be angry with me?" Imari asked, and, yes, dammit, she felt *glum*.

"I'm not angry."

"No?" *Totally could have fooled me.*

"No."

Her fingers tapped on the bar. Once upon a time, she'd worked in this bar. She'd been undercover back then. Some days, it felt as if she'd spent most of her life being undercover. She wanted a different path now. She wanted something real. "If you're not angry, then what are you?"

"On my way to getting drunk."

Not the answer she'd wanted. "Why are you shutting me out? I never wanted to hurt Ramsey. I was technically on your side all along." Shouldn't she get bonus points for that?

He stared at her. Just stared.

And under his intense stare, she shifted uncomfortably. "Cy?"

"I'm shutting you out because I realized that I can't always have what I want."

There it was...a question—one *she'd* asked— seemed to fill the space between them. *Do you want me?* Imari licked her lips. "Cy..."

He drained his shot glass. Let it clink back against the bar. "Good night, Imari."

She grabbed his wrist. "Don't you care at all about what I want?"

"Fine. What is it that *you* want?"

Imari realized she might just be looking at what—who—she wanted...

Oh, damn.

"No answer?" Cyrus taunted. "I thought as—"

She leaned forward and kissed him.

Ramsey wasn't the only one who could get a happy ending.

THE END

A NOTE FROM THE AUTHOR

Thank you for reading REMEMBER RAMSEY.

The Trouble for Hire books have been a blast to write. I loved setting the stories in one of my favorite areas—Pensacola, Florida. The gorgeous beaches there begged for a book...or, a few books. I appreciate you taking the time to check out the Trouble stories!

It was definitely time for Ramsey to get a story of his own. The man needed a happy ending. After writing over 100 books, I think this was actually my first secret pregnancy story. Thanks for giving me the chance to try something new!

If you'd like to stay updated on my releases and sales, please join my newsletter list.

https://cynthiaeden.com/newsletter/

Again, thank you for reading REMEMBER RAMSEY.

Best,
Cynthia Eden
cynthiaeden.com

ABOUT THE AUTHOR

Cynthia Eden is a *New York Times*, *USA Today*, *Digital Book World*, and *IndieReader* best-seller.

Cynthia writes sexy tales of contemporary romance, romantic suspense, and paranormal romance. Since she began writing full-time in 2005, Cynthia has written over one hundred novels and novellas.

Cynthia lives along the Alabama Gulf Coast. She loves romance novels, horror movies, and chocolate.

For More Information

- *cynthiaeden.com*
- *facebook.com/cynthiaedenfanpage*

HER OTHER WORKS

Trouble For Hire

- No Escape From War (Book 1)
- Don't Play With Odin (Book 2)
- Jinx, You're It (Book 3)
- Remember Ramsey (Book 4)

Death and Moonlight Mystery

- Step Into My Web (Book 1)
- Save Me From The Dark (Book 2)

Wilde Ways

- Protecting Piper (Book 1)
- Guarding Gwen (Book 2)
- Before Ben (Book 3)
- The Heart You Break (Book 4)
- Fighting For Her (Book 5)
- Ghost Of A Chance (Book 6)
- Crossing The Line (Book 7)
- Counting On Cole (Book 8)
- Chase After Me (Book 9)
- Say I Do (Book 10)
- Roman Will Fall (Book 11)
- The One Who Got Away (Book 12)

Dark Sins

- Don't Trust A Killer (Book 1)
- Don't Love A Liar (Book 2)

Lazarus Rising

- Never Let Go (Book One)
- Keep Me Close (Book Two)
- Stay With Me (Book Three)
- Run To Me (Book Four)
- Lie Close To Me (Book Five)
- Hold On Tight (Book Six)
- Lazarus Rising Volume One (Books 1 to 3)
- Lazarus Rising Volume Two (Books 4 to 6)

Dark Obsession Series

- Watch Me (Book 1)
- Want Me (Book 2)
- Need Me (Book 3)
- Beware Of Me (Book 4)
- Only For Me (Books 1 to 4)

Mine Series

- Mine To Take (Book 1)
- Mine To Keep (Book 2)
- Mine To Hold (Book 3)
- Mine To Crave (Book 4)
- Mine To Have (Book 5)
- Mine To Protect (Book 6)
- Mine Box Set Volume 1 (Books 1-3)
- Mine Box Set Volume 2 (Books 4-6)

Bad Things

- The Devil In Disguise (Book 1)
- On The Prowl (Book 2)
- Undead Or Alive (Book 3)
- Broken Angel (Book 4)
- Heart Of Stone (Book 5)
- Tempted By Fate (Book 6)
- Wicked And Wild (Book 7)
- Saint Or Sinner (Book 8)
- Bad Things Volume One (Books 1 to 3)
- Bad Things Volume Two (Books 4 to 6)
- Bad Things Deluxe Box Set (Books 1 to 6)

Bite Series

- Forbidden Bite (Bite Book 1)
- Mating Bite (Bite Book 2)

Blood and Moonlight Series

- Bite The Dust (Book 1)
- Better Off Undead (Book 2)
- Bitter Blood (Book 3)
- Blood and Moonlight (The Complete Series)

Purgatory Series

- The Wolf Within (Book 1)
- Marked By The Vampire (Book 2)
- Charming The Beast (Book 3)
- Deal with the Devil (Book 4)
- The Beasts Inside (Books 1 to 4)

Bound Series

- Bound By Blood (Book 1)

- Bound In Darkness (Book 2)
- Bound In Sin (Book 3)
- Bound By The Night (Book 4)
- Bound in Death (Book 5)
- Forever Bound (Books 1 to 4)

Stand-Alone Romantic Suspense

- Never Gonna Happen
- One Hot Holiday
- Secret Admirer
- First Taste of Darkness
- Sinful Secrets
- Until Death
- Christmas With A Spy

Printed in the USA
CPSIA information can be obtained
at www.ICGtesting.com
LVHW030303031223
765362LV00024B/1680